TRISOMY XXI

G. A. MINTON

World Castle Publishing, LLC
Pensacola, Florida
Copyright © G. A. Minton 2016
Paperback ISBN: 9781629894447
eBook ISBN: 9781629894454
First Edition World Castle Publishing, LLC. June 6, 2016.
http://www.worldcastlepublishing.com

Cover: Karen Fuller
Editor: Eric Johnston

DEDICATION

This book is dedicated to my Mother, Shirley—my biggest fan and supporter. Thanks, Mom!

Chapter I
HENRY

Spring had finally arrived in the small town of Tranquil. The winter snow had melted, and all that remained were a few patches of frosty white ice nestled under the shadows cast by some of the loftier pinion pines and alligator junipers. Like clockwork, Mother Nature had once again displayed her magnificence. The newly transformed landscape was now alive with a panorama of plant and animal life, recently awakened from a forced slumber under a blanket of wintry snow.

Drawn by nature's fragrant bouquet, ruby-throated hummingbirds and bumblebees could be seen hovering over colorful spring blossoms, sipping nectar, only to be exploited as naive vectors of pollination. As a white-tailed deer lapped up freshly melted snow from a babbling brook, two rock squirrels emerged from their seasonal nap, giving noisy chase to each other across a sun-soaked, high-desert terrain. Off in the distance, the muffled bugle of a big bull elk was faintly audible.

Tranquil, a rural Arizona town with a yearly population of almost three thousand, was located in the picturesque White Mountains, which boasted an elevation of seven thousand feet above sea level.

Most of the people living in this close-knit community were honest, law-abiding citizens who worked in the large copper, silver, and molybdenum mines dotting the area. The rest of the townspeople were either retired, or small business owners who catered to the assortment of tourists that visited the region each summer.

Tranquil was just like its name, a sleepy mountain community where nothing much ever happened. Yes, there was that incident that had occurred around six months ago, when Henry Pickridge, a local resident and retired miner with a fondness for straight bourbon whiskey—or for that matter, any other spirits he could get his hands on—claimed he had been abducted by a space alien.

According to Henry, the extraterrestrial being he encountered that day wasn't your average run-of-the-mill visitor from another planet. It wasn't a little green man or a Grey. Nor was it cute, furry, or friendly. The otherworldly thing that attacked Henry was a nightmare—a monstrosity that he'd never seen the likes of before, *or* ever wanted to see again. Unfortunately for Henry, the horrific image of that alien creature was permanently etched into his brain.

Henry Pickridge was Tranquil's proverbial town drunk, a crusty old-timer who lived by himself in a little wooden cabin located on the outskirts of town. He grew up there, back when it was just a widened area in the road, missed by most passing motorists if they had blinked their eyes. His father, Foy, was employed by the Midas Mining Company as a miner who worked hard in, at that time, the only molybdenum mine in the area. Foy worked the lode for over twenty years until he died of lung cancer, when Henry was only fifteen.

In order to help his mother out with the bills, Henry was forced to drop out of school in the eighth grade. The boy worked in the mines off-and-on for longer than he could remember, until finally retiring a couple of years ago at the age of sixty-eight. On two separate occasions, Henry ventured out to find work in Texas and New Mexico, but within a few short months found himself back in his beloved Tranquil, homesick and broke.

A rough-and-tough abrasive man, Henry possessed a mouth so foul that it would have knocked the socks off of *anyone's* Aunt Mildred. The old duffer had about as much appeal as a turd in a punch bowl. He was the king of cuss; the prince of profanity; the sovereign of swear; the viceroy of vulgarity. Over the years, Henry amassed a huge repertoire of curse words and expletives—an obscene vocabulary that would have elicited the envy of any seasoned sailor or traveled truck driver. And he didn't limit himself to the use of the same profane phrases over-and-over again, ad nauseum; nope, the wily senior was too sophisticated for that. The patron saint of smut had the unique ability to combine certain words together—creating a descriptive expression that would be

9

offensive to *anyone* around him — one of Henry's favorites was "pig fornicator."

Taking immense pride in his unsavory slang, Henry became a connoisseur of the cuss-word, mixing and matching obscenities that would best accommodate his particular conversation or situation — even to the point of applying the art of alliteration in the deliverance of a choice selection of his vulgar verbalizations. Even though he had barely attained an eighth grade education, Henry must have paid special attention in English class that day when the teacher was discussing the merits of alliteration in sentence construction. To question if old man Pickridge had a foul mouth would be as ridiculous as asking if the Pope were Catholic — or, in Henry's language — if the Trojan Horse had a wooden dick, or if a bear craps in the woods.

The silver-haired speaker of smut did his research. Curious about the origin of cusswords, he visited the town library and learned about some interesting historic accounts pertaining to the derivation of certain obscenities. Take the word *crap*, for example. Henry read in *The History Book of Slang*, that this word is merely a shortened version of the name Crapper, taken from the English plumber and royal sanitary engineer, Thomas Crapper, the inventor of the modern toilet.

Henry's verbal antics were even too much for his wife, Mabel, to handle. She divorced the foul-mouthed fogy many years ago for what her lawyer called *irreconcilable differences*. Differences…yes; irreconcilable…definitely. "Fix me my damn dinner, you bony bitch!" wasn't exactly the most romantic of phrases one could use to greet a wife when arriving home after a hard day's work. And Mabel didn't appreciate Henry's gift

of alliteration either, especially when it was used *that* way —
no woman appreciates being called the "b" word. The old
geezer's lewd language had kept him a bachelor ever since —
no self-respecting female would even think about tolerating
his vocally offensive shenanigans.

Henry was truly the father of filthy four-letter-words. If
the citizens of Tranquil ever decided to hand out an award
for "The Most Potty-mouthed Citizen," he would be its proud
recipient, winning hands down. It would be a dream come
true for Henry — one that he pictured often. The master of
ceremony would heartily announce to a hushed audience,
"This year, the recipient of 'The Most Potty-mouthed Citizen
of Tranquil' award goes to...Henry Pickridge!" The crowd
would erupt into loud clapping, cheers, and cat whistles.

Old Henry, dressed in his best fishing outfit, would
graciously walk across the stage to receive the prestigious
honor. The boozer would step up to the microphone and read
from a wrinkled napkin that he had scribbled his acceptance
speech on earlier. *"I humbly accept this bitchin award and I want
to thank all you a-holes out there who voted for me!"*

The unruly members of the cheering audience would go
crazy — hooting and hollering, screaming and yelling — some
chanting "Hen — ry...Hen — ry....Hen — ry," while others
would cry out, "You da man, Henry...you da man!" Amiably
waving and throwing kisses to his rowdy admirers, Henry
would proudly exit the stage, shining trophy in hand. Like
perpetual constants of the universe; the earth revolves on its
axis every day and Henry Pickridge cusses — that was the
name of that tune.

Around six months ago, Henry camped out one night

next to Fletcher's Pool, a small pond that was located about five miles north of Tranquil. There were some nice trout that resided in the deep fishing hole, and he was going to try to catch a stringer-full. The only way to get there was to travel on Route 44—a poorly maintained, winding mountain road that everyone used before they built the new highway to Tranquil six years ago. Now, the pothole-ridden artery was only utilized by those wishing to fish, swim, or picnic at Fletcher's Pool, although occasionally, a group of backpackers would also take the scenic journey to explore the wooded hills and grassy valleys enveloping the area. Henry fished there many times before, so he was familiar with the surrounding countryside. He parked his old blue pickup truck, and set up camp about fifty feet away from the dirt road that was adjacent to the small body of turquoise water.

Henry was the proud owner of a 1965 Chevrolet pickup truck that still sported its original factory paint job, except that now, as a result of weather and time, the "blue" had degenerated into at least five distinct shades of color—ranging from light gray to dark purple. He would affectionately refer to his well-traveled vehicle as *Betsy—Ole' Betsy* if she wouldn't start. All of the townsfolk in Tranquil were familiar with Henry Pickridge's mode of transportation—it was the ancient, broken-down, bluish pickup truck sporting the white sticker with red printing on the back bumper that read, *IF YOU CAN READ THIS, THEN YOU ARE DRIVING TOO CLOSE TO ME — SO BACK OFF, JACKASS!* And Scotch-taped to the truck's rear window was a sign saying, *When Guns Are Outlawed, Only Outlaws Will Have Guns!* Henry was just that kind of a guy—a free spirit who didn't give a rat's butt about what others thought of him.

After starting a small fire from the kindling he had gathered from a nearby wooded area, Henry sat down next to the warmth in his worn-out folding sports chair — one that he purchased many years ago when living in Irving, Texas. The seat and back supports of his wooden throne were constructed from some type of cloth fabric, now noticeably discolored and tattered from weather and wear. Imprinted on the frayed seat was a faded image of a blue-and-white football helmet, and stenciled on the back of the armchair were the washed-out and barely legible words, *Dallas Cowboys*. For all the years that Henry lived in Irving, he had never attended a Dallas Cowboy's football game, but he *did* use that chair religiously — for all other outdoor events.

Gazing upward, Henry took off his raggedy New York Yankees baseball cap and repeatedly repositioned it on his head until it felt just right. The full moon was out that night, shining brightly in all its splendor, and there wasn't a single, solitary cloud in sight. His eyes followed the somber stretch of dusky sky, dotted with twinkling luminaries that radiated their brilliance in a way that reminded him of countless white sequins reflecting off of a solid black evening dress. As Henry meditated the vastness of the firmament above, an occasional streaming white trail of a distant shooting star would entice his peripheral vision, only to disappear from sight as he turned to observe its celestial journey.

While downing several shots of his favorite brew, Henry noticed some strange blinking lights — darting in a zigzag pattern, much like a misguided bottle rocket — moving across the clear, nocturnal sky.

"Well, crap fire and save your matches," Henry spouted. "What, in the name of fornication, is that?"

As the mysterious flashing beams approached his campsite, he could visually make out the outline of a cigar-shaped metallic object, dark gray in color. A dome-like structure extended upward from the middle third of the craft, and Henry estimated the soaring thing's length to be about fifty feet. There was absolutely no sound emanating from the unidentified flying object, which hovered effortlessly in a fixed position over the gently swaying, neighboring treetops.

In a state of awe, Henry vigilantly rose from his chair—eyes bugged out and mouth gaped open—astounded by the surreal presence and sheer magnificence of this alien mechanical masterpiece. He watched intently as the Mack Truck-sized, sheeny Cuban cigar peacefully glided over the nearby assemblage of towering evergreens. Then in one smooth fluid motion, like a raindrop falling from a leaf, it vertically descended out of sight—into an open meadow located about a hundred yards away from his camp.

"Mamma mia...if that's what I think it is, I'll kiss a rang-o-tang's butt," quipped the old-timer, as he followed the flying saucer's flight through inebriated eyes.

Outwardly, Henry tried to remain calm, but inside the retired miner's chest sat an adrenaline-driven heart that was fluttering faster than a thumping pair of hummingbird wings. His wrinkled flesh crawled with goose bumps, sending a huge wave of chills streaming down the entire length of the weathered fisherman's scrawny back. Momentarily spellbound by this strange and unusual event, Henry slowly took off the scruffy baseball cap and scratched his grizzled head, pondering about what his next move should be.

Sitting down next to the fire, he took a big swig out of the whisky bottle, swallowed hard, and then wiped his alcohol-soaked lips on his dirty shirtsleeve. As he stared across at the crackling flames, a wisp of crisp mountain air coolly caressed his pensive face. Heaving a deep sigh of deliberation, Henry screwed the cap back on his glass container of booze and defiantly stood up.

"A man's gotta do what a man's gotta do!" he crowed.

The effects of the alcohol may have helped, but the determined old imbiber had made up his mind. He walked over to his truck, opened the door, and grabbed the ivory handled Smith & Wesson, three-fifty-seven magnum, snub-nosed revolver lying on the seat, tucking it under his belt, behind his back. There was a history behind this hand-held cannon that fired .357 magnum bullets—hollow-point projectiles with enough power to knock down a Clydesdale horse. It had belonged to his big brother, Fred, who was a member of the Phoenix Police Department—a senior detective with only three months of duty left until his retirement—when he was killed in the line of duty. Needlessly murdered by two new members of a street gang robbing a 7-Eleven convenience store as a part of their initiation. It was around four in the morning, and Fred had walked through the front door to buy a pack of cigarettes, catching the robbers totally by surprise. They had already killed the store clerk, so the pair of punks emptied five caps into the unsuspecting detective— Fred was dead before he hit the ground. Never even had a chance to un-holster his gun. The thieves got away with less than a hundred dollars. This was just one of the thousands of countless, senseless murders that occurs every day when someone is in the wrong place at the wrong time. Henry used to jokingly caution his brother, "Fred, those damn cigarettes are going to kill you someday," and he was right—in a bizarre, *Twilight Zone* sort of way, it was the addiction to the neatly papered cylinders of tobacco that were responsible for the police detective's untimely death—Rod Serling himself could have authored the script, with its unforeseen O'Henry ending. Never in his wildest dreams would Henry have thought that something like this could have ever happened to his only brother. The sterling Smith & Wesson was happily gifted to him by Fred's wife, who never, ever wanted to see a gun again in her life. Henry always kept the firearm close by, treasuring it as a memento, in commemoration of his brave older brother.

Hell-bent on finding out what the metal thing with the aerial acrobatic maneuvers was, Henry slammed the truck door closed, walked back to the fire, and downed another big gulp of liquor. Then he set out toward the UFO's landing site—located due west of his campsite, just beyond the haughty rows of pine, juniper, and fir trees that majestically bordered Fletcher's Pool.

Slowly making his way through the arbor of wooded columns, Henry's eyes caught a glimpse of fluorescent light, shimmering brightly from the settled saucer ahead. As the surplus of coniferous branches gestured in the wind, the rays of illumination radiating from the alien ship twinkled and flickered, like shiny strands of colored tinsel draped loosely over the boughs of a freshly cut Christmas tree.

Exiting a thick grove of ponderosa pines, Henry observed the gargantuan metallic beast with its collection of blinking lights, obscurely nestled in the open grassy field ahead. As he approached the docked spacecraft, the only sounds audible were the high-pitched chirpings of the crickets around him. The jittery old coot slowly and silently walked through the thick grass, cautiously stopping about ten feet away from the mystical flying machine. A sudden gust of howling wind swept across the open meadow, upsetting the rabble of wild flowers clustered around Henry's feet. The perennials thrashed about angrily, making thumping sounds as they unmercifully whipped against the pant legs of his trousers.

Standing motionless and taking in a slow deep breath, the amazed septuagenarian marveled at the exquisiteness of the interplanetary phenomenon from another universe. The smooth outer surface of the saucer was fabricated from a dark gray metallic substance, an alloy that Henry had never seen before. Flashing luminescent lights, which reflected a kaleidoscope of brilliant colors, extended in a horizontal fashion around the centrally placed dome. Five symmetrically placed, teardrop-shaped landing extensions projected from the belly of the craft to the ground below.

Henry had watched enough documentaries about military aircraft on television to know that the complex design of this mechanical creation was far too sophisticated to have come from *this* Earth. Besides, there were no jets that he knew of that could instantly reverse their direction of flight while traveling at such fantastic speeds — physically defying the laws of gravity.

This thing was definitely extraterrestrial.

Henry happened to look down at the gold plated watch strapped to his left wrist — an inexpensive timepiece he had received as a retirement gift from the Midas Mining Company. Its luminous white hands were spinning like an airplane propeller, stopping at the high noon mark that was pointed directly at the spacecraft in front of him. He frowned and grunted, "Suck my sausage...this goddam watch had better not be broken—it's almost brand-spanking new!" The perturbed souse moved his arm at a forty-five degree angle, extending it away from his body, and like clockwork, the hands again spun furiously, this time ending up praying to the three on the dial. Henry shook his wrist and said, "Must be some son-of-a-bitchin magnetic thing...from that freakin flyin contraption over there." In reality, the retired miner was clueless when it came to knowing *anything* about wristwatches, magnetic forces, or for that matter, alien saucers from outer space.

From a distance, the curious elder examined the UFO's outer structure, but could see no seams, rivets, joints, or openings on the exterior of the ship, so he carefully moved in closer to get a better look.

Then something suddenly dawned on Henry. There was no sound coming from the landed spacecraft.

Not a peep.

He cocked his head and listened.

Nothing.

It was disturbingly quiet—*too quiet* to suit Henry. A particular reminiscent thought flashed through the old codger's boggled mind. He recalled the 1951 science fiction epoch, *The Day The Earth Stood Still*, a movie that he had seen countless times before. *Would an invisible door suddenly slide open, exposing Gort, the giant frickin alien metal robot that could beam out disintegration rays from where its eyes should be?*

Unsure if he would be facing friend or foe, Henry slowly and carefully reached behind his back, pulled the snub-nosed firearm from his belt, and held it nervously at his side.

Not knowing what to do next, Henry took a deep breath in and anxiously cleared his throat. His voice quivered as he called out, "Hel...hello, is any...anyone there? Any...body.... home?...I ca...come in peace!"

Silence.

There was no response from inside the metal aircraft that had arrived from another planet.

Attempting to pacify his building anxiety, Henry jokingly recited the outer space vocabulary he had memorized from his favorite old sci-fi movie — the utterances used to keep the giant robot from harming any Earthlings — "Gort...Klaatu... Barada...Nicto!" The old drunk felt really stupid saying that, but those were the only alien words that he knew of, and besides, it couldn't hurt.

Again, no reply was given to the trembling alcoholic.

Henry swallowed hard, gripped the pearl handle of his magnum tightly, and began to slowly raise the barrel.

Without warning, a condensed beam of rainbow-colored light discharged from the undersurface of the craft, seizing the surprised senior citizen in its paralyzing grip. Henry struggled to get away, but was unable to move a muscle or scream for help. The gray hair on the back of his neck stood on end, sending a cold shiver down his bony spine. Henry was so horrified that he thought he was going to lose control of his bowels — *take a crap, pinch a loaf, or dump a deuce* in his pants, as he would fondly say. He was petrified...too petrified to do anything! The terrified tippler wouldn't have been able

19

to drop a load even if he had wanted to.

Son-of-a-bitch! I'm screwed…what am I gonna do now?

Henry was trapped. He was helpless.

The engrossing iridescent shaft of luminosity lifted the senior citizen slowly and methodically toward the ship. Floating ever closer to the mammoth spacecraft, the frightened old-timer sensed that someone or *something* inside was watching him.

From nowhere, and without making a sound, a small oval-shaped panel slid open on the hard metallic covering of the UFO, discharging a yellow cloud of foul-smelling gaseous material into the air. Henry caught a whiff of the vapory miasma, which reminded him of the sour acid reek that he had occasionally inhaled when he was a miner, working in the deep shafts of the molybdenum mines. It was a fetid smell that he would never forget. The stench was overwhelming, so Henry held his breath to avoid inhaling any of the noxious fumes.

As the gas slowly dissipated, he caught a shadowed glimpse of something moving from inside the ship. Rapidly blinking his irritated eyes in order to help clear up the blurry vision, the drunkard could barely make out the gangly figure of an alien being—human-like in appearance—lumbering directly towards him from within the portal opening.

Henry wasn't one to believe in creatures from outer space—the only aliens he knew of were the illegal ones from south of the border—those with black hair and brown skin that spoke no English and worked for below minimum wage. *Old man Pickridge was in for one helluva surprise!*

Holy Jesus! What the hell's that thing?

As the dark anthropomorphic being approached, Henry squinted to try to see its face, but was unable to discern any features — only that it possessed a large, oblong-shaped head.

Don't come any closer, you overgrown alien piss-ant!

A monstrous reptilian-like extremity reached out for him, grabbing at his frayed shirt collar. The limb was bulky and muscular, covered with coarse green scales. Four long flexible fingers with two opposable thumbs, joined together by bands of thick fleshy webbing, extended from the animal's grotesque hand. Projecting out from the end of each lime-colored digit was a thick, black fingernail — a horny claw that was long and curved, with serrations — ending in a razor-sharp point. Henry's heart was pounding like a rock band's drummer, and he could feel the surge of adrenaline racing throughout his quivering body.

Do I still have my…where's my damn gun? Even though he couldn't move his arms, Henry sensed that the revolver still remained at his side, its pearl handle tightly gripped in the sweaty palm of his trembling right hand.

Closing both eyes and using every ounce of strength that he could muster, he moved his right wrist just enough to elevate the snub-nosed barrel of the Smith & Wesson. Unable to accurately aim his gun, he would have to shoot from the hip, just like a quick-draw artist — only minus the quick-draw part.

The saurian hand latched onto Henry's left shoulder, and the frail old man could feel the vise-like grip of the beast's claws painfully tighten down on his bony flesh.

Then a terrifying thought raced through his head.

This motherthumpin thing is gonna kill me…I don't wanna

die…not like this! Henry didn't want to end up like his brother, the haphazard recipient of a senseless murder. *You weren't given no chance to do anything, Fred, but I will…I will, dammit!*

Panicked but determined, the leather-skinned whiskey guzzler concentrated all of his will on his right index finger, which was firmly curled around the contoured trigger of the .357. Even if he could only fire off one round, his hollow pointed slug was bound to inflict some serious damage to whomever or *whatever* it hit.

Come on, you pussy…squeeze your finger…pull the trigger… move the hammer…shoot the freakin gun!

Forcefully flexing his forefinger, he felt the metal trigger slowly begin to budge, then depress.

Screw you and the horse you rode in on, you alien bastard!

The trigger finally yielded to his finger pressure, firing the weapon once—discharging its deadly hollow-nosed projectile in the direction of the alien aggressor.

"Boooom!"

The report echoed through his ears—a deafening sound, as if two symbols had been clashed together next to Henry's head. The recoil of the magnum's barrel was so intense that the gun flew out of the old man's hand and landed on the grassy ground below his levitated feet. A cloud of blue-gray smoke fumed before the alcoholic's terror-filled eyes, and the strong distinctive odor of gunpowder permeated throughout his flared nostrils. Those were the last things that Henry remembered before he passed out.

\#

When Henry awoke, it was daylight, and the sodden old-timer found himself at the campsite, lying on his sleeping bag, fully clothed, with his baseball cap and shoes still on. The elder's revolver, along with his half-full bottle of liquid spirits, lay innocently on the grass next to him.

"What…what in the name of Jesus H. Christ is going on?"

Groggy and disoriented, the rousing rummy slowly lifted himself from the sleeping bag and sat up. His head throbbed, and he felt woozy and weak—like he had been drugged with a Mickey Finn. Henry instinctively reached over for his nearby bottle of hooch, uncapped it, and tossed down a few nips of intoxicant.

"Oh, man…I feel like hammered dog crap."

Wait a minute…how the hell did I get here? Was that all a dream…a damn hallucinatory? I didn't drink enough to pass out… did I?

Henry popped his baseball cap off and swept back his scraggly locks of silver hair with both hands. The old alcoholic had suffered through enough hangovers to know that the sensations in his head were very different from those symptoms that he usually experienced after a night of heavy boozing.

"This is just too friggin freaky!"

The befuddled inebriate felt mighty weird, and knew that something creepy had befallen him the night before— something he was presently unable to explain. Determined to find out what happened, Henry picked up his gun and walked back to the area where the UFO had landed. He meticulously explored every inch of the grassy field and found nothing— the saucer was gone, leaving no trace that it had ever been there before. No footprints, no blood, no wounded monster from outer space.

Jumping in his pickup, the dazed dipsomaniac raced back to town and reported his fantastic story to Buck Evans, the sheriff of Tranquil. Buck was very familiar with the alcoholic antics of Henry Pickridge—he had arrested the old coot several times before for drunk and disorderly conduct. The experienced lawman was extremely skeptical, but still drove out with the protesting boozer to search the area. When they arrived at Fletcher's Pool, Henry led Sheriff Evans to the grassy site where the alleged alien landing had occurred. They hunted for any signs of an extraterrestrial visit, but found nothing—there was no evidence to indicate that *anything* had landed there, much less a flying craft from outer space.

Most of the townsfolk never believed Henry's bizarre account, attributing it either to hallucinations conjured up by his alcohol-demented mind, or to the dream illusions associated with an affliction of sleep paralysis. Besides, no one else saw the flying saucer or any aliens, and the retired miner had no tangible proof to back up his startling story—except for the oddly shaped bruises on his left shoulder, and the fact that one of the bullets in his three-fifty-seven magnum had been fired.

Henry Pickridge was the talk of Tranquil for the past several months—and because nothing that exciting had ever occurred in the town before, the local gossips milked the scary story for everything it was worth. Frequenting the local bars in town, the liquor-loving lush would gladly spin his tale over a wet whiskey for anyone who would listen—especially if they paid for the drinks. Henry really didn't care whether they believed his grisly encounter with the alien or not—in his mind, he *knew* that it had happened.

\#

After enduring months of a snowy, harsh winter, the community of Tranquil approvingly welcomed the onset of beautiful spring weather. In preparation for the upcoming tourist season, the residents hung up a *"Welcome to Tranquil - The Quietest Town in Arizona"* sign over the street entrance to its business district—a city block of about twenty stores, shops, and eating establishments located on both sides of Main Street.

As an orange-red sunset slipped into the western sky, the townspeople prepared for the approaching darkness of night. Scattered puffs of grayish-white smoke could be seen arising from a handful of chimney tops, as the evening chill still had enough bite in it to warrant the welcome of a warming blaze in the household fireplace.

Most of the residents and newcomers had already departed the downtown area and were heading for home, but a few window shoppers could still be seen milling around the outside of some of the quaint gift shops that were interspersed along the row of small business establishments. Even though a spattering of rental cars belonging to a handful of visiting tourists remained parallel parked along the curb located on the north side of Main Street, virtually all of the shops and stores in town had pulled the shades, hung up their CLOSED signs, and locked their doors for the night. For now, everything was peaceful and quiet in the charming little mountain village of Tranquil...but that would all change drastically in the days to come.

Chapter II
NATIVITY

Joshua Allen grew up in Tranquil, the county seat of Juniper County. On a crisp spring night sixteen years ago, he was born at the local community hospital. The boy had always lived in Tranquil, but he wasn't like the other teenagers in town. In fact, Joshua just wasn't your average sixteen-year-old kid.

His father was Luke Allen, the preacher at the only non-denominational church around town. Luke was one of those hellfire and damnation evangelists who believed that he had been chosen by God to fight the Devil — and he was determined to exorcise any demon who attempted to possess any member of his small congregation.

Joshua's Mother, Mary, a meek and devout woman with

a kind and generous heart, was overshadowed by Luke, who believed that a righteous Christian wife should always be subservient to her husband. Mary and Luke had married late in life, and they desperately wanted the Lord to bless them with a child; so after two miscarriages, she became pregnant with Joshua at the age of forty.

Because of their strong religious convictions, Luke and Mary refused any prenatal care—they were determined to deliver their baby at home by natural childbirth—as they believed God had intended. Ignoring the pleas of friends and neighbors, no appointments were ever made with any doctors, and the pair of spiritual zealots adamantly refused to have any laboratory tests, ultrasounds, or amniocentesis performed on Mary. In spite of her advanced maternal age and lack of medical care, the pregnancy surprisingly progressed smoothly, and managed to proceed into the third trimester without any major complications.

Mary was convinced that her child would be a boy—she was carrying the baby low in her womb—a definite indication that it would be a male, according to her mother. In addition, the churchman and his wife had prayed to God to bless them with a son who could continue on with Luke's holy work in the ministry, spreading the gospel and expelling demons.

The boy would be named Joshua, in praise of Moses' successor and leader of the Israelites into the Promised Land. Mary believed that her Joshua was not destined to lead an ordinary life, but would develop into a person of special significance, positively affecting the lives of countless others around him—according to Mary, her son had been preordained for greatness.

Luke and Mary had just finished the baby nursery—a wooden crib purchased from the used furniture store, placed in the corner of the small back room that Luke had painted blue. The ninth month of pregnancy had been uneventful for Mary, and she was happily looking forward to the birth of Joshua, and the ensuing blissful maternity it would finally bring to her.

#

While home alone washing the dishes one evening, Mary experienced an abrupt twinge of tenderness, arising from her stomach as she reached up to place a dried drinking glass into the cupboard.

"Must have been something that I ate," she said to herself.

The pain only lasted a few seconds, and then subsided. Mary thought nothing of it, and continued on with her household tasks. A few minutes later, the discomfort menacingly returned to her lower abdominal area, this time exhibiting a much greater degree of intensity than the first encounter.

"Is that you, my sweet Joshua…why are you kicking me so hard?"

Suddenly, a violent jolt of excruciating pain gripped Mary's lower torso, forcing the pregnant woman to grab her swollen belly as she spontaneously doubled over in agony. It felt as if something inside of her was intensely pushing outward—frantically trying to tear its way through her womb—like a trapped malevolent entity endeavoring to madly break out of her body from within.

Oh, God, please make it go away! Mary had never experienced a paralyzing pain like this before, and she was

29

truly frightened—worried that it was a sign—an evil omen of bad things to come.

Unable to catch her breath, the unforgiving torture radiated throughout Mary's frail, wilting body—so unbearable and unrelenting that she feared she would pass out. Overtaken with lightheadedness and blurred vision, Mary closed her eyes and tried to breathe in a deep lungful of air. As she inhaled a mouthful of oxygen, the muscles in her legs began to convulse uncontrollably, progressively weakening to the point of being unable to support her wavering, fragile frame. Powerless to keep her balance, the wobbling woman collapsed like a house of cards, making a loud *thud* sound as her head hit the kitchen floor.

Dazed from the crumpling fall, Mary curled up into a fetal position, remaining as still as possible in an attempt to alleviate some of the intolerable pain she was suffering. As Mary lay motionless on the floor, she felt a surge of enormous pressure pounding against her pelvic wall. Without warning, the distraught woman's water burst, spouting out a waterfall of amniotic fluid down her legs and onto the kitchen linoleum tiles around her.

All alone, and in the quiet, Mary could feel and hear the hastened rhythm of her adrenaline-pumped, pulsating heart. "Please, God, don't let my baby die," she whispered.

Mary Allen wasn't just scared…she was terrified.

Luke, returning home from working late at the church, found his wife sprawled out on the kitchen floor in a pool of pinkish-colored fluid—barely conscious—muttering, "Save my boy, Joshua…save Joshua." He carefully picked Mary up into his arms, and carried her to their bed, gently laying her limp body down on the soft mattress. The apprehensive pastor positioned a big pillow behind her neck, and then rushed into the bathroom and returned with a wet washcloth. Tenderly brushing her long amber hair aside with one hand, he gently placed the cold rag onto her pallid forehead.

Invigorated by the stimulating sensation elicited from the cool wetness on her brow, Mary slowly opened her lovely hazel eyes. Aroused from a state of semi consciousness, she could barely make out the blurred image of her husband's visage above her head. As the revived wife blinked her blurry eyes, Luke's facial features gradually drew into sharper focus, imparting a serious expression of worry and concern on his face. The minister's hairy eyebrows, wrinkled forehead, and squinting blue eyes acted in concert to create a noticeable frown, indicative of the anxiety that he harbored over her ailing condition.

"Mary, honey, what happened?" he asked.

"I was at the sink, doing the dishes...I fell...I must have fainted...and then my...my water broke," she sighed.

"We need to pray to God to help us deliver our baby," said Luke, solemnly.

"Yes...yes...of course," mumbled Mary.

The clergyman kneeled down next to the head of the bed and grasped both of his wife's willowy hands, holding them securely in his.

"Let us pray," he said, closing his eyes tightly. "Our Father, who art in Heaven...."

Mary joined in, "Hallowed be thy Name...."

As she lay motionless on the bed, reciting the Lord's Prayer with her husband, Mary was abruptly made aware of a strange, disturbing sensation emanating from her pelvic area.

Looking down, the expectant mother made a frightening observation.

"Oh, God, no!' she screamed.

The white maternity stretch pants that she was wearing were rapidly changing into a burgundy color, right before her very eyes. The pregnant woman had begun to hemorrhage—profusely and rampantly. Blood was furiously leaking out everywhere.

Witnessing this horror, Luke grabbed a large towel from the bathroom, placed it between his wife's legs, and exerted pressure—futilely attempting to impede the rushing flow of red fluid that had already saturated her clothing. Like a snake that had been struck a deadly blow, Mary began writhing in agony, the recipient of an ominous abdominal injury.

"Try to hold still, Mary!" cried Luke, as he struggled to reposition the towel to stop the gush of dark blood spilling from between her legs.

"Ooohh…Oh, dear Lord, *the pain!*" she moaned.

Flailing her arms and legs wildly over the bed, Mary's entire body began to jerk spasmodically—like an uncontrollable puppet dangling from a string. In order to prevent his distressed wife from heaving herself off of the mattress, Luke laid on top of her, almost as if he were a wrestler pinning his opponent—positioning his body directly over Mary's spastically convulsing torso, in order to keep her from injuring herself. As the thrashing woman lost consciousness, her eyes rolled back in her head, and her lurching body suddenly turned noodle-limp.

Using the drenched towel to reapply pressure to the area

of bleeding, the evangelical extremist rambled through his recitation of holy prayers and religious readings. Seeing that his wife was progressively getting worse, a frightened and distraught Luke once more summoned God's help. Extending his arms upward, he cried out, "Dear God…omniscient and omnipotent creator of Heaven and Earth…I beseech thee to extend your powerful hand down and cleanse my mortal wife from the evil sickness that has taken over her body!"

After several minutes of prolonged prayer by the concerned cleric, Mary regained consciousness and tried to speak, but the words delivered from her mouth were distorted and foreign to Luke—she was using a language unfamiliar to him.

"*Lu sa te bay…me jash…hell em…mi bay,*" she mumbled deliriously.

Luke listened intently, but could make no sense out of her bizarre utterances.

"*Te bo…milaba se bo…je mira.*"

Mary has never spoken like this before, he thought.

To Luke's dismay, his aphasic wife continued to spew out rambling locutions of unintelligible dialect.

Is Mary speaking in tongues…has some unearthly spirit taken possession of her soul? he wondered.

Disturbed by her peculiar vocalizations, Luke believed that his only hope to save Mary rested in an exorcism, or a *deliverance from evil,* as he called it. God willing and with Bible in hand, the evangelist was determined to purge his wife's body of the vile demon responsible for her rapidly deteriorating condition. With the palm of his right hand firmly pressed to Mary's perspiring forehead, Luke exhorted, "In the name of

Jesus Christ, Son of almighty God, I command you evil spirit to depart this body! Leave this God-fearing Christian woman, and return to your fiery pit in Hell, never to return to Earth to invade the innocent souls of God's children!"

For the next hour, while she slipped in and out of consciousness, the unremitting reverend sustained his acts of soul-saving exorcism, resolute to complete the deliverance of his beloved wife, Mary. Every religious incantation and prayer that the man of God could think of was verbalized on her behalf, yet in spite of his pious convictions and eternal persistence, Luke was unable to heal her. He watched helplessly as the love of his life lapsed into a state of oblivion, unresponsive to the world around her. Lovingly caressing her ashen face, he cried, "Wake up, Mary, please wake up! You can't leave me now...I love you...I need you!"

Mary's comatose body continued to lay lifeless on the bed, impassive to her frantic husband's compassionate pleadings. Luke's disheveled black hair dangled limply over his wrinkled brow, as he stared down at his dying wife. The distressed preacher looked upward, a swelling of tears filling both eyes. "I don't know what to do, God...please give me a sign...anything...just tell me what to do!"

The patient parson waited, but no sign from the Almighty appeared. In an act of desperation, he finally phoned one of his congregation, who quickly summoned help to the preacher's house. Upon entering the bedroom, the midwife encountered a disturbing and horrifying image—Mary's unconscious body lying motionless on the blood-soaked covers of her bed, with Luke kneeling nearby, quoting verses from the Bible. The midwife nurse recognized the seriousness of the situation and immediately called 911.

By the time the ambulance finally arrived, Mary, in shock from profound blood loss, had descended into a deep somnolence, unresponsive to any external stimuli. As they loaded her traumatized body onto the gurney, the paramedics observed the inert woman exhibiting an abnormal breathing pattern—a rhythmic waxing and waning of her depths of respiration, with intervals of apnea—one of the classic signs of coma. En route to the hospital, Mary's heart suddenly stalled out, plunging the unfortunate woman into a disastrous cardiac arrest, necessitating cardiopulmonary resuscitation. One of the members of the emergency medical team hurriedly thrust an endotracheal tube down her throat, attached a squeezable rubber bag to the end of the plastic hose that extended from her mouth, and began ventilating her lungs. Using the exposed palm of his clasped hands, the other EMT straddled Mary and initiated chest compressions to her oxygen-starved heart. The expeditious paramedics worked in repetitive synchrony—five quick chest compressions followed by one big squeeze from the black bag containing fresh air. They toiled feverishly over the preacher's wife, doing everything in their power to keep the poor woman alive.

#

By the time Mary reached the Tranquil Community Hospital emergency room, her vital signs were absent, and there was no electrical activity observed on the heart monitor.

Dr. Ted Tisdale, the emergency room physician, speedily positioned the gelled defibrillator paddles on Mary's bare chest and shouted, "Clear!" He thumbed the red button on one paddle, discharging the thousand volts of electrical

35

current that would instantly surge through the woman's fluid-depleted heart.

Tha-thum!

Mary's upper torso lurched from the table and made three rhythmic spasmodic jerks, as if she were suffering from a grand mal seizure. Dr. Tisdale glanced over at the EKG. There was no electrical activity. No blips. No sound. Nothing. He repositioned the paddles around her left breast.

"Clear!" he yelled.

Ka-thum!

Mary's back arched, bouncing her chest momentarily upwards—only to rigidly slam back down on the hard table.

Still motionless.

Ted viewed the monitor again…flatline. He palpated her carotid artery for a pulse…no sign…empty…lifeless.

Bright hazel eyes that once reflected joy and happiness were now dull and gray. Only a cold, vacant stare into nothingness could be observed in Mary's fixed and dilated pupils. Her ravaged body and contorted facial expression reflected an anguished, agonizing torment that no God-fearing human should ever have to endure.

Dr. Tisdale and his staff were helpless to do anything for Mary at this point in time. In the game of craps called life, the roll of her dice had turned up snake-eyes, and she had tragically died before giving birth to her son, Joshua.

"We did everything we could to save her," sighed Bill, one of the paramedics who had feverishly worked on the moribund woman in the ambulance.

"I know you did, Bill," responded the doctor, in a comforting tone. "We'll have to pronounce her now."

"Time of death is 11:57 P.M.," lamented Ted, as he scribbled down the juncture of her demise on the hospital chart.

Peering up at his staff with a newly found look of resolution in his dark blue eyes, the emergency room physician barked, "By God, we couldn't save this woman, but let's see if we can rescue her unborn baby! Prep and drape off her abdomen, and get me a surgical tray, *stat!*"

An emergency C-section would have to be performed immediately on Mary's dead body in order to have any hope of saving her child's life.

Ted donned a mask, then hurriedly scrubbed his hands in the sink and snapped on a pair of surgical gloves. He grabbed the scalpel from the surgical tray, and in one smooth motion made a sweeping, fifteen-inch transverse incision in Mary's lower abdomen — penetrating through the skin, underlying fat, fascia, and peritoneum. There was virtually no bleeding since rigor mortis had already begun to manifest its telltale signs; the dead woman's crimson-colored liquid of life had been grotesquely transformed into a coagulated black sludge, negating the need for extensive cauterization of any blood vessels.

Like a hot knife through butter, the sharpened steel blade continued to penetrate through Mary's cadaverous flesh. Entering the peritoneal cavity, Dr. Tisdale exposed the underlying uterus that had been the home to Joshua for the past nine months. The emergency room physician promptly grasped the uterus with hemostats and made a horizontal incision in its lower portion, uncovering the top of a tiny hairy head. As Ted liberated the newborn through the surgically-made uterine opening, the nurse rapidly suctioned the baby's nose and throat to help prevent any aspiration of fluid into its pristine lungs. Now, fully extracted from the confines of his mother's dead body, the baby could be easily visualized by everyone in the room.

"It's a boy," said Ted.

A baby boy—just as Mary and Luke had predicted—a son named Joshua...but something was seriously wrong.

Instead of the rosy pink skin color exuded by most healthy newborns, the infant's integument was a disturbing deep blue color, indicative of severe hypoxia—there was no telling how long he had been deprived of oxygen in his mother's dying womb. In addition, the baby was motionless and exhibited no outward signs of life.

Troubled about the child's condition, Ted cautioned, "He's not breathing, and there's no pulse."

The emergency room was silent.

With no palpable heartbeat and no respiratory efforts appreciated, the emergency room physician pulled down his mask and immediately attempted to resuscitate the lifeless, plum-skin colored baby. Using his right index and middle fingers for chest compression, Ted alternately expelled small, controlled puffs of air into the newborn's mouth, delivering the energy of life to Joshua's oxygen-famished lungs. All that was heard in the room was the sound of the doctor's exhaled breath entering the baby boy's mouth every three to four seconds.

"Phew...phew...phew...phew...phew."

After about a minute of what seemed to be an eternity, one of the nurses exclaimed, "Look, he moved his hand!"

The rest of the emergency room staff piped in. "Come on

little guy, you can make it!" cheered a paramedic.

"Yes…yes…he's starting to come around!" cried another.

The doctor was exceedingly encouraged that Joshua's cyanotic skin color had now adopted a more robust pink tone. He stopped the chest compressions momentarily and placed the tip of his index finger on Joshua's elfin neck. The delicate throb of a subtle heartbeat was palpated by Ted's discerning digit; faint initially, but getting stronger with each systole. There was also a rising motion of the sternum and rib cage — Joshua was breathing on his own now, without any assistance. Movement of the arms and legs followed, and a soft kitten's cry emerged from the newborn's tiny trembling lips.

Joshua was alive! The odds had been heavily stacked against him, but he had made it. The neonate opened his blue eyes for the first time and looked around the emergency room, where he was greeted with smiling faces and happy voices. One of the nurses quickly wrapped the shivering baby boy in a warm blanket, and placed him in a heated bassinet.

On the bloodied table next to Joshua lay the lifeless, disfigured corpse of his beloved mother, Mary, whose surgical violation had resulted in her son's miraculous salvation. She was wearing what was left of her favorite blue and pink flowered blouse, a gift from her first baby shower. In all the mayhem, the garment had been ripped apart and most of its buttons were missing. Even though the fabric had been stained a deep crimson color from the blood splatter, you could still make out the three words that had been artistically sewn on the front of the blouse — *Baby On Board*.

Joshua turned his tiny head toward Mary's dead body. As if controlled by some supernatural force, his eyes eerily fixated on her somber face. After carefully studying his mother's features for a set period of time, the boy's initial joyful look of recognition rapidly deteriorated into an empty expression of sadness — like he had possessed an extrasensory awareness of what had just happened to his birth-giver. Tears welled up in both of Joshua's baby blue eyes, then overflowed and rolled gently down his pink cherub cheeks.

The nurse pulled the sheet up over the dead woman's frozen face — it would be the first and last time that Joshua would ever lay eyes upon his sweet mother again. Mary Allen was cruelly denied the fulfillment of her dreams of motherhood, and Joshua would never have the opportunity to experience the love she had carried for him. Incredibly, the newborn boy had beaten the odds and inexplicably survived a most horrible ordeal — this time he had escaped the finality of death — but not the uncertainty of life.

Chapter III
JOSHUA

"...happy birthday, dear Joshua...happy birthday to you!" sang the ninth grade students.

Patrick Murdock patted Joshua Allen on the back and said, "I can't believe you're sixteen today."

"Yeah," said another classmate.

"Hey, Joshua, do you feel any older?" asked Patrick.

The sixteen-year-old shook his head from side to side.

"You can blow out your candles now, Joshua," said Mrs. Ravens, the biology teacher who had arranged his school birthday party.

"*Ass-hum!*" replied Joshua, exhibiting a toothy smile.

Everyone in the class roared.

Joshua didn't suffer from any speech impediments per se,

but had the peculiar habit of parroting the slang sayings and colloquialisms of his best friend, Patrick. Just recently he had picked up the word *awesome*, but still didn't exactly know how to properly pronounce it.

"What did you say?" inquired the teacher.

"Ass-hum!" repeated the boy.

Again, the students reacted with a loud hoot.

Ass hum. It sounded like some rare, exotic disease that only a proctologist could treat.... *"Mrs. Smith, please hold very still — I've positioned the proctoscope, and I see what the source of that annoying humming sound is — I'll have that kazoo out of your butt in no time!"*

Mrs. Ravens wiped the smile from her face and said, "Joshua, you meant to say *awesome*...it's pronounced ah'sŭm."

"Yeah, ass-hum, totally ass-hum," said the birthday boy.

Uncontrollable laughter erupted once more — this time, Mrs. Ravens even got a chuckle out of it. Joshua's malapropisms were always humorous.

The teenager looked down at his birthday cake, covered with gleaming white frosting applied in irregular swirls — it reminded him of curled waves in a stormy sea. On top of the cake were the words, *Happy Birthday Joshua*, written in cursive with decorative blue frosting. Sixteen burning, pink wax candles, placed in four evenly spaced rows, stood flickering below the acknowledgment.

Joshua took in a deep breath of air and pursed his lips tightly. Before he could exhale, he heard a loud whooshing sound coming from behind him — over his right shoulder. To his astonishment, the flames of all sixteen birthday candles were extinguished instantly by the unwelcome gust of air.

"Hey!" yelled the birthday party's guest of honor.

As Joshua turned around, he caught sight of one of his classmates, Niles Slovinsky, standing behind him, flaunting an ugly smirk on his freckled, acne-ridden face. The leering boy's ragged red hair was sloppily parted down the middle, with his forelocks combed forward, draped randomly over both eyebrows.

"Why'd you blow out my candles?" asked Joshua.

Niles reached over and stuck his finger in the frosted birthday cake, and then licked the creamy icing off the tip of his withdrawn digit.

"Too slow on the draw, retard," laughed Niles.

"You just bought yourself a detention, Mr. Slovinsky," said Mrs. Ravens.

"Whatever," replied the redheaded teen, nonchalantly.

Niles Slovinsky was not the sharpest pencil in the box, but he took pride in being the token bully of Tranquil High School, a *persona non grata*, targeting Joshua for many of his callous jokes and cruel pranks.

Joshua turned and glared at the acne-faced troublemaker, his facial features reflecting an expression of annoyance and anger. Prominent epicanthal folds adjacent to Joshua's blue eyes, along with a flat, wide nose, projected the menacing appearance of an angry cobra, ready to strike.

Using the index finger of his right hand, Joshua pointed at his tormentor and said, "I don't like you. You're not nice… no…you're not nice at all."

"What are you looking at, mongoloid?" Niles shot back. "And I don't like you either, because you're a stupid idiot."

Joshua's best friend, Patrick, rushed over and pushed the

carrot-topped teen in the chest. "What's your problem, dude?" yelled Patrick.

"Yeah, what's your problem, *douche*?" mimicked Joshua.

The kids in Mrs. Raven's class all exploded into hysterical laughter over Joshua's inadvertent word play.

"Mind your own business," said Niles.

"This *is* my business," retorted Patrick.

Mrs. Ravens walked over to the juvenile delinquent, and in a stern voice reprimanded him. "That's enough, young man. I've had just about enough of your antics...go to the principal's office right this minute!"

Niles shrugged his shoulders and said, "Whatever."

He sneered at Patrick and Joshua, and yelled, "I'll settle up with you two spazzes later...you'll wish you'd never been born!" Then Niles stormed out of the classroom, slamming the door loudly behind him.

Retard, mongoloid, stupid idiot. Joshua knew what all the words meant—he had been called those names many times before.

Joshua Allen was the unlucky recipient of one of the most common genetic mishaps known to man, occurring approximately once in every one-thousand births—unfortunately, his mother's advanced maternal age of 40 had increased Joshua's odds of inheriting the defect to one in one-hundred.

In 1866, a physician and superintendent of an asylum for children with mental retardation in Surrey, England, published an essay that described a group of progeny with common features distinctly different from other offspring afflicted with mental retardation. At first, individuals with

44

this genetic disease were referred to as mongoloids, because according to the medical investigators, the shape of their eyes resembled those of an Asian. This disorder was later referred to as Down's Syndrome, more recently shortened to *Down Syndrome*, in honor of its discoverer, Dr. John Langdon Down.

Sixteen years ago, Joshua was born with Down Syndrome, a genetic condition caused by an extra twenty-first chromosome.

Most people have twenty-three pairs of chromosomes, but individuals afflicted with Down Syndrome have three chromosomes instead of the normal two at the twenty-first chromosome level — hence the scientific name, *Trisomy XXI*. During fertilization, the chromosomes do not split properly, so a nondisjunction occurs, resulting in an extra copy of the twenty-first chromosome being passed on to the baby. The extra genetic DNA from chromosome twenty-one is responsible for certain characteristics seen in Trisomy XXI, resulting in some degree of mental retardation, cognitive disability, or developmental delay.

With a measured IQ of 70, Joshua was only mildly mentally retarded. Even though his mental capacity was equivalent to that of a first or second grader, he attended classes with the other ninth grade students at Tranquil High School. The town couldn't afford to have any special educational programs available for someone like Joshua, so he was placed in regular courses of study along with the other kids, only given a much easier curriculum.

Since Joshua had grown up in Tranquil, he was acquainted with most of the other classmates that attended his high school, and they all knew him, as well. Everyone got along very nicely with Joshua except for the Slovinsky boy—a kid with a mean and cruel personality who taunted and teased Joshua, constantly ridiculing his mental and physical handicaps. Niles derived pleasure from making fun of those less fortunate.

Mrs. Ravens' biology class had all voted to celebrate Joshua's sixteenth birthday by having a party, so today was *his* day, and Niles had tried to ruin that. Patrick could tell that Joshua was upset by what had happened, so he put his hand on his mentally compromised friend's shoulder and said, "Don't worry about him, Joshua…Niles is the one who's a stupid idiot. We're not going to let anybody ruin our fun, are we? Now, let's eat your birthday cake!"

Joshua's frown quickly turned into a smile. "Okay…yeah, you're right," he answered. "We're not gonna let Niles mess things up. You can have the biggest piece cuz you're my best friend!"

"No, I think I'll eat the whole thing," laughed Patrick.

"Are you joshin me?" giggled Joshua. The Down Syndrome boy would always use the line, "are you joshin me" when anyone would kid or joke with him. Since his name was Joshua, he thought that it was pretty funny that someone would be *joshing* him.

"Yeah, I'm just joshing you," answered his smiling friend.

Patrick was Joshua's next-door neighbor, and they had grown up together in Tranquil. As far back as Patrick could remember, he and Joshua had always been the best of buddies— inseparable. The two boys were even blood-brothers. One day after elementary school, while playing "Indians," they each pricked the tip of their forefinger with a sharp thorn from the neighbor's rosebush. Touching their bleeding pygmy digits together, they chanted in unison, "Blood-brothers to the end… blood-brothers until we die…blood-brothers forever!"

At a very young age, Patrick had realized that Joshua was different from the other kids, and would be looked upon as abnormal; he also knew that his genetically-altered friend would suffer from their cruelty, as well. As Joshua's guardian and protector, Patrick vowed that he would never let anything harmful happen to his blood-brother friend — so over the years, he had been involved in several episodes of fisticuffs, protecting Joshua from the malice of others. The two boys had a lasting bond that couldn't be broken.

Mrs. Ravens cut the adorned birthday cake into small appealing pieces, and placed each wedge on a colored paper plate. One of her students passed the slices out to the kids in class, while another poured punch into miniature plastic cups. The teacher looked over at Joshua and Patrick, standing alongside one another, hungrily gobbling down their tiny tidbit of delectable pastry. Patrick, easily a six-footer, dwarfed the diminutive Joshua, who barely stood five feet tall. The Trisomy XXI recipient had a stocky build — broad shoulders, a barrel chest, and a wide waist that was attached to thick, squatty legs. Patrick sported a lean, yet symmetrical physique — a well-developed, chiseled upper body that gradually tapered to join long, muscular legs.

Joshua imparted a facial appearance characteristic of Down Syndrome; a short thick neck, low-set ears, marked epicanthal eye folds, and a flattened bridge of the nose. His deep blue eyes and cropped blonde hair contrasted sharply with Patrick's dark brown eyes and thick black, curly locks.

Mrs. Ravens was very fond of Joshua, and like many of

the people around Tranquil, harbored a genuine heartfelt sympathy for the handicapped boy. The town gossip was that Joshua's father, Luke, had never emotionally recovered from the loss of his darling Mary, so the preacher bitterly resented Joshua—the retarded son he held responsible for his dear wife's death. According to Luke, Mary had been possessed by an evil spirit from Hades—causing her untimely demise, and resulting in the birth of Joshua, a demon-child of the dark angel.

As a preacher, Luke's religious fanaticism and distorted views of the scriptures were so bizarre that many of his small congregation had left the church. He had turned to the bottle for salvation, and Joshua's worst beatings occurred when Luke was on a drunken binge. In his fits of intoxication, the zealous diviner would literally try to beat the Devil out of his weak-minded son. Mrs. Ravens had witnessed the boy's bruises in class many times before. On several occasions she had queried Joshua about the injuries, but his rehearsed response was always the same—"I fell down and hurt myself."

Joshua was a happy-go-lucky, mentally challenged kid who possessed a kind and caring nature; there wasn't a mean bone in his body, and he would never harm anyone. He was an unfortunate child who sadly grew up missing the unquestionable love and heartened praise of a nurturing mother—an innocent boy, forced to endure the callous abuse of a vindictive father. Joshua deserved better than this.

The students quickly devoured every last crumb of Joshua's birthday cake, and were milling around the classroom, enjoying the free time off. As the school bell rang, Mrs. Ravens announced, "Please clean up around your desks and throw all of your trash in the waste basket. Oh, and by the way, this Monday, remember to bring the handout that I gave you on invertebrates — we're going to dissect an octopus tentacle. Class dismissed…have a nice weekend…and have a happy birthday, Joshua."

"Gross me out or what…a slimy octopus," said one disgusted-looking girl.

"That's enough to gag a maggot!" blurted out another.

"Happy birthday, Joshua…thanks for the cake Mrs. Ravens…see you on Monday….we won't forget the handout," yelled a small group of students as they left the classroom.

"Thanks for my birfday party, Missas Ravens…me and Patrick are goin to ride bikes after school today…and I can't wait to *infect* that *testicle* on Monday!" said Joshua.

Mrs. Ravens glimpsed over at Patrick, then shook her head and smiled. *Where did these sexual connotations come from?* She was starting to wonder if maybe Joshua had a little bit of Tourette's Disease intermingled with his Down Syndrome.

"You're more than welcome, Joshua…have fun on your bike ride," replied the teacher. "And Joshua, it's 'Patrick and I,' not 'me and Patrick,'…and we're going to *dissect*, not infect, a *tentacle*…it's pronounced ten'ta'kul…*not* testicle!"

Patrick looked over at Joshua and said jokingly, "Come on, Mr. Testicle, let's go."

With a quizzical expression glued to his face, Joshua peered up at Patrick and asked, "Are you joshin me?"

"Only joshing you," smiled Patrick. "It's time for us to go ride bikes now."

"Ass-hum!" giggled the Trisomy XXI boy.

Whenever Joshua laughed, his almond-shaped eyes

transformed into narrow slits, and his thick lips spread apart, revealing noticeably large teeth and gums. Buckteeth that looked like a row of Chicklets, anchored to over-developed gingiva, reminiscent of Mr. Ed, the talking horse. Even though the mentally challenged teen's outward appearance was disturbing to some, his inner joy and happiness was contagious; seeing Joshua giggle would bring a smile to the most solemn of observers—the type of infectious laugh that would even force the Mona Lisa to reveal her pearly whites.

Chapter IV
WRATH

Patrick and Joshua rode home in the yellow school bus that always picked them up and dropped them off at the same place—next to the white picket fence that surrounded the small, red brick house on the corner of Willow and Oak Streets. While waiting for the bus, they often played with the dog that lived there, a miniature shorthaired dachshund named Gertrude. Each morning and afternoon, like clockwork, Gertrude would nervously watch for them next to the ramshackle railing, patiently holding one of her rubber toys in her mouth, anxiously primed to play a fun game of fetch.

Joshua sat by the window on the bus, next to Patrick. For one of the few times in his life, he was happy—extremely happy. It was his birthday, there was no school tomorrow, and he looked forward to the upcoming bike ride with his best friend.

"Hey, Patrick, where we goin to ride today?" asked Joshua.

"How about we bike over to Green Valley...maybe we'll see some elk or deer," suggested Patrick.

"Ass-hum!" squealed the insipient boy, bouncing up and down elatedly on the cushioned bus seat.

Patrick reached into his pants pocket and pulled out a small box covered in shiny red wrapping paper. He turned to his stocky friend and said, "Oh, by the way, Joshua, I've got a little present here for you."

"For me?" replied Joshua, grinning from ear to ear like the Cheshire cat from *Alice in Wonderland*.

"Yeah, open it up," said Patrick.

Joshua hastily ripped off the ornate red paper covering and carefully opened the lid to the tiny box. Reaching down with his stumpy thumb and index finger, he gently lifted the enclosed gift of jewelry from its protective container. Draped over his wrinkled palm lay a necklace made from golden hemp twine that had been interwoven into a beautifully thatched pattern. Dangling from the straw necklace was a polished silver emblem—a Y-shaped peace sign contained within a closed circle.

"Totally ass-hum!" marveled Joshua. "What is it?"

"It's a peace sign. I made it myself...not the peace sign, but the necklace part...out of yarn," said Patrick proudly. "Here, I'll help you put it on."

"I love this *piss sign*," remarked the malapropist.

"For God's sake, Joshua, don't ever call it a piss sign, it's a peace…spelled p…e…a…c…e — a peace sign.

"Peace sign…peace sign," parroted Joshua.

"Right!" answered Patrick. "Now, lean your head forward so I can put it on for you."

Joshua slowly tilted his large head downward, proudly exposing the back of his bull neck. Patrick delicately placed the string necklace around Joshua's neck, securely fastening the two clasps together in the back. The argent symbol, perfectly centered on the loop of hemp, rested impressively on Joshua's broad chest. Patrick leaned back proudly on the bus seat to admire his handy artwork.

"Sweetist," marveled Patrick.

"Yeah, *sweet tits!*" mimicked Joshua, trying to repeat the sounds of the words phonetically.

Patrick, caught totally off-guard by his companion's hilarious bastardization of his colloquial expression, burst into a fit of wild, gut-wrenching laughter. Everyone has experienced this at one time or another in his or her lifetime — something tickles your funny bone and you lose it completely. Everything. All control. Say good-bye to your composure. Adios, brain. Arrivederci, body. The type of laughter that gives you a red face, makes your eyes water, and keeps you from catching your breath. And not only do you *look* like an idiot, but you *know* that you look like an idiot. Even though your belly throbs afterward, you still feel good — almost euphoric, in fact. Must be nature's way of giving an emotional overhaul to that jumbled mass of electrical impulses that we fondly refer to as a brain…a quick lube-job, as it were.

Patrick's hilarity was highly contagious, like a communicable yawn. Joshua enunciated the syllables again, "sweet tits," then joined in the hysterics, even though he had no idea of what he was laughing at—making everything seem that much funnier to his amused friend.

"Sweet tits!" screeched Patrick, pointing to Joshua with one hand, while using the other to clutch his overworked stomach muscles, which ached from his unrelenting laughter. After a few minutes of hysterical spasmodic gyrations on the bus seat, the two boys finally regained their composure enough to pacify their boisterous behavior. Mopping the tears of happiness from his eyes with his shirtsleeve, Joshua looked down at the necklaced symbol, then hugged his pal and gleamed, "I love it! Thank you so much for my *pees* sign!"

"Anytime," said Patrick coolly, wiping the streams of wetness from his flushed cheeks.

The brakes emitted a high-pitched squeal, as the bus slowed to a grinding halt. Patrick looked out the window and said, "Let's go, Joshua, here's our stop."

Peering out through the glass, Joshua excitingly proclaimed, "Hey, Patrick, look…there's the weenie doggy!" Sure enough, there sat Gertrude, eagerly waiting by the rickety fence for her two human playmates—tail wagging like a metronome on high speed, and holding a big rubber bone in her sweet little canine mouth.

As the two boys stepped off the bus, they caught sight of Joshua's father, Luke, impatiently awaiting their arrival on the mismatched sidewalk that ran alongside Willow Street. The pastor rapidly approached them, briskly pacing past the white picket boundary marker that was a part of Gertrude's guarded domain. When the dachshund sighted Luke, she perked up her floppy ears, dropped the squeaky play-toy, and started growling and barking at the man in black. Luke kicked one of the fence slats with his shoe and yelled, "Get out of here, you mangy mutt!" The frightened animal let out a loud yelp and scampered across the yard, her wilted tail positioned timorously between her two hind legs.

"Hi, Mr. Allen," said Patrick. "That's Gertrude…she won't hurt you…she's a nice dog."

The churchman responded with a guttural grunting sound.

"Hello Father," said Joshua, his eyes staring downward.

Ever since he could remember, the boy had been forced by Luke to always use the word "father," when addressing him. Not dad, daddy, pop, or pa…but father. And it didn't just stop there, either. The preacher had programmed Joshua to reply to any figure of authority with the respectful "yes sir" or "yes, ma'am." If the Down Syndrome son ever disobeyed any of his father's rules, he would have to answer to a painfully brutal whipping from Luke's belt.

Rudely refusing to acknowledge either one of the boy's greetings, Luke eyed his son and said sternly, "Joshua, you need to go over to the church now—I want you to clean the pews, sweep the floor, and wash the windows."

"But Father, today's my birfday and Patrick and I were goin to ride bikes."

"I don't care if it is your birthday, the church needs tidying up."

"Can't I do it after we ride bikes…or tomorrow?"

"No, you'll do it right now."

"But…but…Father…please."

"Don't backtalk me, boy…you do as you're told!"

"Yes sir."

Joshua could sense that his father was in a bad mood, so he didn't argue. He certainly didn't want to do anything that would initiate another beating—especially on his birthday.

"Can I help Joshua with his chores?" inquired Patrick.

"No!" snapped Luke, erupting into one of his homilies. "Cleaning the church is Joshua's job, not yours. He needs to learn to do things by himself. God intended for all of us to work hard so that we can learn responsibility. Work *always* comes before play...don't ever forget that, boy!"

Luke was in constant denial over Joshua's Down Syndrome affliction. According to him, God would never have allowed the son of a devout Christian preacher to be born feeble minded—therefore, it must be the work of Lucifer. That's why he insisted that Joshua attend public schools; Luke would never have sent him to an institute for the mentally handicapped. The man of God was too haughty—too embarrassed to ever have his son ride on the *short* school bus. Luke was a sanctimonious hypocrite of the worst variety—a religious fanatic who preached love and forgiveness, but practiced hate and condemnation. He also suffered from a God complex. In his alcoholic-deranged mind, the minister felt that he was superior to others, holier than thou. "You are all lost lambs, and I am your shepherd," he would tell his congregation. The evangelist should have practiced what he preached; "judge not lest ye be judged," was one of his favorite admonitions. His distorted, perverse interpretations of the Bible were used to intimidate and emotionally harm others. Luke was the king of rationalization—any happening or event that could not be explained or understood was either the work of God or the Devil. If the reverend's interpretation of the occurrence was good, then it was the Lord's blessing; if bad, then Satan was responsible for it. The parson's tirades may have professed benevolence toward others, but in reality, Luke only felt contempt for his fellow man.

"Joshua, go home and change into your work clothes and I'll meet you at the church," his father ordered.

"Yes sir," answered the son. Luke then stormed off across the street, a wicked scowl etched on his weathered face.

Eyeing the clergyman's departure, Gertrude jubilantly pranced back to the wooden fence, clutching the oversized toy dog-bone in her mouth, as if it were Linus's security blanket. Patrick and Joshua played a rousing game of fetch with their furry canine friend for several minutes, and then followed the creviced concrete walkway back toward home.

\#

Joshua's entire wardrobe consisted of three functional outfits—his school clothing, made up of blue jeans, a few shirts, and a pair of cheap tennis shoes; his church attire, a compilation of a two-piece suit, white shirt, dark tie, and black loafers; and his work clothes, comprised of torn blue jeans, an old ratty shirt, and a pair of his father's worn out army boots.

After he had changed out of his school clothes and put on his working attire, Joshua left the house and walked toward his church, which was located about two blocks away. A heavy gathering of dark thunderclouds had rolled in, significantly obstructing the overhead azury sky, so he took the shortcut—a winding dirt trail that emptied onto a stone footpath, leading to his father's place of worship. As Joshua strolled along the walkway, the teenager recalled the disconcerting events of his baptism that had been performed on him the previous year.

Luke believed that a Christian baptism—essential in order to be saved by God—should only be performed on individuals old enough to understand the meaning of the Holy Scriptures. That's why Joshua had to wait until he was fifteen—old enough to understand what a sin was, and why he, like all other people, was a transgressor in the eyes of the Almighty.

From the time that Joshua was a small boy, his overly orthodox, pious father had been delivering him from evil—through exorcisms that would go on for hours—or until Luke was totally satisfied that the malicious spirit had departed from his poor son's body. The religious fanatic firmly believed, God willing, that Joshua's baptism was a way to prevent the malignant demons from re-entering the boy's physical form and possessing his embodied soul.

Joshua vividly remembered his baptismal ceremony as if it had happened yesterday. Dressed in a white shirt that had been sloppily tucked into the waist of his black pants, he stood before the entire congregation of his father's church—nervous and embarrassed. Next to him on the hardwood floor of the tiny chapel sat an old rusty bathtub, supported by its four tarnished clawed feet, and filled three-quarters of the way up with blessed holy water.

The Down Syndrome boy's father stood at the pulpit and recited several Biblical scriptures, fervidly espousing the sanctity of baptism. With the help of one of the elders, Luke positioned his unaware son into the tub, submerging Joshua entirely underwater except for his head, which the cleric supported with one hand. A procession of shivers marched over Joshua's skin as the icy water flooded around his exposed body parts, totally saturating all of his clothing.

Gazing upward, Luke vociferated, "We beseech you, almighty God in Heaven, to cleanse this mortal of his sins and to guide him in the direction of salvation. Please keep and protect him from the temptation of the Devil, so that he may continue on with your righteous work. Help us to live our lives in remembrance of your only son, Jesus Christ, who sacrificed his life for us so that we may live. I baptize thee, Joshua Allen, in the name of the Father, Son, and Holy Spirit. Hallelujah...praise the Lord."

Then, without warning, the preacher forcibly dunked Joshua's head completely under the still surface of the chilly liquid. Cold water poured unmercifully into the alarmed boy's eyes, ears, and nose, as slapping waves of water sloshed over the rim of the old bathtub. The submerged teen peered upward through the watery prism, only to witness a grossly distorted, rippled caricature of his father's impassive face. He couldn't lift his head. He couldn't breathe. He thought he was drowning.

Joshua panicked.

The mentally challenged adolescent tried to scream—but the sounds emanating from his mouth were foreign to him—bubbles of oxygen containing low-pitched muffled howls that reverberated through the water, like an echo in a bottomless pit. Joshua kicked his legs and flailed his arms around wildly, but his father's grip was too strong. The boy was running out of air, and he felt like he was going to pass out. Finally, Luke lifted Joshua's head out of the water. Coughing and choking, the drowning teenager gasped for air. What had seemed like an eternity to the traumatized boy had actually occurred in only a matter of seconds. Dripping wet from head to toe, Joshua quickly and ungainly exited what he feared could have been his watery, porcelain grave.

Immediately after Joshua had freed himself from the confines of the water-sloshing, bathtub baptism, sounds of spontaneous giggling erupted from several members of the church congregation. *How could anyone find my near-drowning funny?* thought the perplexed boy. The assisting elder wrapped a blanket around the drenched, shivering teenager and escorted him into a back room. Joshua thanked God that the religious ceremony was over — happy and grateful that he only had to do this baptism thing once.

As the reminiscent boy ambled up the meandering stone pathway, his father's tiny non-denominational church came into full view. In the front yard of the dwelling stood a wooden sign with stenciled black lettering that read:

CHAPEL OF GOD
Luke Allen, Pastor
43 West Elm Street

The bold ebony print had slowly faded over the years, and the signboard's white paint background exhibited noticeable blistering and flaking — like the peeling epidermis of recently sunburned skin. A makeshift planter, constructed from four hastily cut logs arranged in a crude square on the ground, surrounded the chapel's signpost on all sides. Multicolored artificial flowers that chaotically pointed skyward extended from the decomposing layer of pine chips that filled the timber box. The remainder of the unkempt front lawn was in a state of total neglect — checkered with a hodgepodge of overgrown grass, invading weeds, and bare areas of dirt.

Behind the humble sign and planter sat the house of worship—an unadorned single-story wooden structure that had always been Joshua's sanctuary—his home away from home. The exterior wood siding of the church had been painted a bland, off-white color. Two blue shutters, situated adjacent to a framed glass window, faced reverently toward the street. The laid track of rock that Joshua stood upon abruptly ended at the entryway to the converted cottage, its front door also painted blue in order to match the shutters.

Originally one of the first homes built in Tranquil back in the early 1900s, the diminutive one-bedroom residence was now a tiny chapel. Using money donated by his small flock of parishioners, Luke had purchased the old home about twenty years ago. He and Mary, along with other church members, worked day and night to transform the simple domicile into a place of prayer.

Joshua stopped at the front porch of the Lilliputian house of God and scanned the heavens above him. Without warning, a jagged bolt of lightning arced out from a majestic cumulus and zigzagged ominously across the blackened, overhead sky. Soon thereafter, a noisy explosion of thunder clamored down from the approaching storm, its sound reverberating off the modest sanctuary's wooden structure. Frightened by the loud clap, Joshua quickly twisted the tarnished brass knob with his stubby fingers and opened the old door to his father's chapel.

Squeeek…creeek!

When opened, the weathered door-hinges always made those high-pitched noises—creepy sounds that reminded Joshua of Halloween, with its witches, ghouls, and monsters.

He was never allowed to go trick-or-treating, because Luke believed that Halloween was the work of the Devil, a celebration of evil.

The apprehensive adolescent timidly walked in and shut the squealing door behind him. Inside the church, it was pitch black, so he felt along the wall for the plastic switch and flipped on the overhead lights. Then he stood motionless, attentively listening for any sounds. It was quiet. Luke hadn't arrived yet, and no one else was there.

Joshua was alone...and afraid.

Out of the corner of one eye, the jittery teenager caught a glimpse of something moving, a dark misshapen shadow hiding behind his father's pulpit. He turned and looked, but nothing was there—only his imagination. A strong gust of wind suddenly howled at the roof, whistling through its eaves, forcing the building's walls to creak and moan. The soft pitter-patter of falling rain gently knocked at the front window, as another bang of thunder crashed violently overhead. Joshua's fear was mounting, and his mind was playing scary tricks on him.

"There's nothin to be afraid of," he reassured himself.

The uneasy juvenile cautiously moved past the four rows of dark wooden pews that faced a magnificent golden cross, which hung gloriously on the back wall of the church. He grabbed the straggled straw broom that stood alone in the corner of the rear closet, and began sweeping the old hardwood floor. After a few minutes of whisk-waltzing, Joshua had rearranged the dust and dirt into a neat pile next to the front entrance. A heavy burst of breeze, wailing like a haunting banshee spirit, savagely attacked the old door as he reached for its handle. The terrified boy hesitated for a moment, waiting for the scary sounds to dissipate. As Joshua nervously swung open the front door to sweep out the mound of collected debris, he encountered a tall, formidable figure dressed in dark clothing, standing in the entryway. A brilliant flicker of lightning momentarily illuminated the gloom behind the mysterious black shape. Startled, the youngster dropped his broom and jumped back.

The intimidating silhouette moved forward into the light. "Watch what you're doing, stupid. You almost hit me with that door!" bellowed Luke.

Now, Joshua really *did* have something to be afraid of.

Gaining his composure, the shaken boy lowered his head and replied in an apologetic tone, "Ye...yes sir...I...I'm sorry." Joshua breathed in and immediately recognized the stench—it was the familiar pungent odor of alcohol on his father's breath that he had smelled countless of times before. Joshua didn't even need to look up—he could *feel* the hatred surging from Luke's glaring eyes.

Piercing bloodshot eyes.

Eyes surrounded with dark circles.

Eyes that were cold and mean.

Evil eyes.

Having seen his father in a state of drunkenness many times before, Joshua had become fully aware of the atrocities the cruel man was capable of inflicting upon him. The intoxicated preacher swayed through the front door and harshly demanded, "Done with your chores yet?" There was a hint of slurred speech in the words delivered from his lips—an alcoholic enunciation that the son had heard many times before.

"No sir...I just got done sweepin," replied Joshua, "and now, I gotta clean the pews and wash the windows."

"Well, hurry up and finish, I don't have all day, you know," said the sarcastic minister.

"Yes sir."

As he bent over to pick up the fallen broom, the teen's silver peace sign pendant slipped out from under his shirt and dangled unpretentiously from his neck, in full view of Luke.

"What in God's name is *that?*" thundered his father.

"It's a pees sign. Patrick made it for me...for my birfday...a present!" said Joshua, proudly.

With eyes glowering, the pastor suddenly reached over with an open hand and grabbed the shiny symbol. With one quick yank, the holy man menacingly ripped the piece of jewelry from his dumbfounded son's neck, severing the attaching clasps of the woven hemp necklace.

"You broke it!" cried Joshua.

Luke examined the silvery pendant that lay in his wrinkled palm. "This isn't a peace sign. It's blasphemy...the work of the Devil himself...a sacrilege of the holy cross that our Lord and Savior, Jesus Christ died on for your sins!" he screeched.

"But—"

"How dare you!" shouted the reverend, flinging the necklace across the chapel's wooden floor.

"But Father—"

"And you were wearing it around your neck, like it was a blessed crucifix—in praise of some false idol. My son, you have committed a transgression against the laws of God, and you must pay for your sins," screamed Luke, vehemently.

"But, Father, it's a birfday present!"

"Bow your head, Joshua...get on your knees *now* and bow your head down to the Almighty!"

The intimidated teenager immediately dropped to his knees and lowered his head.

The drunken evangelist lifted both hands upward and prayed, "Oh, heavenly Father, please forgive this sinful boy...tempted by our enemy, Satan, to disobey your divine commandment. He will be punished. With your help, I will purge the evil demon from his body and cleanse his soul... praise Jesus...Amen."

Looking over at his pitiful son, who was still in the head-bowed position, Luke, in a tone of regret, expressed, "I thought that your baptism might protect you from the evil ones, but it obviously hasn't!"

Joshua continued to maintain his silence, remaining frozen in his pose of prayer.

Pointing his finger toward the pulpit, the parson ordered, "Go kneel before the holy cross that you scorned, and pray to God for your forgiveness." The docile, mentally challenged boy obediently scurried over to the pulpit and crouched down before the lofty gold crucifix that was affixed to the wall above him.

Like a child's wooden rocking horse, the confused adolescent swayed his genuflected body back and forth, repeating, "Dear God, I'm so sorry...please forgive me."

The man of the cloth momentarily stood over Joshua, then unbuckled his belt and growled, "This is for your own good, son!"

An intense clatter of thunder rang out, as sheets of rain

machine-gunned down on the shingled roof of the house of worship. Luke freed the belt from his trouser loops and doubled it over, holding the two free ends in his fisted right hand. Then the sadistic disciplinarian reared back the leather bludgeon and powerfully swung it forward, striking a heavy blow to Joshua's back with the instrument of punishment. The rawhide strap made a loud slapping noise as it unmercifully ripped into the innocent teen, ravaging his flesh and bone. An intense burning sensation radiated down the schoolboy's spine, as if he had been seared with a hot poker, but the stoic adolescent didn't make a sound.

"In the name of God, I send you, Lucifer, back to the flaming depths of Hell!" the inflictor of pain roared.

"I'll be good, Father...please don't hit me no more," pleaded his ravaged son.

The shepherd of God continued his scourging of Joshua, "Be gone, demon from Hades...be gone, evil one!"

The praying boy tensed up his entire body, then clenched his teeth tightly together, bracing himself for the next unwanted lashing. Suddenly, the loop of cowhide swished through the air and bit into the teenager's backside once again, launching another paroxysm of unbearable pain and torment.

Joshua screamed out, "He's gone, Father, I felt him leave my body! God told me he's gone...God told me the demon's gone...praise the Lord!"

"He's gone? How do *you* know that?"

From his place of kneeling, Joshua raised both cupped hands upward toward his father and said, "The devil's not inside me no more...God told me he's gone. I'm okay now, so you don't have to beat me no more. We can't question the word of God...can we, Father? Hallelujah, praise Jesus!"

The cunning youth may have been mentally retarded, but he was still able to muster enough brainpower to outsmart his drunken dad. And his ploy worked—Luke stopped the thrashing.

"Praise the power of God!" the holy man shouted.

"The power of God!" reiterated Joshua.

"Finish your chores and get on home," ordered the religious zealot as he staggered toward the front door, fumbling to thread his belt back through its loops.

"Yes sir."

The alcoholized reverend exited the tiny church and unsteadily jogged to his parked car, while a torrential downpour of rain pelted him furiously along the way. After his father had departed, Joshua crawled over, picked up the broken necklace from the church floor, and stuffed it in his back pocket. *Maybe my friend Patrick can fix it,* he thought. The raw skin on his flailed back burned unremittingly, as the tortured teenager slowly rose to his feet.

Leaning over slowly, Joshua grabbed the wooden handle of the broom and then angrily swung it through the air several times. The mentally challenged boy was too incensed at the moment to notice the pain radiating throughout his back and shoulders. "Why's he always mad...why's he so mean... why's he hate me?" screamed out Joshua.

Then the distraught adolescent looked down and mumbled, "He'll be sorry someday!"

By the time Joshua had finished his chores at the church, it was nightfall, and the drenching storm had already passed through the area. The expansive blister of precipitation that had enveloped the house of worship and surrounding neighborhoods had completely dissipated. Using the same dirt trail—now muddied by the heavy rains—Joshua quickly scrambled home and entered through the front door. As he tiptoed by his father's bedroom, he peered in through the opening and observed Luke, fully clothed, passed out on the bed, snoring sounds rhythmically emanating from his open mouth. The fingers of the preacher's right hand were tenaciously clutched onto a black book, the Bible. A large bottle of auburn-colored liquor, half-empty, stood on the nightstand next to the bed.

Joshua silently walked down the hall to his own bedroom, turned on the light, and quietly closed the door. As he removed his shirt, the pummeled skin on his shoulders and back throbbed in excruciating pain. He looked in the mirror, witnessing the reflected angry-red slash marks of injury that had been inflicted on him by his father's leather belt. Joshua reached into the back pocket of his blue jeans and withdrew the treasured gift that his best friend had given him. The sterling metal peace sign still shone like new—only the hemp necklace had been damaged. Hiding the pendant in the back of his sock drawer, Joshua mumbled, "Patrick can fix this…I know he can!"

The mistreated youth pulled off his shoes and blue jeans, and then slipped on the baggy Batman pajamas that were lying in the chair next to his bed. He flipped off the wall switch to his overhead light, slowly made his way back to his bed in the darkness, and blindly climbed under the covers. As he carefully positioned his aching body on the hard mattress, the soft coolness of the sheets helped to comfort the burning skin of his battered back and shoulders.

I'm sixteen years old today, he thought.

"Happy birfday, Joshua," he whispered quietly to himself. Then the Trisomy XXI boy closed both of his slanted blue eyes and drifted off into a deep sleep.

Chapter V
LOSS

The following morning, Joshua was abruptly awakened to the tapping sounds of someone knocking on his bedroom window. He jumped out of bed and opened the blinds, revealing Patrick's smiling face.

"Hey, Joshua...let's go bike riding," his friend proposed.

"I gotta ask Father first...meet you out front," answered the aroused boy.

Joshua hurriedly made up his bed, while simultaneously jettisoning his Batman pajamas onto the bedside chair. The mentally handicapped teen jerked out the bottom drawer of the old wooden dresser, grabbed his play clothes, and hastily positioned the tattered garments over his squatty body. Fortunately for Joshua, his excitement about riding bikes with

Patrick overrode the pain signals sent to his brain from the fiery flesh wounds he had received the evening before.

Joshua scurried to the bathroom and haphazardly squeezed out a big blob of white toothpaste onto the smashed-down bristles of his green toothbrush. He intensely focused on the reflection of his chubby face in the mirror sitting above the sink, and slowly separated his blubbery lips. The adolescent carefully placed the head of the toothbrush into his mouth, and momentarily jiggled the creamy bristles across the front of his buckteeth and gums, while still staring attentively into the mirror. The teen scrubbed his ivories for about twenty seconds, then twisted the old, pitted metal handle marked with a "C," sending a gush of cold water from the tarnished faucet into the rust-stained sink. Leaning his head downward, Joshua spit out a mass of whitish gunk into the liquid pool, and watched as the glop of goo slithered down the gurgling drain. He walked timidly out to the kitchen, where Luke was drinking coffee and reading scriptures from the Bible.

"Good morning, Father...Patrick's outside...can I please go bike ridin with him today?"

Without looking up from the Good Book, the preacher replied, "Did you finish your chores at the church...is your bedroom straightened up?"

"Yes sir...I done everything."

"After you eat breakfast, then you can go bike riding with Patrick, but make sure you're home by lunchtime. I'm going over to the church now."

"Yes sir...thank you, Father."

Luke got up from the kitchen table, walked over to the entryway and opened the front door. "And don't forget to wash your dirty dishes," ordered the preacher, slamming the door behind him.

Joshua gulped down a small bowl of his favorite cereal — Sugary Stars — then rinsed out his bowl and spoon. When he opened the front door, there stood his friend Patrick, patiently waiting for him on the concrete porch.

"My father said yes!" cried Joshua, sporting a goofy grin.

"Sweetist! Let's go, man, we're wasting time…get your bike, we're going to Green Valley!" Patrick announced.

"Sweet tits!" mimicked Joshua.

The Trisomy XXI boy rushed over to his father's open garage and excitedly wheeled out his bicycle — a used ten-speed that had been donated to him by one of Luke's church members. Painted a dark blue color, the bike was decorated with red pin striping, and had candy-apple-red flame decals on its front and back fenders. Its silver handlebar sported a white plastic grip on each of its two ends, and was equipped with brake and gearshift attachments. From each ivory handle dangled a flashy assortment of red and blue streamers, which made loud rustling sounds when the bicycle was ridden against the wind.

Patrick owned a fully equipped, new black and gray mountain bike he received as a gift from his parents last Christmas.

"Follow me, Joshua," said Patrick, "and be careful."

"Okie dokie!"

The two boys energetically pedaled both of the multicolored bikes down the street, headed in a beeline toward their favorite scenic spot to explore, Green Valley. Everyone around town was familiar with the area called

Green Valley—hundreds of acres of lush valley land, fed by foothill streams, and surrounded on all sides by mountains of emerald forests. It was property owned by the State Department of Land Management, so any form of hunting or fishing was strictly prohibited. Abundant wildlife roamed the area there, taking refuge and seeking protection from seasonal hunters, who were hungry to bag a prized trophy animal. It was commonplace for visitors to see large groups of elk and deer grazing on the tender shoots of tall grass that covered the verdant, valley floor. Huge flocks of colorful migratory birds inhabiting the wetlands could also be easily observed flying over the area, in search of food, shelter, and water. In addition, a healthy population of rainbow, brown, and brook trout could be found in virtually every picturesque waterway that flowed through the fertile dale. Like Shangri-la and the Garden of Eden, Green Valley was truly a paradise.

"Hey, look at me!" shouted Joshua, as he propelled his bicycle faster down the middle of the wandering, narrow dirt road that led to the entrance of Green Valley.

Patrick turned around to see his friend gaining on him.

"Catch me if you can," yelled Patrick, speeding up.

"Here I come!" hollered Joshua. He squeezed the white handlebar grips tightly and continued to pedal furiously, thoroughly enjoying the feel of the cool breeze against his face. The Down Syndrome boy's tires made an assortment of whistling sounds, as they sped over the road's bumpy surface.

Joshua's bike was no match for his friend's, so Patrick purposely slowed his ride down to allow Joshua to overtake him. As his retarded pal passed him by, Patrick called out, "You win, buddy, you're just too fast for me!" Joshua glanced back over his shoulder at Patrick, his face radiant with exhilaration. The inseparable pair of biking enthusiasts continued merrily on their journey, riding side-by-side—talking, laughing, and enjoying the scenery—just having a blast on this beautiful spring day.

The boys spotted a small dust devil, whirling harmlessly across the road ahead of them. A mass of spinning leaves and flying debris was trapped inside the wind funnel, making clicking sounds as they ricocheted off each another. The enthralled teenagers fixated their eyes on the swirl of breeze, until it mysteriously disappeared into the air above them.

Suddenly, Patrick heard the loud rumble of an automobile engine, approaching them from behind. He relayed to his friend, "Hey, Joshua, pull your bike over. Here comes a car." Both he and Joshua carefully maneuvered their wheeled mode of transportation onto the constricted shoulder, which sharply dropped off into a deep ravine that ran alongside the narrow road. The two teens slowed down, and cautiously steered their bikes along the unforgiving edge of the dirt passageway.

They were suddenly startled by the shrill sound of honking—the trailing vehicle had pulled up behind them, and was bleeping its horn loudly. Patrick and Joshua whipped their heads around, and instantly recognized the car. It was a yellow Ford Mustang with green stripes on the hood—Niles Slovinsky's yellow Ford Mustang! The obnoxious teen blared the horn repeatedly, then stuck his head out the window and yelled, "Hey, dickheads...move it or lose it!" In the gusting wind, the juvenile delinquent's jumbled tufts of scraggly red hair looked like the nest of writhing snakes on Medusa's head. The two annoyed bike riders faced forward again, immediately focusing their attention on the perilous path in front of them.

When Patrick looked back again at Niles, who persisted to honk the horn with his head poked out the window, he encountered a pair of cold, dark staring eyes—wild and scary. Cruel and sadistic eyes that reflected a disturbing hatred generated from deep within. Malevolent eyes that no one liked to make visual contact with. The telltale eyes of a sociopath.

Patrick repositioned his head frontward, paying close attention to his steering and the abrupt drop-off of the narrow road he and his friend were traveling on. He waved his hand back and forth, motioning for Niles to pass them. Joshua copycatted his friend's peculiar arm movement.

"Screw you guys...I'm not going anywhere!" bellowed the carrot-haired smart aleck.

Patrick turned his head to the side and shouted into the wind, "Just go around us, Niles...this isn't funny!"

The terrorizing bully continued to follow closely behind them with his car. "Oh, I think it's *real* funny. Hardy-frickin-har-har...I told you pricks I'd get even with you!"

The pair of cyclists tried not to look over at the menacing gorge below them, attempting only to concentrate on keeping their tires away from the edge of the road. And they couldn't dare stop, for fear that the tailgating car might hit their bikes from behind, sending them crashing over the bluff. Patrick called back to his buddy, "You're doing fine, Joshua...don't let him get to you...just follow my path with your bike."

"Okay," answered Joshua.

Niles downshifted and gunned the engine, lurching his yellow horse to within inches of Joshua's rear tire. The panicking teenagers pedaled furiously to stay ahead of the shiny chrome bumper that was snapping at their heels.

"Leave us alone, you bastard," yelled Patrick, "or I'm going to kick your ass!"

"Yeah, leave us alone, you *bass turd!*" echoed Joshua.

Niles spread his lips apart, molding his crooked teeth into an evil grin. Then he sneered out his window, "I'm *so* afraid, Patrick. Please don't kick my ass. You two retards messed with the wrong guy!"

From nowhere, a tiny rabbit emerged from beneath a nearby bush and darted out in front of Joshua's bike. The mentally deficient boy panicked, squeezing down on his handbrake lever to avoid hitting the young cottontail with his front tire. Niles's car bumper slammed into Joshua's tail fender, vaulting the old ten-speed forward, high into the air. The force of the impact hoisted the rear tire up, causing the front of the catapulting bike to nose downward. Like a Kamikaze's airplane descending on its target, Joshua and his airborne bicycle violently crashed headfirst into Patrick.

The furious impact unmercifully thrust both riders off their seats, plunging them headlong over the roadside, and into the valley depth below. As the jettisoned teens traveled skyward, a physiologic surge of adrenaline pumped instantaneously throughout their bodies, supernaturally boosting their perception. This allowed them to visualize everything as if it were in slow motion—an evolutionary protective mechanism that permits the mind to function more quickly under stressful situations. And it couldn't have gotten any more stressful than this. Like two rag dolls floundering through the air, the boys' flexible bodies tumbled and flipped as they rapidly descended downward—eventually landing in a twisted heap on the hard floor of the rocky canyon.

Niles squealed the brakes of his car to a stop, and then ran back to the side of the road where the unfortunate incident had occurred. The mangled bodies of Joshua and Patrick lay in the valley below — bloodied and motionless. Spotting their position on the bottom of the ravine, Niles shouted, "Hey, down there…can you hear me…it wasn't my fault…it was an accident…say something!"

There was no response. There was no movement. Like a still photograph, the frozen images of Patrick and Joshua remained in a fixed position on the stony floor of the canyon below.

"The hell with you then!" yelled Niles. The devious redhead thought about driving away and leaving them there, but even Niles was smart enough to know that the special tires he had on his car would leave their identifying prints in the dirt. Besides, he was the only one in town who owned a yellow Mustang with green stripes, and someone could have easily spotted him traveling on Green Valley Road that day.

Taking his time to prepare a plausible story, Niles turned the car around and casually drove back to town. When he arrived in Tranquil, he fetched Sheriff Evans, who immediately dispatched an ambulance, which followed them back to the place where the tragic incident had occurred. In the patrol car, Niles explained to Buck that he was merely sightseeing on Green Valley Road when he witnessed the biking accident — a rabbit had bolted in front of Joshua's bike, causing him to crash into Patrick, sending them both tumbling over the roadside and into the gorge. Niles conveniently failed to provide any information about *his* part in the horrible mishap.

While relaying his account of what had happened, the boy seemed unusually nervous to the sheriff, and the version he was giving just didn't seem to ring true. There was definitely something fishy about the teen's story, so being a lawman, Buck was naturally suspicious.

Sheriff Evans pulled the patrol car over to the side of the road, jumped out, and then hurriedly made his way down the steep, bumpy ramp that led to the canyon below. From a distance, it looked as if both of the boys were dead. Patrick was lying face down, and Joshua had ended up on his side. As Buck approached them, he could see that Joshua was still breathing, but was unable to ascertain any chest movements for Patrick. Carefully turning Patrick over, Buck observed the teen's once handsome face — now, it was a blotchy gray color, with blue lips, and glassy, colorless eyes. The glorious spark of life that had once lit up the boy's attractive adolescent face was gone. He also observed that the young man was making no efforts to breathe, either. Buck cautiously positioned Patrick's head into the proper position for mouth-to-mouth resuscitation. When his fingers felt a bony protuberance, jutting out from the boy's nape, and he heard the grating sounds of crepitation, the lawman was concerned. Both signs were indicative of fractured cervical vertebrae. Patrick had broken his neck in the fall!

The paramedics made their way down the steep hill and tried to help Patrick, but it was too late. He was dead. Joshua's best friend and blood-brother was gone...forever. Though Joshua was still alive and breathing, he had sustained severe head trauma. The boy inflicted with Trisomy XXI was in a deep state of unconsciousness, unresponsive to the world around him. They placed Joshua's comatose body onto a gurney, and loaded him into the back of the ambulance, next to Patrick's sheet-covered corpse. With sirens wailing, the trauma truck speedily made its way back to Joshua's place of birth — the emergency room at Tranquil Community Hospital.

#

When they arrived at the hospital, one of the paramedics provided a medical evaluation to the emergency room physician, as Joshua and Patrick were taken out of the ambulance. "These are the two boys involved in the bicycling accident off of Green Valley Road…according to an eyewitness, their bikes collided, and they fell off into the ravine. One of the boys is Patrick Murdock, a sixteen-year-old white male who suffered a badly broken neck. When we found him, he had no vital signs and his pupils were fixed and dilated…he's DOA. The other white male, also sixteen…he sustained some head trauma…his vital signs are weak, but stable, and he is still unconscious….unresponsive to any stimuli. His name is Joshua Allen…a Down Syndrome kid."

"What did you say his name was?" asked the doctor.

"It's Joshua Allen," replied the paramedic. "Do you know him, Dr. Tisdale?"

Ted stroked his salt-and-pepper beard and said, "I sure as hell do! I delivered him by an emergency C-section after his mother had died…right here in this same emergency room… sixteen years ago…it was a miracle that he survived!"

The paramedic shook his head and said glumly, "Well, doc, it looks like he could use another miracle."

Ted pulled back the sheet that covered Patrick's unsightly body. His neck appeared grossly distorted — hideously bowed over to one side. The fractured cervical vertebrae had been traumatically dislocated, displacing the bones laterally, grotesquely distending the overlying muscle and skin outward. It reminded the emergency room physician of the Old West— gruesome pictures he had seen of horse thieves and cattle rustlers hanging from the end of a rope, with their contorted necks bent over at a sharp angle.

"What a shame," said Ted. "Only sixteen years old...my daughter's age...he had his whole life ahead of him...I'll never understand why this happens."

"Should I take him to the morgue now, Dr. Tisdale?"

"Yes...please do," replied Ted, sadly.

The doctor walked over to Joshua, who lay in a state of unconsciousness on the examining room table, attended to by one of the female ER nursing staff.

"How's he doing?" queried Ted.

"His vital signs are all stable and he's continued to maintain an adequate airway...breathing on his own just fine, Dr. Tisdale...but he's still comatose...there's no response to any type of stimuli."

Ted performed a cursory physical exam on Joshua— listening to the teenager's heart, lungs, and abdomen with the stethoscope, feeling his belly and flanks for any abnormalities, visually inspecting his body for trauma, testing his extremities for any suggestion of bone fractures, and evaluating his general neurologic status by checking for any signs indicative of brain damage.

"Find anything?" questioned the nurse.

"The boy's skin reflects an appreciable amount of ecchymoses—heavy bruising all over his body...and he has

81

received his fair share of scrapes and cuts...but surprisingly, I don't think he has any broken bones. He exhibits some neurological deficits consistent with his closed head injury and insentience, but his respiratory center doesn't seem to be adversely affected. The long-acting intravenous steroids he's receiving should help to minimize his brain swelling... his comatose state is nature's way of shutting down, while his cerebral cortex tries to repair itself. Take him over to X-ray and get a CT scan on his head...we need to rule out any bleeding in the brain, like a subdural or epidural hematoma. Then we'll hook him up to the EEG...hopefully he's got some brain activity and isn't totally *gorked out*...I've got too much time and effort invested in this young man to see him end up like that."

Worried that Joshua may end up as a mental vegetable, Dr. Tisdale reflected back to when he was a resident in emergency medicine at Parkland Hospital, a major trauma center in Dallas. He was working on the neurosurgery ward, and had lost count of the number of patients diagnosed as "brain-dead" from head trauma—usually the consequence of a motor vehicle accident. The worst brain damage that Ted had ever witnessed occurred in those Evil Knievel wannabes, who, while wearing no protective helmet, crashed their motorcycles when driving at dangerously high speeds. Sorry, Charlie, but there are no air bags on those bad boys. The neurosurgery residents jokingly referred to the traumatic incidents as *murdercycle* or *donorcycle* accidents.

Ted remembered the joke he had heard as a rotating resident on the neurosurgery service—the one about the carrots. It goes something like this. Mr. and Mrs. Carrot were walking on the side of the road, when all of a sudden, a car came out from nowhere and ran over Mr. Carrot. The ambulance took him to the hospital, where he had to undergo an extensive surgical procedure in the operating room. A distressed and concerned Mrs. Carrot remained in the waiting room, anxiously awaiting the results of the surgery. After several hours, the surgeon finally emerged from the operating room.

"Doctor, how's my husband?" Mrs. Carrot asked.

"Well, Mrs. Carrot," said the doctor, "I have good news, and I have bad news...the good news is that Mr. Carrot is alive!"

"Thank God!" cried Mrs. Carrot.

"But the bad news," explained the surgeon to Mrs. Carrot, "is that your husband will be a *vegetable* for the rest of his life!"

Although sick jokes like that may seem heartless and insensitive to others, it was one way that doctors and other medical personnel, who had encountered the most horrific images imaginable—mutilating injury, deforming disease, pain and suffering, death and dying—could psychologically deal with those disturbing memories. Ted hoped and prayed that Joshua wouldn't suffer the same fate as Mr. Carrot.

The results of the computerized tomography scan revealed moderate swelling of Joshua's smaller-than-normal brain, but no skull fractures or intra-cranial bleeding was noted. Joshua's electroencephalogram results were discouraging, though. His brain wave patterns—alpha, beta, theta, and delta—were almost flatline, indicating little to no brain activity. Even though Joshua had Down Syndrome and was mentally retarded, he should have had some type of higher brain activity registered on the EEG.

Dr. Tisdale assumed the role of treating physician and admitted Joshua to the Intensive Care Unit. On Joshua's hospital chart, he wrote:

Admit to ICU from ER

Admitting Doctor: Dr. Ted Tisdale

History: 16 y.o. Down Syndrome white male involved in bicycle accident

Diagnosis: Closed head injury — Coma

Condition: Stable

Prognosis: Guarded

Routine ICU head trauma orders with periodic crani-checks Ted placed a big asterisk in front of the last written order, underlined it, and then signed his name:

For any questions, ONLY contact Dr. Tisdale — ALL orders and treatments must be approved through me first!

T. Tisdale, MD

After the physician finished writing Joshua's orders, he set down the hospital chart and in a compassionate tone whispered, "I'll do everything in my power to see that you make it, Joshua...you have my word on that!"

#

Oblivious to everything around him, Joshua, dressed in a blue patient gown, lay flat on the hospital bed—isolated in a small room of the Intensive Care Unit. In order to keep him stationary, the side rails on the bed were elevated, and his arms had been tightly secured with soft cloth restraints. A flexible plastic oral airway had been inserted into his mouth to keep his breathing passage open, and emerging from Joshua's nares were the prongs of a nasal cannula, delivering fresh oxygen to his lungs. The translucent hollow tubing delivering the clean air to Joshua's nose extended out from the wall panel behind his hospital bed, and was wrapped circumferentially around his head.

An intravenous line, taped firmly to his skin, emerged from the antecubital vein in Joshua's left arm. The thin plastic, hollow line extended upward from the boy's upper extremity to join a mounted plastic bag that contained D_5LR—five percent dextrose combined with a Lactated Ringer's solution that was made up of salt water and electrolytes—all vitally needed to sustain his body. The IV line was also used to administer any medicines that the teen might need as well. A calibrated urinary catheter bag hung at the foot of the bed to assess Joshua's fluid output and kidney function.

Box-shaped, beeping monitors with blinking lights, mounted on tall, thin metal poles with tripod stands, surrounded the unconscious adolescent's bed. Flexible strings of multicolored electrode leads extended from the electroencephalogram and electrocardiogram units to accurately record his brain waves and heart rhythm—reaching out like tiny sucking tentacles to attach themselves to the skin of Joshua's head and chest.

It was around midnight, and the ICU nurse had just checked in on him. She turned off the room light and closed his door, before returning to the nurse's station to record his medical information on the hospital chart. Dr. Tisdale had visited the teen only an hour ago, and was deeply disturbed about his minimal brain wave patterns. Joshua's father, Luke, had showed up earlier during visiting hours, staying only long enough to recite a brief, unemotional prayer for his son.

Everyone was gone now, and the comatose juvenile had been left in the dark room all by himself. In the still of the night, the only sounds audible were the sleeping boy's deep breathing, and the intermittent bleeping noises of the monitors.

The door to Joshua's room slowly opened, and a dark shape quietly entered and walked over to the left side of his bed. In the dimly lit room, the shadow stood next to the unconscious teenager, lurking over his inanimate body. A syringe full of red luminous liquid was meticulously injected into the portal of the intravenous line, steadily propelling its way down the pliant plastic tunnel that had become an extension of Joshua's left arm. Moving steadily as a bolus of fluid, the shimmering solution emitted a ruby-red glow, as it methodically descended the chambered tubing—a prisoner of gravity. Like luminescent juice through a straw, the red radiant substance continued on its downward flow, until it disappeared completely into Joshua's dilated arm vein. The young recipient of the strange infusion elicited no response to the infringement, and continued to lie motionless on the bed. Withdrawing the emptied syringe from the IV portal, the mysterious figure waited a few moments, and then turned and silently walked out of Joshua's room...unseen...disappearing into the blackness of the night.

Chapter VI
CHANGELING

When Ted arrived at the ICU the following morning to check on Joshua, he was greeted by Shirley Gates, the head nurse of the Intensive Care Unit.

"Dr. Tisdale, you're *not* going to believe this!" she exclaimed, "Come with me...this is really eerie!"

Shooting the nurse a surprised look, he asked "What is it, Shirley?"

The nurse faced the baffled doctor, lifted her right hand and spread her middle fingers apart, gesturing the Spock sign, and then started humming the theme to *The Twilight Zone* – "Dew-de-dew-dew...dew-de-dew-dew...dew-de-dew-dew!"

Ted was *extremely* intrigued now. Following her down the hall to Joshua's room, he queried, "What the hell's going on...

how is he…tell me…what happened?"

"*You'll see*," she replied.

When Shirley opened the door to the boy's room, Ted observed Joshua, wide-awake and alert, sitting up in his bed.

"Hi, Dr. Tisdale, how are you today?" the teen asked cordially.

"I found him like this on my morning rounds…look at the EEG," said Nurse Gates, pointing to the monitor.

Ted walked over to the EEG monitor to get a closer look. Joshua's brain wave patterns were oscillating up and down like a theme park roller coaster.

"That's incredible! Yesterday, his cortical signals were almost non-existent…now look at the amplitude pattern of those beta and delta waves! This is great! I've never seen anything like that before!"

Shirley moved next to the excited physician and whispered, "That's not all, doctor. Look closely at his face… you may think I'm crazy, *but I think it's changed!*" The tone of her voice, along with the nurse's puzzled expression, told Ted that she wasn't joking. Dr. Tisdale walked over to the side of the bed and closely observed Joshua's face. Using his hand, Ted turned the adolescent's head from side-to-side, thoroughly examining every facial feature.

Joshua's visage *was* different — it *had* been transformed. The characteristic or "mongoloid" traits uniquely seen in someone afflicted with Down Syndrome had vanished. The prominent epicanthal folds that gave Joshua's eyes a distinctive slanted appearance were gone. His previously flat, wide nose now assumed a proportionate shape and desirable form. The boy's lips and tongue weren't oversized anymore, and his low-set ears had been raised up—currently sitting in their correct symmetrical position on the sides of his head. No more Mr. Ed either—the horse teeth and gums had disappeared, replaced with a perfectly aligned dentition. Incredibly, all of Joshua's facial features were presently in balance and aesthetically pleasing—instead of possessing the distinctive face of a Down Syndrome boy, he displayed the countenance of a handsome young man.

Dr. Tisdale continued his examination and made another remarkable finding. The numerous contusions and abrasions inflicted on Joshua's body by the accident had disappeared—the scrutinizing physician was unable to find any bruising or skin scrapes anywhere. It was as if Joshua had healed himself overnight. "The extensive ecchymoses and skin excoriations...all gone...replaced by normal, healthy tissue... this is unbelievable!" Ted mumbled to himself.

Shirley grabbed the doctor's arm and led him over to the corner of the room. "You ain't seen nothing yet!" she whispered excitedly. "When Joshua was admitted to the ICU, we measured him and he was sixty inches long—now he's seventy inches. And look at his hands...his fingers...they're not short and stubby anymore...*he's* not short and stubby anymore!"

"Remarkable...truly remarkable!"

"Any ideas on what's happening here?" asked Shirley.

Ted stroked his hairy chin. "Maybe his head injury triggered the release of human growth hormone from his pituitary gland and it affected his development...and other immune chemical substances were somehow stimulated to account for his rapid healing time."

"In one day?"

"I don't know…maybe it's a medical miracle. I don't have all the answers, I'm just delighted…and amazed…that he's come out of the coma and doing so well!"

Nurse Gates looked over at Joshua, and then at Ted. "All I know is, something really weird is going on here," she said softly. "This is strange as hell!"

Ted put both of his hands on top of the nurse's shoulders, looked her squarely in the eyes and whispered, "Listen, Shirley, I don't know what the hell is going on here either, but we have to keep this a secret — low profile — until we have more information. I don't want a bunch of news reporters or nosey townspeople sniffing around here…Joshua has been through enough as it is. I'll talk to his dad and you talk to the other nurses. In the meantime, let's get a battery of blood tests — especially a DNA profile. Send him down for a multichannel EEG recording and a repeat CT brain scan…maybe something will show up that will explain all of this!"

Shirley smiled and replied, "Sounds good to me, doc."

Joshua looked up from his bed with a concerned look and asked, "Dr. Tisdale…what are you two talking about? Please tell me what's happening!"

"Shirley, would you be so kind as to get me a mirror?" Ted requested. The nurse walked over to a white cabinet, opened one of its drawers, and pulled out a large round looking glass. She handed it to Ted, who held it up in front of Joshua. Seeing his new reflection for the first time, the changeling lifted both hands up to his reconstructed face and closely inspected every altered feature with ten trembling fingers.

"What's happened to me, Dr. Tisdale…I'm scared…please

help me!"

"There's nothing to be afraid of, Joshua," said Ted. "Your facial appearance has somehow been changed, and your injuries have all healed. I don't have the answers yet, but I assure you, it's nothing to worry about."

"That's right, Joshua, you're doing great! We're just amazed at your progress," said Shirley.

Feeling reassured, the preacher's son continued to stare into the mirror, mesmerized by his new comely appearance. He suddenly looked up at Ted and said, "Dr. Tisdale, the last thing I remember is Patrick and I falling off of our bicycles, into the ravine. Was Patrick seriously injured...how's he doing... when can I see him?"

It finally dawned on the physician. Ted had been too preoccupied — too excited by the boy's altered appearance and healed wounds to notice it before. What had happened to Joshua's simple grammar and poor sentence structure? The mentally compromised teenager had never spoken this eloquently before. This was amazing. Turning to Shirley, Ted winked and said, "Better get an IQ test too."

"It just keeps on getting weirder by the minute...will do," replied his nurse.

Ted felt that he should honestly address the boy's questions about Patrick, so he set the mirror down and sat on the side of the bed. "Son, I have some bad news to tell you...Patrick didn't make it...he's gone...he was killed in the accident."

Tears welled up in Joshua's eyes. "Oh, no...Oh, dear God, no...please...not Patrick!"

Ted squeezed his patient's shoulder reassuringly. "He didn't suffer at all...he went quick."

Joshua began to cry. With tears rolling down both cheeks, he sobbed, "But he was my only friend...the only *true* friend I ever had...we were blood-brothers!"

"I'm so sorry," said Ted. "Everyone loved Patrick...I know that he meant a lot to you... we'll all miss him dearly."

"Patrick will always be alive...in your heart," said Shirley.

"Yes...he will," wept Joshua.

Dr. Tisdale patted the boy on the back and picked up the medical chart that hung at the foot of the bed. He quickly scribbled down a long line of orders for all of the tests he wanted to run on Joshua, handed the chart to the nurse, and then walked toward the door.

"Shirley, I want these tests done *stat*...I need the results back today...*capiche*?

"*Capiche!*" she answered.

"Thanks, Shirley, you're a real pal," said Ted, "and a damn good nurse too!"

"Fuhgeddaboudit!" quipped Nurse Gates, in her best Italian accent.

Ted's beeper suddenly went off—it was the emergency room calling for him again. He had been overwhelmed with patients that morning, busier than a one-armed man in a juggling contest. "Shirley, I'll be in the ER...be sure to call me as soon as you get the results of those tests back." Then the physician looked over at Joshua and said, "See you later, son. Take it easy and don't worry about what has happened... everything is going to be okay."

Forcing a weak smile, Joshua said, "Thanks, Dr. Tisdale, I don't know how I'll ever repay you...you've saved my life *twice* now!"

Ted smiled. Walking out the door, he joked, "That's right, Joshua, let's not make this a habit...you can repay me by continuing to get well."

"We're going to be running some more medical tests on you today, Joshua, and I need to go order them. Are you going to be okay if I leave you alone for a while?" Shirley asked.

"I'll be fine," answered Joshua. "Go order the tests, I need some time by myself anyway."

"Be back soon...if you need anything, just punch that red button on the control panel next to your bed, and I'll be right here." Securing Joshua's medical chart under her arm, Shirley pushed the door open and walked back to the nurse's station.

Joshua couldn't quite figure it out. It was a strange and weird sensation. When he awakened that morning, the teen felt as if he were a different person—like he had been reborn. Except for memories associated with the accident, Joshua's recollection of long-term and past childhood events was intact. Yet now, all of the changeling's retained memories were vivid and full of color, whereas before, they had been black-and-white and fuzzy—like pictures out of focus. Since that morning, the adolescent's mental powers, thought processes, and cognitive abilities had developed immensely—compared to the mind of the "old" Joshua, his views of the world around him, understanding of the abstract, and capacity to conceptualize, were clearer, sharper, and more highly advanced.

Before the accident, the capabilities of Joshua's mentally impaired mind were severely limited. Now, for some unknown reason, Joshua had acquired a powerful intelligence that could assimilate and formulate all of his past life experiences into a cohesive understanding, placing everything in its proper perspective. Like piecing the parts of a jigsaw puzzle together, the gifted adolescent was finally able to understand the intricacies of life, and to appreciate the interdependent relationships of all things, both living and inanimate. The locked door of Joshua's brain had been opened, freeing his mind to ponder the universe. He had changed. The Trisomy XXI, mentally retarded, Down Syndrome boy was now a precocious prodigy — slowly metamorphosing into a highly evolved intelligent entity.

#

Nurse Gates picked up the phone and dialed the three-digit extension number to the emergency room. "Hi, this is Shirley up here in ICU...please tell Dr. Tisdale that the tests on Joshua Allen are back...thanks." After a few minutes had passed, she eyed Ted, walking at a rapid pace toward the nurse's station.

"Where are the results?" he anxiously asked.

"Good afternoon to you, too," answered Shirley, sarcastically.

"Sorry, I didn't mean to be rude, but I've been waiting all day just to see those findings."

Shirley handed him a big manila envelope and said, "Here they are...the lab delivered them only a few minutes ago. I've got to go start an IV now, but I'll be back soon...tell me what you found out."

"Yeah...thanks," said Ted. He quickly pulled up a chair, sat down at the station counter, ripped open the sealed flap, and pulled out a stack of computerized printouts detailing the results of Joshua's lab tests.

Flipping through the pages, the doctor scanned the results

like a crazed speed-reading champion let loose in a bookstore. "Let's see what we have here...

...blood count...

...differential...

...gases...

...pH...

...electrolytes...

...urine...

...enzymes...

...all perfect."

Reading a printed summary of the radiologist's diagnosis of Joshua's brain scan, Ted mumbled, "Compared to patient's first brain CT, areas of moderate cortical edema are totally resolved, but remarkably, gray matter of brain has enlarged approximately twenty-five percent in contrast to atrophic brain appearance in first CT. *Unknown medical phenomenon responsible for this increased growth in brain tissue.*"

"Whoa!" said Ted, laying the radiology report down on the table.

Drawn to the remaining sheets of paper like a moth to a bright light, the fascinated physician continued to read on, "Admission EEG revealed virtual flatline appearance of alpha, beta, theta, and delta waves, demonstrating little to no brain activity. Multichannel EEG now shows extremely elevated patterns of waking beta and delta waves, along with prominent alpha and theta waves, indicating a much more highly enhanced brain function. Strangely, gamma rhythms, which were previously undetected in the admission EEG, are now present and maximally peaked, indicative of highly advanced mental activity associated with superior cognition.

I have no plausible explanation for this drastic change in brain activity."

"This is awesome…totally awesome!" Ted said.

He turned to the next page, and read aloud the hospital psychologist's summary of Joshua's intelligence quotient test.

"A standardized Stanford-Binet Intelligence Scale Test that assesses intelligence and cognitive ability was administered to Joshua Allen, a sixteen-year-old male patient with a history of Down Syndrome and borderline mental retardation. This test has an average, or mean score of 100, with a standard deviation of 16. Joshua achieved the remarkable score of 142, which is more than two standard deviations above the mean, ranking him in the top one percent. This correlates to an IQ that is very superior, indicating gifted brain function. In lieu of his previous IQ of 70, which is consistent with mental impairment, I administered a Wechsler Scales Test to confirm the validity of his score of 142 on the Stanford-Binet—to rule out any factor of chance that may have been involved in taking that test. To my amazement, Joshua scored a 140, placing him again in the very superior, or 'gifted' category. To my knowledge, there have only been a handful of reported cases in the medical literature about individuals sustaining brain trauma that ended up with higher cognitive abilities, but nothing to compare with this puzzling finding. *I consulted with a neurologist, and we have no idea of the etiology behind this extraordinary intelligence enhancement."*

Ted lifted his eyes from the paper, leaned back in his chair, and exclaimed, "Ho—ly shmoly!"

Shuffling through the last pages of the lab results, he found the report he had been most interested in—an analysis of his patient's DNA profile. Ted had ordered a simple genetic test on Joshua, a *karyotype*, in which a blood sample is checked for the number and type of chromosomes found in the cells. He had the lab compare the boy's chromosomal pattern of his previous admission blood test to the findings taken that day in the ICU.

"Here's what I want," said Ted, looking down at the page demonstrating the two representations of Joshua's set of chromosomes, which had been dyed and photographed under a light microscope.

ALLEN, JOSHUA
KARYOTYPE - ADMISSION

1 2 3 4 5 6 7 8 9 10 11 12

13 14 15 16 17 18 19 20 **21** 22 x y

ALLEN, JOSHUA
KARYOTYPE - ICU

97

𝕀𝕏 𝕏𝕦 𝕒𝕟 𝕒𝕏

1 2 3 4 5 6 7 8 9 10 11 12

𝕒𝕟 𝕒𝕦 𝕒𝕒 𝕩𝕪 𝕩𝕏 𝕒𝕒 𝕩𝕏 𝕟𝕒 𝕒𝕒 𝕪 𝕟

13 14 15 16 17 18 19 20 **21** 22 x y

At the bottom of the page was a typed explanation of the genetic differences seen between the two chromosomal patterns:

In the karyotype obtained from the patient's blood drawn in the emergency room on the day of hospital admission, there are three chromosomes that are easily visualized at the twenty-first level, consistent with Trisomy XXI, the cause of Down Syndrome. The xy chromosomes found at the end indicate that this karyotype is from a male. The karyotype from the patient's blood that was taken the following day in the ICU demonstrates that now, there are only two chromosomes at the twenty-first level, which is a normal finding. This DNA profile test was run twice to rule out any laboratory or human error, and the end results were the same both times: an admission karyotype that exhibits an extra chromosome at the twenty-first level, or Trisomy XXI, versus a karyotype of the same patient the subsequent day that reveals the perfectly normal chromosomal pattern of a male. *In my twenty years of being a laboratory technician and geneticist, I have never witnessed anything like this, and I have no scientific reason or theory to explain how or why this genetic aberration occurred.*

"Bingo!" said Ted, smiling.

Shirley returned to the nurse's station and strolled over to where Ted was sitting.

"What's the verdict?" asked the R.N.

Ted looked up at Shirley from the stack of papers and opined, "This is one of those medical phenomena that will probably *never* be explained…at least in my lifetime. The only rationale I can give is that Joshua's head injury must have affected his frontal-cortico-neuronal synaptic biochemical relays responsible for higher cognitive processing…somehow stimulating and expanding his mental and physical growth potential…that's the only scientific explanation that I can come up with…it's *way* beyond my comprehension."

The totally bewildered nurse looked at the esoteric doctor and said, "In English, please?"

"In other words, before the accident, Joshua's brain was a four-cylinder Geo — now, he's a supercharged V-12 Ferrari."

"I gotcha now." Shirley grinned.

"The big picture, though, is that Joshua is alive, and now, the boy has a fully functioning and wonderfully *gifted* mind…a mind that he can use to start a fresh, new life," said Ted.

Shirley flashed a smile and then announced, "Who cares how it happened? I'm just so happy for Joshua!"

Chapter VII
TARA

Ted walked into his patient's hospital room, pulled up a chair next to the bed, and said, "Joshua, I've reviewed all of your medical tests, and the results are astonishing...some of them unbelievable...but the bottom line is that you are as healthy as a horse, and you can go home tomorrow. I'll have the nurse take out your IV and unhook you from all these monitors, so you can get a good night's sleep."

"Dr. Tisdale, do you have any medical information that would explain what has happened to me...the physical and mental changes that I've undergone?"

"Not at this time, Joshua...maybe later. I don't know if you are aware of this or not, but my daughter, Tara, was diagnosed last year with an inoperable malignant brain tumor—a glioblastoma—and she had to undergo a series of chemotherapy and radiation treatments. The oncologist told me that she would be lucky to make it to her sixteenth birthday. Well, Tara's sixteenth birthday has come and gone, and there's no evidence of the tumor anywhere...she's had a complete remission! Just like you, my daughter was blessed with an unexplainable miraculous cure. I would like you to meet her...you two have a lot in common," said Ted.

"Sure...I would be honored," answered Joshua.

Ted knew the importance of a family. He had lost his lovely wife, Doreen, in a freak car accident when Tara was only six years old. It had started to snow, and Doreen was returning home from the hospital—she did volunteer work every Thursday on the pediatric ward, helping sick kids. Ted's wife was driving across an icy bridge, when the rear wheels of her car started to slide. She boldly steered into the skid, but the vehicle overcorrected, sending her across the median into a head-on collision with an oncoming pickup truck. Doreen was killed instantly. Ted never got over losing his cherished wife, but knew that he would have to play with the cards that life had dealt him. Now, all he had left in the world was his precious daughter Tara—and he would do *anything* for her.

Unannounced, Joshua's father, Luke, dressed in his black preacher's garb and carrying the Bible, burst through the door and walked into his son's hospital room. He smelled of liquor. Immediately observing his boy's changed physical appearance, Luke lifted up the Bible and shouted, "What in God's name is going on here...what have you done to Joshua? This is the work of Satan...blasphemy...God will surely punish..."

Ted interrupted the rambling evangelist, "Just calm down,

Luke, Joshua is fine...as a matter of fact, he is better *now* than he ever was before. I don't have all the answers, but the head injury he received in the accident has somehow incredibly repaired the physical and mental defects that he suffered from having Down Syndrome. No, Luke, this isn't the work of the Devil...if anything, this is a miracle from God!"

Joshua joined in, "Father, Dr. Tisdale *is* correct...my mental handicaps and physical disabilities have all disappeared... healed...it *must* be an act of God!"

"Or from Beelzebub himself," retorted Luke.

The intoxicated pastor grimaced, then placed the Bible over his heart and said, "I must go and pray now...the Lord will provide me with the answers to all of this."

As Luke opened the door to leave, he angrily looked back at Ted and said, "You had no business bringing him into this world...the boy should have died inside his mother, Mary. What you did was immoral...a sin against nature...may God have mercy on your lost soul!"

After his father left, Joshua looked over at Ted and said, "He doesn't know what he's saying...he's just drunk."

Dr. Tisdale nodded his head reassuringly and answered, "I know, I know." Then the physician stood up and announced, "Well, Joshua, it's time for me to leave. You've been through a lot these past two days...I know you can use the sleep. It's been great talking with you...see you tomorrow!"

Joshua smiled. "Thanks for coming in, Dr. Tisdale, I also enjoyed our conversation, and I'm looking forward to meeting your daughter, Tara!"

Ted waved back to his patient as he walked out the door. A few seconds later, Shirley ambled in and said, "How would you feel about severing your ties to all of this medical paraphernalia?"

"I could definitely handle that," grinned Joshua.

After the nurse had disconnected the intravenous line, urinary catheter, and monitor wires, she asked, "Need anything else?"

"No, ma'am, thank you very much...this feels great."

Shirley smiled brightly and said, "*I* know of something that you need." She walked out the door and quickly returned with three boxes stacked on top of each other, carefully cradled in both of her arms. They were gift wrapped, with colored paper and a bow, like the ones you get at Christmas time under the tree. The nurse placed them on the boy's lap and said, "Happy belated birthday, Joshua!"

The surprised teen had a dumbfounded look on his face, and didn't know what to say.

Shirley pointed to the boxes and said, "Go ahead...open them up!"

Joshua took the bow and wrapping off the first box, opened it, and to his amazement, found two new pairs of blue jeans and a pair of slacks, along with two belts; a brown one and a black one. The second box contained three new short sleeve shirts, color coordinated to match the pants, and the third had an assortment of underwear, undershirts, and socks—all enclosed in clear plastic packages.

"Sweet tits...uh...sweetist!" exclaimed Joshua, extremely excited about the presents. The disadvantaged teenager hadn't worn anything new in a long time, nor owned any clothing as nice as this before.

"None of your old clothes will fit you anymore," said

Shirley, "so Dr. Tisdale and I figured that you could use some new threads...we took up a collection at the hospital. Tomorrow, after you're discharged, I'll take you over to Harland's Shoe Store and let you pick out some new stompers."

This was the nicest thing that anyone had ever done for Joshua, aside from the peace sign necklace that his best friend had personally made for him. Patrick had spent hours up in his bedroom working on Joshua's gift, re-weaving the hemp until the design was perfect.

The act of kindness touched Joshua emotionally. His eyes moistened, and with a shaky voice he said, "Thank you so much, Nurse Gates...you've been so kind to me...please thank everyone at the hospital for the gifts, especially Dr. Tisdale." The sight of the poor boy in the hospital bed with tears in his eyes was moving, and even tugged at the heartstrings of a veteran nurse who had seen just about everything.

How would that look if a tough-as-nails nurse broke down in front of her patient? thought Shirley.

Nurse Gates didn't want to get misty in front of Joshua, so she stifled her quivering lip and swallowed back the emotional tickle in her throat. She put the clothes back in their boxes and placed them in the corner of the room. Clearing the sentiment from her pharynx, Shirley said, "We enjoyed doing it for you, Joshua...you're a great kid, and an even greater patient...we'll try on the clothes tomorrow to make sure they fit, okay?"

"Okie dokie," answered Joshua.

The choked up nurse opened the door, flipped off the light, and in a shaky voice softly said, "See you bright and early tomorrow morning, Joshua...sleep tight." He watched as the door closed slowly behind her. The tired teenager yawned widely, shut both eyes, and momentarily thought about everything that had recently happened, before dozing off into a sound slumber. Even though Joshua greatly mourned the loss of his best friend, Patrick—for some reason, he wasn't lonely anymore.

#

It seemed like the entire town of Tranquil had arrived at the city cemetery to pay their respects to Patrick Murdock. Joshua, dressed in his new clothes and shoes, rode with Patrick's parents to the funeral because Luke was too sick to attend—more like too hungover to get out of bed. Patrick was to be buried in the Murdock family plot, next to where his grandparents lay. It was an open coffin affair, and the embalmer at the Pinetop Funeral Home had done a wonderful job in preparing the body—Patrick's broken neck had been manipulated into a more normal position, and flesh-tone makeup was strategically applied to cover up the abrasions and bruising that had been stamped on the boy's neck and face.

Joshua, being Patrick's closest friend, was one of the first to view the contents of the casket. The lid of the coffin was hinged open, and the inside surface of the pine case was cushioned in a satin-like material, regal-red in color. Patrick lay supine in the long, ornate wooden box, both arms positioned over his chest, with his hands clasped tightly together. The deceased teenager was nicely adorned in a dark suit with matching vest, a light blue shirt, red tie, and black patent-leather shoes. Joshua instantly recognized the clothes that his friend had on—it was the same black suit that Patrick had worn to church every Sunday. Even though they belonged to different congregations, the two boys would goof around together on Sunday mornings before leaving for their respective houses of worship. Joshua specifically remembered the red tie, because it was the same necktie that Patrick had used to teach him how to fasten a Windsor knot. After many patient days of repetitive practice, Joshua had become somewhat proficient at tying it.

Joshua used the powers of his newly reconstructed mind to reflect back over time. He vividly reminisced about all of the wonderful things that his blood-brother, Patrick, had done for him—teaching him to ride a bike, protecting him from the cruelty of bullies, making him laugh—Patrick was always there for Joshua. Patrick was a rarity, truly a one-of-a-kind individual...an unselfish friend that put others before his own wants or needs. Joshua would miss him greatly.

The preacher's son stood alongside the coffin and stared down at the resting body of his dead comrade. Patrick's eyes were closed, and he had a peaceful, calm, contented expression on his face. Pulling the peace symbol necklace from his pocket, Joshua held it up over Patrick and said, "I fixed it, it's as good as new now...I'll always wear it in memory of *you*, Patrick...my best friend. Tears of sorrow filled his eyes as he bent over the casket and whispered into his companion's ear, "Blood-brothers to the end...blood-brothers until we die...blood-brothers forever...goodbye, Patrick." Joshua then gave his deceased pal a kiss on the cheek. The saddened teen wiped the drops of grief from his face and with head bowed, shuffled slowly away from the wooden casket, never to see his wonderful friend again.

As the melancholic adolescent physically distanced

himself from his dead cohort, he was approached by Sheriff Evans. In order to shake Buck's extended hand, Joshua took the clutched peace sign he was holding and placed it into his suit pocket. "Joshua, I'm so sorry about Patrick," said Buck. "I know it's not a good time now, but do you mind if I ask you a few questions about what happened?"

"No, I don't mind," answered Joshua.

"First of all, congratulations on your extraordinary recovery...everyone in town is talking about it. We only wish that Patrick could have been saved, too. Now, what do you remember about the accident on Green Valley Road?"

Joshua paused for a second, and then said, "I do have some memory loss associated with the accident itself, but as far as I can tell, I suffer from no significant retrograde amnesia. To the best of my recollection, Patrick and I were riding on our bikes, when Niles Slovinsky drove up behind us in his Ford Mustang, honking his horn and yelling obscenities. Niles was trailing very closely behind us, when a rabbit suddenly darted in front of my bike. I remember applying the hand brake to avoid hitting the animal, and I believe that his car bumper struck my rear tire, hurling my bike into Patrick's. We both flew off the shoulder of the road and plunged into the gully below. That's all that I can recall...I must have been knocked unconscious from my fall."

"Did you see the Slovinsky boy's car bumper strike your tire, or did you just 'feel' it?"

"I was focusing on the rabbit at the time, so I didn't actually *see* his bumper hit my bike. I just heard a thump sound, and felt the jolt of something striking my rear tire."

"Could that thump sound have been caused by the

rabbit...a rock...or Patrick's bike?"

"It could have, but—"

"Don't get me wrong, Joshua, I've already questioned Niles, and I think that *he* caused this accident and is guilty as sin, but in a court of law, it would have to be proved beyond a reasonable doubt that his negligence was responsible for Patrick's death...it's basically your word against his."

"I understand...and what jury would take the word of a mentally retarded boy over the fabrications of a 'normal' kid like Niles?"

"Exactly," said Buck. "Unfortunately, our legal system is plagued with all sorts of problems, but since it's the only law that we have, we must abide by its rules. I haven't given up on this yet, Joshua...I'm doing what I can to get this matter before a grand jury hearing, so let me know if you remember anything else."

"I will...thank you, Sheriff Evans."

Buck and Joshua made their way back over to the rows of seats to hear the pastor deliver the religious service, and to listen to the family eulogies for Patrick. After the ceremony was completed and Patrick was laid to rest, Joshua rose from his chair to leave. As he stood up, he was overcome by a fantastic optical sensation—brightly colored lights flashing and flickering before his eyes, like an assemblage of strobe lights at a discotheque. Joshua shut his eyes, but the aura only intensified. Suddenly, and without any warning, the teen experienced an excruciatingly painful, pressure sensation, accompanied by a high-pitched humming sound, originating from the inside of his head. Everything around him was spinning—not like the dizziness felt from riding the tilt-a-whirl at an amusement park, but something much more bizarre. It was more like a tornado vertigo and hurricane tinnitus, followed by grotesque hallucinations. Joshua had the weird feeling...a strange perception...that his brain was growing, expanding...trying to break out of its bony encasement!

The intensity of pain and crescendo of sound became too much for Joshua to bear. Grasping his head with both hands he cried, "Oh my God, what's happening?" A small drop of bright red blood trickled down from his right nostril. In the blink of an eye, Joshua's visual field dimmed to blackness, as if someone had turned off a television. Like a felled tree, he toppled to the ground, landing in a heap, totally unconscious.

"Joshua...wake up...Joshua...open your eyes," the voice said. Joshua recognized the tone. *It was a deep voice...a man's voice*, thought Joshua, *sounds like...Dr. Tisdale.*

"You're going to be all right, Joshua...you just fainted," said Ted, in a comforting tone.

Groggy and disoriented, Joshua slowly opened his eyes, looking like he had just been aroused from a deep sleep. The first image that came into focus was the angelic face of a stunningly beautiful young girl. All she needed was a halo and wings. *I must be in Heaven...I have never seen anything so gorgeous*, thought Joshua. He blinked his eyes twice to make sure it wasn't a hallucination.

A lovely oval-shaped face, surrounded by long blonde hair that shimmered in the sunlight, posed above him. The goddess possessed perfectly proportioned features: a flawless peaches-and-cream complexion, tiny nose, and rich smiling lips. A pair of bright blue eyes, covered with long, thick lashes, stared down at Joshua. The girl opened her petite mouth, revealing orthodontically-aligned white teeth, and spoke in a melodic tone with a voice that could melt butter.

"Hi, Joshua, I'm Tara," she said. "Are you okay?"

"I think so," answered Joshua, keeping his eyes fixated on the maiden's pretty face.

"I wanted you two to meet, but I didn't exactly have this scenario in mind," said Ted. "Sit up slowly, Joshua, you're going to be lightheaded and feel a little bit disoriented, until you get acclimated."

"What happened?" queried the confused boy.

The doctor helped raise Joshua to a sitting position, and then explained, "You had a syncopal episode...you passed out...probably from all of the emotional drain of today, along with just being released from the hospital. Son, you've been through some tough times these past few days. I'll run some more tests on you tomorrow just to be on the safe side, but don't worry about it, you'll be fine.

"Oh...yeah...right," replied Joshua.

Like Ulysses and the sirens, Joshua was mesmerized by the mere presence of this nymph named Tara—unable to take his eyes off of her foxy face. It was as if he were in a hypnotic trance, under her spell. Tara was exquisitely attired in a light-yellow print sundress, made of cotton, and dotted all over with tiny, pink-colored roses. The beauty's garment was embellished with an embroidered full collar, and was gathered in at the waist with a thin yellow, patent leather belt. The dress ended just above the knees, and fell demurely over her slender, well-proportioned figure—delicately accentuating every curve of her femininity.

Ted and Tara helped the dizzy teen to his feet, and walked

him over to one of the nearby chairs. Joshua could feel Tara's soft arm around him — her gentle touch was comforting and energizing. The love-struck boy looked over at the angel's smiling face and thought, *what a beautiful creature she is.* Joshua had been bitten by the love-bug *and* shot with Cupid's arrow. A magnetic chemistry was developing between the two teenagers, and both could feel its dynamic power. From the time their eyes first met, the couple had connected, and Joshua felt drawn to Tara by something intangible — an indescribable bonding. A heart that was once forced to beat to the tempo of cruelty and sadness was now pulsating to a rhythm of love and ecstasy.

"Come on, Joshua, we'll give you a ride home," said Ted. "I've already contacted the principal at Tranquil High School, and informed him about your new mental capabilities, and the results of your intelligence tests. You've been transferred to the honors program for gifted kids."

"You'll love it, Joshua...now we'll be in the same classes together," said Tara.

Unable to hide his excitement, the smitten teenager smiled at his newly found girlfriend from Heaven, and said, "Ass-hum...I mean...uh...awesome... totally awesome!"

Chapter VIII
RETRIBUTION

It was Joshua's first day of class in the honor's program at Tranquil High School. The handsome teenager looked pretty spiffy in his new clothes, and walked confidently onto the campus grounds, where the other kids were hanging out—awaiting the buzzing clang of the morning bell that signaled the beginning of first period. As Joshua scaled the steps that led to the front doors, he was greeted by Tara, who had been anxiously awaiting his arrival.

"Hi, Joshua," beamed the gorgeous Tara, her radiant blue eyes glistening in the morning sun. She had her hair pulled back into a ponytail, and looked as cute as a pixie—with pristine features and an unblemished complexion that required essentially no makeup embellishment.

Joshua, looking quite stellar himself, smiled and answered, "Hi there, yourself."

"Our first class is biochemistry, taught by Mrs. Ravens," said Tara.

"Mrs. Ravens...cool...she was my biology teacher...before the accident," said Joshua. "But if it hadn't been for the accident, I never would have met—"

Baaa-rriinngg!

At that very moment, the class bell went off, clamoring out its characteristically annoying sound, deafening to the ears, rudely interrupting Joshua's comment.

"Never would have met...who?" smiled Tara. She had *such* a beautiful smile—the kind of smile that could stop the flow of heavy downtown traffic during an afternoon rush hour.

Joshua smiled down at the adorable face of the golden goddess and said, "Why...you."

Tara took her boyfriend's hand in hers and said, "Come on, Joshua, we don't want to be late for our first class!" Hand-in-hand, the two lovebirds pranced through the swinging front doors of the high school.

In the hallway, Joshua encountered his old nemesis, Niles Slovinsky, who had spotted him walking with Tara toward Mrs. Ravens' classroom. Niles, with a puzzled look on his face, called out, "Hey...is that you...the retard, Joshua? What the hell happened to you? Man, you've really changed...you're different. What did you do with that dumb face of yours, get plastic surgery or something?"

The old Joshua would have tried to strangle the no-good, son-of-a-bitch that had killed his best friend, Patrick, but the reborn Joshua—the superiorly intelligent clone—composed himself, and with no expression calmly said, "Yes, Niles...it's me, Joshua...what do you want?"

"Listen, dickweed, you better not've told the sheriff that I had anything to do with your accident," said Niles, in an obnoxious tone of voice. "It's your fault that Patrick's dead...if you hadn't slammed on your brakes to avoid that rabbit, you wouldn't have crashed into his bike."

Prior to the accident, Niles had easily been able to intimidate Joshua, but now, the smart aleck was definitely no match for the genius's superior mental powers. The prodigy angrily looked at the redheaded troublemaker and charged, "Niles, you *know* that you were the one responsible for our accident. *You* bumped my rear tire with your car fender, causing me to lose control of the bicycle. How can you live with yourself knowing that your negligence caused Patrick's death?"

The words rang true, and they seemed to have had an effect on Niles's feeble mind. Whenever the acne-faced teen became nervous, he had the habit of reaching into his pocket and playing with his car keys, which, along with his penlight, were attached to his key ring. Niles's facial sneer quickly changed into an expression of shame, and the accused boy started to stutter. "B... bu...bull...bullshit," he stammered. Even a sociopath like Niles still retained a small remnant of a guilty conscious, hidden deep in the distorted matrix of his dysfunctional brain.

Joshua's psychological mind game with Niles was working, so he continued further. Making direct eye-to-eye contact with the fidgeting fool, Joshua said, "The truth really hurts, doesn't it Niles...aren't the feelings of guilt overwhelming for you...don't you have nightmares at night...how can you look at yourself in the mirror, knowing you were responsible for the death of another human being?"

Niles initially hesitated, then flashed a quizzical look—like he was actually thinking about what Joshua had said. Displaying a face riddled with guilt, the carrot top looked down at his shoes and said sheepishly, "I don't have to listen to this crap," and walked away.

"Who is *that* Neanderthal?" Tara inquired.

"Niles Slovinsky...the one who caused Patrick's death, and almost mine," said Joshua.

Tara was silent for a moment, then she pulled on Joshua's hand and said, "We're going to be late!" They hurried down the hall and rushed through the classroom door, just as the bell rang.

Mrs. Ravens walked over to Joshua and gave him a big hug—the kind a mother would give a son. The teacher immediately noticed the changes in the boy, but didn't want to say anything that would embarrass him in front of his classmates. "Joshua, it's so good to see you again...you look wonderful...so tall and handsome!"

"Thank you, Mrs. Ravens, it's great to see you too!" replied Joshua.

"I've got to start class now, but later, you've got to fill me in on everything," said the teacher.

Joshua smiled and answered, "Mrs. Ravens, I don't even know myself what happened, but I'll be happy to tell you what I do know."

The two teenaged sweethearts took their seats, located next to each other in the back of the room, and prepared for the biochemistry course. Mrs. Ravens stood at the front of the class and announced, "Today, we are studying the Krebs Cycle. Does anyone know what the purpose of the Krebs Cycle is?" No one responded to her question, so Tara raised her hand.

"Yes, Tara?" said Mrs. Ravens.

"The Krebs, or Citric Acid Cycle, is a series of biochemical reactions used in cellular aerobic and anaerobic metabolism," answered Tara. "It converts pyruvate to carbon dioxide and energy."

"Very good, Tara," said the teacher, "I'm glad that *someone* did their homework. Can anyone come to the chalkboard and draw a simple diagram of the Krebs Cycle?

No one in the class raised their hand

"Any volunteers?" asked the instructor.

Joshua leaned over and whispered to Tara, "I can't explain how, but I can do this."

"Don't be bashful, Joshua...raise your hand, and go do it!" said his girlfriend.

Joshua hesitantly lifted his hand and said humbly, "I'll give it a try, Mrs. Ravens."

Trying to hide the astonished look on her face, the teacher said, "Okay, Joshua, come up to the front, please."

The mentally and physically transformed boy timidly got up from his seat, walked up to the board, and picked up a piece of white chalk. Joshua looked out at the rows of faces staring curiously back at him, and then turned to confront his assignment. *Don't be nervous, Joshua... you can do this*, he thought to himself.

The determined teenager placed the chiseled tip of the

scrawling utensil against the black surface of compressed shale and began to write furiously. As if his hand were possessed by some unearthly power, Joshua moved the white limestone stick with purpose and intent, moving at a superhuman pace over the flat plane of the blackboard. The chalk squeaked and banged as it made steady contact with the smooth ebony slate, leaving legible impressions of its telltale white powdered residue behind. In only a matter of minutes, and to the amazement of the entire class, Joshua had drawn the following detailed schematic of the Krebs Cycle on the chalkboard:

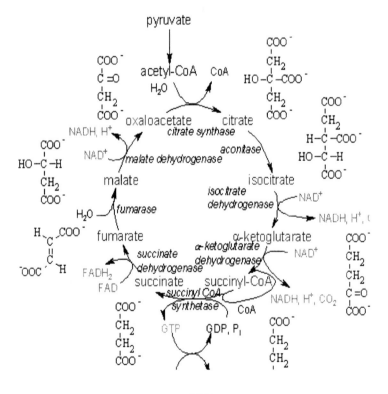

After he had completed his work of art, Joshua set the worn piece of chalk down on its holder, and nonchalantly walked back to his seat. Sitting down in his chair, he observed Tara, who smiled cutely and winked at him, as if to say, *"Way to go, Joshua, that was sooo impressive!"*

Other than a few *Oohs* and *Ahs*, the classroom was dead silent—the clichéd "hear a pin drop" type of quiet. One of the students whispered to her friend, "I think I know who this new boy is...my mom works at the hospital and I heard her talking on the phone...he's that retarded kid that got in a bad accident and almost died...now, he's like a genius or something."

Mrs. Ravens couldn't believe her eyes, either. *What in the name of Mary, Mother of God, was going on? How could Joshua have known the chemical formula, structure, and pathway of these compounds?* What the boy had so eloquently illustrated on the chalkboard was a product of organic chemistry—something that the teacher had learned in her college upper-level biochemistry classes. Mrs. Ravens had probably memorized the Krebs Cycle over a hundred times before, only to forget most of it in a matter of days—whereas Joshua drew a detailed rendering of the entire complex thing in record time, cold turkey!

"Joshua, is this a joke? Who put you up to this...was it the other science teacher, Mr. Hampton?"

"No, ma'am, no one put me up to it. Don't ask me how, but I just knew the answer...it was already there in my head," explained Joshua.

The educator was still skeptical. Trained as a biologist, Mrs. Ravens had learned to approach things scientifically and objectively—using logic and deductive reasoning to

119

determine the validity of the information presented. In order to make sure she wasn't the unsuspecting recipient of a well-rehearsed joke, Mrs. Ravens replied, "Okay, Joshua, that *was* remarkable...*quite* remarkable. Would you please briefly explain your diagram to the class?"

"Certainly!" answered the brilliant boy. "The Krebs, or Tricarboxcylic Acid Cycle, converts pyruvate to carbon dioxide gas, producing energy — namely NADH and $FADH_2$, and also phosphorylated energy in the form of GTP. Using the electron transport chain and oxygen, NADH and $FADH_2$ can be used to generate ATP — another source of energy. The substrate pyruvate is broken down into Acetyl CoA by oxidative decarboxylation, which occurs inside the mitochondria. The Acetyl CoA combines with oxaloacetate to form citric acid, which is subsequently converted into a number of other chemicals, eventually resulting in the cyclical regeneration of oxaloacetate. The entire reaction sequence results in the production of NADH, $FADH_2$, GTP, and ATP, with the release of carbon dioxide. Mrs. Ravens, would you like me to explain the specific chemical reactions for each of the..."

"No thank you, Joshua, that was all very well done," interjected the flabbergasted Mrs. Ravens. "Does anyone have any questions?"

One of the kids in the room raised his hand and cracked, "Is it too late for me to transfer back to the *retarded* science class?" Everyone, including Joshua, got a chuckle out of that witty remark.

Joshua was right; he had *seen* the answer in his head, and visualized its image, just like a photograph. Before the accident, the photograph was a black-and-white snapshot that was blurry and grossly distorted—now, it was a fully developed, color image—clear and sharply focused. Joshua's mind wasn't a black, light-box anymore—the teen's brain had evolved into a high-resolution, digital camera. *Everything* that Joshua had been exposed to prior to his bicycle crash—words he saw or heard, but didn't comprehend their meaning; books he previously read, yet unable to understand their contents; television programs or news reports he listened to or watched; any unusual sounds he heard; or, for that matter, any external stimuli he ever received before—all of these images had been indelibly stored, locked away somewhere in the endless communication of electrical synapses in his brain, only to be miraculously awakened after his accident.

Joshua was now blessed with an all-encompassing, photographic memory—a superhuman rote recall that could recite or recount anything that he had ever been exposed to—and then some. As luck would have it, this phenomenal gift arrived without any other disabling, accompanying baggage. Fortunately for Joshua, his amazing powers hadn't been saddled with any of the other handicaps that many times plague savants, such as autism or mental retardation.

#

The noon bell rang and Joshua and Tara, inseparable from each other since the school day had begun, decided to eat lunch in the park located next to Tranquil High. It was another beautiful spring day, one that could be appreciated the most by being outdoors. The two teens picked out a wooden picnic table that was partially shaded by an old oak tree, and then sat directly across from each other on its attached benches. While eating lunch, their mundane conversation turned into queries of a more personal nature.

Joshua ripped off a big bite of his ham and cheese sandwich, chewed it several times, and then chased it down with a hearty swig of coke. "Tara, we have a lot in common—both of us have had to overcome great obstacles in our still young lifetime. I battled mental retardation and the stigma associated with it, and you fought off an inoperable brain tumor," he said. "If you don't mind me asking, what was it like to have cancer?"

"I don't mind, Joshua...you can ask me anything," smiled Tara. "It's horrible, a disease that destroys you from within, not only your body, but your heart and soul as well. Even though I am now in complete remission, there is always that nagging voice in the back of my brain that periodically asks me, *Is it gone...did the chemotherapy and radiation treatments kill all of it...or is there still some left? Has it spread to another part of my body? Even if only one malignant, isolated mutant cell has survived, it can nevertheless continually divide to reproduce itself and grow into a killer cancer once again!*"

Joshua reached over and held Tara's hand. "It must have been very tough on you, having to undergo all of those chemotherapy and radiation treatments."

"It wasn't a cakewalk, by any stretch of the imagination. Your hair falls out, your skin turns pale and bruises easily, you're always nauseous, and you get up each morning feeling horrible. There were many times that I wanted to give up...to let those cancer cells take over my brain...to just fall asleep and never wake up again."

"But you didn't give up, and look at you now, Tara," said Joshua. "I'm really proud of you!"

"Thanks...you've been on quite a roller coaster ride yourself, Joshua...how did *you* cope with everything?"

"It's funny...people feel sorry for the mentally retarded, but usually, the person with the limited brain function is happier and more content than the average individual—because of their limited mental capacity, they don't have all of those worries and responsibilities. If happiness is the key to life, then most mentally challenged people have found the answer—sometimes simple *is* better. I guess that I was able to cope with misfortune because I'm a fighter...and my faith... I never lost my faith."

Tara gently squeezed her new boyfriend's hand and said, "Well, now we have each other to rely on, don't we, Joshua?"

"Yes, we sure do," smiled the savant. He thought about his deceased blood-brother, and the void in his life that Patrick's passing had left. Tara, thank God, was filling that void, and Joshua could feel himself drawing closer to this lovely creature who had the best of both worlds—a gorgeous body and pretty face, combined with the most important thing of all—a beautiful mind.

"Oh, by the way, Joshua, the carnival is in town this weekend and Daddy and I are going...would you like to join us?"

"Sure, that sounds like fun!"

"Great, we'll pick you up at seven this Friday."

Joshua beamed a smile over to Tara and said, "Ass...uh... awesome!"

The two sweethearts finished lunch, and then headed back to attend their third period math class, Advanced Calculus. The rest of the week zoomed by, and before they knew it,

Friday had rolled around—indeed, it *was* true that time does go by fast when you're having fun. And Joshua *was* having fun—the teen was having the time of his life spending the week with Tara. Whether it was studying, talking, walking, or just being together, they both thoroughly enjoyed each other's company—Joshua and Tara, it seemed, were a match made in Heaven.

Joshua had impressed all of his teachers and fellow students, quickly becoming somewhat of a celebrity at school—he was known as "The retarded kid turned genius after a bicycle accident." It sounded just like one of those fantastic headlines printed on the front page of a tabloid newspaper rag that you see while waiting in line at the grocery store.

\#

Kent's Carnival arrived early Friday morning, and the "carnies" were working hard all day, putting up the big tents, assembling the game booths, and preparing the rides. The carnival was held at the same place every year—on the big vacant lot located at the corner of Fir and Spruce Streets, just two miles east of downtown Tranquil.

It was a little after seven-thirty at night when Ted, Joshua, and Tara arrived at the carnival. A sizeable crowd of people were already gathered and wandering around, enjoying the sights and sounds of the festive occasion. Dr. Tisdale was lucky enough to find a parking space in the open field across the street, only a short walk away from the front entrance. Kent's Carnival contained the usual collection of attractions and entertainment—a row of game booths, several amusement rides, a small sideshow displaying animal and human freaks of nature, along with a variety of food and drink refreshment stands. After they had squeezed their way through the crowded admission gate, Tara's father pulled out his wallet and handed Joshua a twenty-dollar bill.

"That's okay, Dr. Tisdale, I brought some cash," said Joshua. The money the boy carried came from what he had earned doing odd jobs for neighbors.

"Here, take it, son," said Ted. "It's my treat tonight."

The teenager stuffed the money in his front right pocket and said, "Thanks...thanks a lot, Dr. Tisdale."

"Just don't blow it all in one place," joked the physician.

"I won't, Dr. Tisdale," smiled Joshua.

"Let's meet up in about an hour," said Ted, studying his watch. "Say nine o'clock, over by —" He peered over the slew of people's heads, and then pointed to one of the rides, "over by Doctor Blood's Castle."

"Thanks, Daddy...see you at nine...at Doctor Blood's... love you!" peeped Tara.

"Love you too...you kids have fun."

The pair of infatuated teens answered in near-unison, *"We will!"* and then strolled off toward the game booths, hand-in-hand.

Dr. Tisdale headed over to the "back end" of the carnival, to the tents located in the rear, where they housed the sideshows and freak exhibits. Carnivals usually don't want to gross out their customers by putting the two-headed calf next to the front entrance, so they tend to keep the creepy monstrosities a good distance away. Being a physician, and having a strong interest in genetics, Ted was especially fascinated by medical anomalies, both human and animal. The doctor had extensively researched many famous human aberrations, such

125

as: the original Siamese twins, Chang and Eng Bunker; Feodor Jeftichew, known as Jo-Jo the Dog Faced Boy; Frank Lantini, the three-legged man; Johny Eck, the human torso; Prince Randian, the human caterpillar; the Crab Boy; Popeye; and a host of others — but his all-time favorite was Joseph Carey Merrick, the legendary Elephant Man.

Ted's fascination with the *lusus naturae* – people born with demonstrable physical differences — wasn't just a consequence of morbid curiosity. The man of medicine wasn't at all like those rubberneck drivers who would snail by the scene of a car accident, eager to see a severed head, a dismembered body, or at the very least, some bloody entrails extruding from a slashed open belly. Hopefully, there would be enough worthwhile gore for the gawkers to scrutinize — their instant gratification should offset the inconvenience of having to slow down their vehicle, thank-you-very-much. No, on the contrary, Ted had seen enough blood-n-guts in the emergency room to last him over several lifetimes. The doctor actually possessed a genuine scientific and medical interest in the study of the human oddity.

Once, several years back, Ted had visited a carnie sideshow, and was taken aback by the bold lettered sign, *MAN-EATING CHICKEN*. He eagerly donated his dollar to see the ferocious foul, and was pleasantly amused when he entered the claustrophobic tent and observed a man sitting behind a tiny table — eating fried chicken. Gotcha! *This Way To The Egress*, said the sign with the arrow, prompting the gullible crowd to unknowingly stroll out the exit door of Barnum's American Museum. P.T. Barnum got a helluva good laugh out of that one — it's actually true, there *is* a sucker born every

126

minute!

Joshua and Tara passed by the "pop-the-under-inflated-balloon-with-a-dull-pointed-dart," the "toss-the-coin-and-make-it-stay-on-the-slippery-waxed-plate," and the "knock-the-pins-not-over-but-off-the-table-with-the-crappy-bean-bag" rip-off games, when they heard the loud, gruff voice of a man.

"Hey, sonny, step right over here and try your luck... you can't lose...a winner every time!" shouted the individual behind the game booth counter. The stubbly-bearded barker was dressed in an old, worn, ratty outfit—dappled, moth-eaten black wool trousers with no belt, a wrinkled, blue long-sleeved shirt with a torn collar, a tight-fitting red cloth vest with missing buttons, and a beat-up purple derby hat with a peacock feather sticking out of its band—clothes in such poor condition that they looked like rejects from a Salvation Army Store.

"Come on, only one dollar to win a dollar!" the carnie called out, smirking widely. It was evident that this chap had never seen the dentist, much less owned a toothbrush. All of his central and lateral incisors—the four front upper and four front lower teeth—were completely missing, leaving a large gap in the middle of his mouth. The open dental space was surrounded on all sides by decaying canines—bestowing the man a scary-but-comical appearance—much like a homeless vampire. Joshua and Tara avoided looking at each other, for fear that they would both burst out into uncontrollable laughter.

"Sure, I'll give it a try," said Joshua, fighting back a chuckle. "How do I play?"

The carnival man's lips formed into a smug grin, as if he had snagged an unsuspecting fly in his web of deceit. "It's very simple, sonny...it's called the pea game. See these three red colored cups in front of you? I place this white pea under one of them. Then I move the cups around into different positions. After I'm done switching the cups, you have to tell me what cup the pea is under."

"Okay," said Joshua, "I think I can handle that."

The con-artist held out his hand, palm up, and said, "One dollar, please."

The boy reached into his left pocket and pulled out one of his own dollars—he didn't want to waste Dr. Tisdale's money on something as frivolous as a pea game—then politely handed over the George Washington to the man. An interested group of spectators started to gather around Joshua and Tara, curiously awaiting the outcome of the game.

With the thumb and forefinger of each hand, the unshaven carnie pulled his shirtsleeves up to his forearm and began his well-rehearsed barker parlance. Playing to the small crowd, he raised his hands and rotated his wrists—like a blackjack dealer who had just finished his shift— and announced, "As you can see, ladies and gents, I have nothing up my sleeves." Next, he held up each of the three cups, exposing the empty inside surface to the pack of attentive onlookers, and then placed them facedown on the plastic countertop. Making sure that everyone could see his movements, the scruffy-appearing dude slowly lifted the center red cup, and delicately placed the white pea under it. He then turned his attention to Joshua, and said, "Watch carefully, sonny...remember that the hand is always quicker than the eye."

Tara affectionately patted her boyfriend on the back and whispered, "Good luck, Joshua, you can do it!"

Joshua concentrated on the game in front of him, fixating his visual field on the fraudster's hands, the pea, and the three red cups. With surprising dexterity and lightning speed, the old trickster maneuvered the cups—switching and repositioning the red blurs in only a matter of seconds.

"Wow, that guy is fast!" said one of the kids in the crowd.

"Those sleight-of-hand movements are mind-blowing," remarked another.

Everyone in the audience had a differing opinion as to which cup the pea was under. Confident that his agility had completely fooled the youngster, the prestidigitator wearing the derby hat smirked and said, "Times up, sonny...which cup is the pea under?"

Joshua pointed to the center cup. "This one here...the pea is under the middle cup."

The con-man's cocky smirk was quickly transformed into an ugly scowl. He lifted up the red center cup, and sure enough, to everyone's surprise, there lay the white pea. "A winner every time!" the conjurer announced to the gathering. Then under his breath he grumbled, "Damn beginner's luck."

"Way to go, Joshua!" said Tara.

"You got two dollars coming to you, sonny...wanna try for double or nothing?"

"Sure," answered the teen.

The disgruntled gamer hid the pea again, then went through his dexterous manipulation of the three red cups. "Okay, sonny, where do you think it is now?"

"This time it's under that one," said Joshua, pointing to

the container on the left.

When the cup was lifted, a loud burst of applause and cheering erupted from the group of observers. "You win again...you sure are lucky," moaned the barker. "How about another double or nothing?"

"Okay," smiled the winner.

Again, the toothless carnie slid the cups furiously over the slick plastic counter, only this time he used an overwhelming number of deceptive hand movements, unfairly prolonging the completion of his demonstration.

"Hey, that's not fair!" yelled a concerned crowd member. "Give the kid a chance."

"He had his chance," barked the showman. "Okay, kid, where is it?"

"The pea is under the same cup as last time...this one," said Joshua, picking up the covering on the left, revealing the tiny round object underneath.

Tara, along with the rest of the supporters, cheered loudly.

"How the hell are you doing that?" growled the con artist. "Nobody's that lucky. Listen, kid, you're eight bucks up. Do you have the backbone to go against me one more time for sixteen smackers or nothing?"

"Don't mind if I do," answered Joshua, self-assuredly.

"Beat him at his own game!" a viewer yelled out.

"Yeah...go get him, kid...kick his butt!" screamed another.

"I'm taking the gloves off this time," said the angry loser, in a threatening tone.

The hustler placed the tiny pea under the center cup, and frantically juggled the three red containers over the polished white surface of the countertop. The cups made squeaking sounds—like sneakers on a basketball court—as they skated over the level plane of polymerized plastic. After a continuation of eye-boggling maneuverings, the gruff old sham lifted his hands from the overturned red containers, leaving them spaced equally apart and in perfect alignment— as if they were a trio of communist soldiers standing at attention. The deceiver then wiped the perspiration from his forehead and looked at Joshua. "Let's see how well your luck holds out now, kid...where's the pea?"

"I *know* that it's not under any of the cups...it's in your right hand!" replied the teen.

A bearded, burly bear of a man standing next to Joshua reached out and turned over all three of the cups—revealing that there was no pea under any of them. "Listen, you cheatin son-of-a-bitch! Where's the goddam pea? You better have a good explanation, or we're gonna call the sheriff...*after* we kick your ass!" roared the angry onlooker.

Totally caught off guard, the accused carnie's surprised face flushed a deep crimson. He suddenly bent down behind the counter, as if he were picking up something, and said, "Oh, here it is...the pea must've fallen off the table when I was moving the cups...my mistake. You win by default, sonny." The swindler pulled a wad of bills from his pocket and counted out sixteen dollars, one ten and six ones, and handed them over to Joshua. "Here ya go, sonny-boy...here's your sixteen greenbacks...now run along and let someone else play." Joshua folded the money and placed it in his front left pocket.

"No one wants to play your rigged game anymore, you dirty cheater!" heckled someone in the crowd.

"Yeah, let's get the hell out of here!" hollered another.

The large gathering of people observing Joshua's uncanny ability to find the hidden pea quickly exited the grounds in front of the game booth, rapidly dispersing themselves to the other areas of carnival attractions.

"I guess you showed him a thing or three," laughed Tara. "How did you do it?"

Joshua thought for a second and then answered, "Since the accident, I have acquired a gift...an ability to use the power of my mind like never before. I even amaze myself...and the force keeps getting stronger! Don't ask me how, Tara, but I was able to visualize in slow motion—like a movie camera—all of the movements that carnival hustler was making with his hands while manipulating the cups. In the last game, he only pretended to place the pea under the middle cup, when in reality, he had used sleight-of-hand to palm the pea, giving the illusion that it was still under the cup."

"That's amazing!" responded Tara.

"This also may sound crazy," he confided, "but I could swear that I heard the man's mind saying that he was going to try and cheat me on that last game."

Tara smiled at her boyfriend and said, "Totally amazing!"

Joshua looked around, and then pointed to a big billboard that had a color painting of a ghoulish-looking monster with blood dripping from its mouth. Below the creature's face were the words, BEWARE! DOCTOR BLOOD'S CASTLE — ENTER AT YOUR OWN RISK. "Hey, Tara, want to ride on that?"

She made a scary face and then said, "Yeah, looks really spooky...let's buy our tickets and get in line."

As the two sweethearts walked toward the ticket booth,

they heard the loudspeaker recording of a man's deep raspy voice. "Welcome to Doctor Blood's Castle...a house of horrors... you won't believe your eyes...enter if you dare...it was nice knowing you...heh-heh-heh-heh...welcome to Doctor Blood's Castle...a house of horrors...you won't believe your eyes..."

Joshua visually scanned the number of people already in line and said, "Tara, I just had a brainstorm...I'll go get our tickets while you save our place in line."

"What a clever idea, Joshua," joked the girlfriend. "You're sooo smart!"

Tara took her place in line while her boyfriend walked around the corner to purchase their ride tickets. As he was waiting, a voice from behind him remarked, "Well, look who it is, mister retard himself. What are you doing here buttwipe... where's that blonde bitch of yours?" Joshua didn't even have to turn around — he had recognized the voice instantly — it was Niles Slovinsky. The boy genius didn't mind Niles calling him names, but he certainly didn't appreciate the rude reference to his girlfriend, Tara.

"The sheriff has been snooping around, asking me a bunch of questions about Patrick's death. He's talking about a jury hearing or something, and you being a witness against me. I'm warning you now...you'd better keep your damn mouth shut, if you know what's good for you and that little slut girlfriend of yours!"

Thinking that the threats were all bark and no bite, Joshua turned to his aggressor, and in a serious tone of voice quipped, "Did you know that the carnival people are looking for you? They want you back in your cage...it's the one with the sign on it that reads, *"Niles Slovinsky - The Boy Born Without A Brain!"*

Most of the time, Niles *was* brainless...his anencephaly was not too far removed from the headless fetus the carnies kept in the pickle jar on the "back end" of the lot. In reality though, Niles did have a brain, but just never bothered to use it. For him, brainless and shit-for-brains were synonymous.

"Screw you and your sleazy girlfriend," snapped back the juvenile delinquent.

The mouthy redheaded teenager had crossed over the line once again. There was no reason for that derogatory remark — Tara had done nothing to Niles. Joshua looked straight into the boy's evil eyes and said, "Killed anybody lately, Niles?" Then he turned back to face the front of the line. Suddenly, Joshua's mind perceived the phrase *"just you, retard."* The words themselves had not been spoken or heard, but had somehow been picked up psychically by his highly advanced brain. Joshua heard a clinking noise behind him — it was Niles, nervously jingling the keys in his front pocket.

A few seconds later, Joshua actually *heard* the words, "Just you, retard" — this time coming from behind him — out of the mouth of Niles Slovinsky. Before Joshua had a chance to turn around, the red-headed hellion reared back with his fist and unloaded a swing, hitting Joshua on the back of the head — a blind-sided, cheap shot that the boy was helpless to defend against. The blow sent Joshua crashing forward to the ground, landing him in a face down position, alongside the back of the concession stand. As the felled adolescent attempted to lift his head, he was incapacitated by a barrage of flashing lights and humming sounds — bizarre auras, like the ones that invaded him at Patrick's funeral. Only this time, besides the auditory and visual hallucinations, he experienced gustatory

134

and olfactory sensations as well — a strong bitter metallic taste on his tongue, and the rancid smell of spoiled meat in his nose. The veins on his forehead and neck bulged outward, pulsating and undulating like blue earthworms exposed to a hot afternoon sun. A gush of blood suddenly erupted from Joshua's nose. He grabbed his head to try to subdue the upsurge of pounding in his brain, but it only worsened. The pain was too unbearable and unforgiving — Joshua tried again to pick himself up, but fell unconscious to the ground...down and out for the count.

Tara heard the commotion, and came running over to where her boyfriend lay. She looked up into Niles's cold eyes and didn't like at all what she saw. "Did you do this?" she demanded angrily.

Niles turned up the corners of his mouth into an annoying smirk and replied, "It was the damnest thing...retard just tripped over his own two feet." Then showing no emotion, the acne-faced teen walked up to the booth, purchased his ticket, and stood in line for the Doctor Blood's Castle ride. "I'm gonna get that bastard...his days are numbered," Niles mumbled to himself.

Tara gently cradled her boyfriend's head in her arms and whispered, "Are you all right, Joshua?"

The dazed teenager opened his eyes half-mast and muttered, "Yeah, I'll be okay."

"What happened...did Niles do this?"

"Hit me while I wasn't looking...that Niles...he's a real prize," uttered the disoriented teen.

Tara helped him to sit up, resting his back against the outside wall of the concession stand. "Can you stay here while

I go get Daddy?"

"Sure, I'll be okay in a few minutes...after I get the license plate number of the truck that ran over me."

"I'll be back with Daddy soon. Just rest here quietly, Joshua, you'll be fine...I promise!"

"I don't know what I'd do without you," smiled the dazed boy.

Tara gave him a quick affectionate kiss on the lips and said, "I feel the same way about you, too, Joshua!" She waved goodbye, and then headed off into the large crowd of people, disappearing into the hodgepodge of balloons, stuffed animals, and cotton candy — in search of her father, Ted.

#

Niles handed his ticket over to the unkempt operator running the Doctor Blood's Castle amusement ride, then stepped onto the electric-driven carriage and sat down. Judging from appearances alone, Niles looked more like a carnie than the ride-guy did. The aged attendant lowered the security bar over the teenager's thighs, and locked it into place. "It's one hell of a spooky ride, boy...I hope you can make it all the way through!"

Niles smirked up at the baseball cap-wearing old man, then remarked in a wimpy, sarcastic tone, "Me too...I'm *so* friggin scared...but now, I feel much better knowing that *you're* here to protect me!" Under his breath, but still audible, he added, "Stupid old dildo."

The ride-jock's jovial expression quickly changed into a countenance of irritation. "I heard that, boy. Don't make me open up a can of whoop-ass on you!"

"Whatever," replied the carrot-headed scoffer.

"Wise-ass, peckerheaded, toilet-mouthed kid," muttered the peeved attendant.

In the background, Niles could hear the gravelly voiced soundtrack reiterating, "Welcome to Doctor Blood's Castle...a house of horrors...you won't believe your eyes...enter if you dare...it was nice knowing you...heh-heh-heh-heh...welcome to..."

"Won't somebody please shut that frickin thing off?" complained the misfit teen.

The ride lurched forward on its tracks, sending the front bumper of Niles's buggy banging jarringly through a swinging wooden gate that had a big black medieval door painted on it—the entrance to Doctor Blood's Castle. Pre-recorded, and playing loudly in the background were the bloodcurdling sounds of screams, moans, and cries, mixed together with the noises of chains clanking together. Intervening with the deafening cacophony was the intermittent crashing clatter of thunder. After Niles's coach entered the small building, the entrance gate immediately slammed closed behind him, shutting out the bright carnival lights.

Suffice it to say that the special effects on this particular amusement ride weren't exactly mind-boggling. Dangling down from the ceiling was an extensive collection of black thread, just long enough to brush up against the face of the unsuspecting rider—hopefully eliciting a case of the heebie-jeebies. Plastic motorized frightening monsters, mechanical mannequins disguised as Doctor Blood and friends, giant spiders on strings, a huge fiendish rubber hand reaching out, bright lights flashing on and off, loud bells, horns, and whistles were all strategically placed to frighten the unwary traveler. The ride featured the mundane carnival, scary sort-of-stuff, which was boring to some, but still fun to others, in a hokey sort of way.

Niles really had no friends to speak of, so to him, the ride was just a way to pass time— another thing that he could ridicule and make fun of. Instead of trying to enjoy the amusement, he could only criticize. The complainer started his condemnation immediately—as soon as the gateway had closed behind him. "What the...how cheesy...that's just string hanging down...look how fake that blood is...what a goofy looking spider...this ride is a piece of crap!" he shouted.

Suddenly, and with no warning, an unexplained power outage occurred, knocking out the supply of electricity to the carnival. The flashing lights, the animated monsters, and the noisy sounds—everything—died abruptly. Niles's de-energized runabout took a sharp turn and continued on its tracks for a short period of time, finally decelerating to a squeaky halt.

"What the hell is going on? I can't see a damn thing...turn the friggin ride back on!" yelled out the frightened teen. The darkness was *so* black that Niles couldn't even see his hand in front of his face. Long projections of dark thread dangling above him tickled his forehead as he nervously turned his head to look around. The stranded teenager thought that he was all alone in the gloom. Niles was afraid—*very* afraid. Whether it was his imagination getting the best of him or not, as he sat there in the quiet, the freckle-faced boy suddenly had the strange feeling that he was being observed. The terrified teen sensed eyes—somebody was watching him—someone was standing there in the blackness, next to his coach. Niles, frozen with fear, sat motionless in his seat, not making a sound or moving a muscle.

Within a short period of time the electricity mysteriously returned, restoring needed power to the busy carnival. The flashing lights, recorded sounds, and flailing creatures all came back to life, as did the motorcars, which continued forward on their serpentine path through the scary amusement ride. Including the blackout time, Niles's journey through Doctor Blood's Castle—from beginning to end—took less than five minutes to complete. As his four-wheeled cart bumped through the swinging gate that was marked EXIT ONLY, the pimply-faced teenager was sitting upright in his seat, facing forward. His carriage coasted for a short distance, and then quickly decelerated, slowly inching forward to a complete squeaky stop.

"Stay in your car until I have lifted the security bar," announced the ride operator, "then please exit to your left."

The elderly attendant flipped a lever on the teen's halted buggy, releasing the protective bar that extended down over Niles's lap, and then lifted it up. "Exit to your left, please."

There was no movement or response elicited from the redheaded rider. "Okay, boy...you can get out now...rides over!" barked the old man.

Niles, with an expression of horror pasted on his face— eyes frozen open, forehead wrinkled, and mouth agape, like he was trying to scream—continued to sit motionless in his seat.

"Very funny, kid. I know...don't tell me...you're scared to death," joked the old-timer. The mime continued to stare straight ahead, speechless and pasty-faced.

The carnival worker gave a glancing study of the teenager's face and then said, "Hey, wait a minute, you're that same assclown who smart-mouthed me earlier. Get your goddam carcass the hell out of this car...you ain't funny, you little bastard!"

There was no response from Niles, just the blank horrified stare and mocking pantomimed scream that were grotesquely displayed on his acne-covered face.

"Listen here, numbnuts!" bellowed the annoyed employee as he tugged on the adolescent's striped shirt. Niles slumped sideways toward the old man, his upper torso stiffened and rigid, as if rigor mortis had already set in. Locked in a sitting position, the teen tumbled out the side of the coach, looking somewhat like a scuba diver who had entered the water backwards from a boat. Niles's head made a nauseating *thud* sound when it impacted the hard, dirt ground—the remainder of his body came to rest in a fixed fetal position, lying completely motionless. Two young girls waiting in line to board the ride shrieked and screamed hysterically after witnessing the horrific scene.

"Well, tongue my tallywhacker!" cried out the aged attendant.

The elder carnival employee rolled over Niles's body, took one look at the boy's frozen face, and then yelled, "Help! We need some help over here fast...is there a doctor in the house? Somebody get a...we need a goddam doctor, pronto!"

Tara and her father were over by the concession stand looking for Joshua, when they heard the loud pleas for assistance and came running over. "I'm a doctor, what happened here?" asked Ted, leaning over to examine the juvenile's lifeless body.

"Hell if I know, it was unfrickinbelieveable. The kid came off the ride...he was a real smartass...I thought he was playing a practical joke. He just fell out of the coach and landed like a goddam sack of potatoes...I think the little prick's dead," rambled the old buzzard.

The physician flashed his penlight into Niles's eyes, observing fixed and dilated pupils that were expressionless — reflecting no life whatsoever. Ted felt the teen's neck for a carotid pulse, but there was nothing there. No breathing sounds or chest movements either. Dr. Tisdale tried to position the teenager's head for mouth-to-mouth resuscitation, but was unable to flex the rigidly fixed neck — it was as frozen as the terrified expression on Niles's face. The boy's jaws were hideously propped open as well. Ted examined the teen's extremities and found hard unyielding flesh, with no mobility at the elbow or knee joints. He was also unable to move the boy's wooden fingers, which extended stiffly outward like the dead branches of an old tree. Niles's anatomy was completely petrified — exactly like a mummy. In medical school, the doctor had dissected old cadavers that possessed more suppleness than was seen in this adolescent's body. *It's as if the boy had been dead for weeks*, thought Ted.

Not wishing to alarm anyone around him, Dr. Tisdale announced, "Excluding a drug overdose, this young man probably died from an arrhythmia or a congenital heart anomaly."

"A whatsit or a...what the hell you talkin about, doc? I don't know what them friggin words mean...please speak human!" requested the potty-mouthed attendant.

"An abnormal heartbeat, or a defect...a disease, or a problem with his heart," said Ted.

"Well, why didn't you say that in the first place!" groaned the old geezer. "I'm not some dumb-ass, ya know!"

Ted gazed out into the nosy crowd of people gathering around them and shouted, "Somebody please call an ambulance...and Sheriff Evans!"

The physician looked over at the feisty carnie and asked, "Do you have something around here that we can use to cover up the boy?" The wrinkled ride-jock looked around and found an old dusty tarp that he threw over Niles's dead body, covering up the mummified corpse that wore a stony mask of horror.

"Let's move him over there...behind that booth," said Ted. The physician and the old man tucked the ends of the tarp up under the adolescent's stiff body, and then picked up the rock-hard corpse and carried it behind the ticket stand. There, the men carefully laid the deceased teen down on a grassy area that was hidden away from the growing mob of morbidly curious bystanders.

Ted eyed the wiry amusement ride operator and said, "Thanks for your help, Henry, I really appreciate it."

"You're welcome, doc...hey, how did you know my name? he inquired. "Can't recall ever meeting you before."

Ted hesitated, then extended his hand and said, "I'm Ted...Ted Tisdale. I must have met you in town...or at the hospital...I'm an emergency room doctor at Tranquil Community."

The elderly codger shook the physician's hand and replied loudly, "Last name's Pickridge—you know the Henry part already. I'm a local here. You probably seen me in town, or at the carnival...I stay away from the hospital — that's where you go to die! Every year I work the rides here...a way to make some extra dough, and meet some pretty women!" Henry eyed Tara out of the corner of his eye and lowered his volume. "There's lots of bearded clam walking around out here, and I need my carrot waxed just like the next guy, if you get my drift — it sure beats *flogging the log*," winked the lecherous old man.

"I understand," said Ted, hoping it was the end of *that* particular conversation.

Henry had an abundant slew of phrases relating to the art of male masturbation: *whipping the wire, beating the meat, petting the pony, spanking the spam, paddling the pickle, wetting the willie, slapping the salami, pounding the pud, choking the chicken, holding the sausage hostage, tugging the slug, pumping the python,* just to mention a few — but his favorite expression — the *pièce de résistance* — the one that had rewarded him with a black eye from a left hook delivered by the big guy whose girlfriend he was sitting next to at the bar, was *mangling the midget.* The lascivious old man had a slightly different idea in mind when he asked the cute brunette if she would like to *mangle his midget* — he didn't know that her six-foot-six inch boyfriend would do the mangling, and Henry hadn't planned on being the midget!

Having had the honor of meeting Mr. Henry Pickridge, and knowing where the old man's lewd dialogue was headed, Ted quickly changed the subject and inquired, "Does anyone know who this dead boy is?"

"It's Niles...Niles Slovinsky," said Tara. "He goes to our

143

school...he's the one who caused the accident that killed Patrick.

Joshua noticed the large gathering of people and walked over to where Dr. Tisdale and Tara were. "What's going on?" he asked.

"Where have you been?" asked a concerned Ted. "We've been looking all over for you. Weren't you supposed to stay where Tara left you, sitting up against the concession stand? How do you feel?"

"Still a little groggy, but I'll be okay. I left because I had to go to the restroom," answered Joshua. The teen peered over at the lumpy tarp, "What is that? Looks like a body under there."

"It's Niles," said Tara, "Daddy thinks he had a heart attack or something when he was on the Doctor Blood's Castle ride."

Couldn't have happened to a nicer guy, thought Joshua.

"We won't know anything for certain until the autopsy is completed," said Ted.

"The one thing we *do* know for certain, though," said Tara, "is that Niles won't be bothering anybody else anymore!"

Chapter IX
DOBBS

Sheriff Buck Evans drove up in his truck, arriving at the crowded carnival at the same time as the ambulance — its sirens squealing and red lights blinking. The two paramedics, along with Buck, exited their vehicles and converged on the area of commotion — a huge throng of people who had congregated by Doctor Blood's Castle ride. The sheriff, followed closely by the pair of paramedics, slowly worked their way through the congested horde. "Emergency police business...please move out of the way...let us through, people...we have an emergency!" shouted Buck, as he pushed through the mass of bodies. After about a minute of slam-dancing with the shoulder-to-shoulder mob of busybodies, they came upon Ted and Henry, standing guard over the covered corpse of

Niles Slovinsky.

"Okay, people, break it up...official police business here... go back and enjoy the carnival...there's nothing here for you to see," voiced the sheriff loudly.

"Hi, Buck," said Ted. "We've got a dead boy here." The doctor lifted up the end of the tarp to reveal the expression of intense fear that was still gruesomely plastered on Niles's face.

"It's the Niles Slovinsky kid," said Buck. "What the hell happened to him...it looks like he's trying to scream. Is it possible for someone to be scared to death?"

"It *is* possible, but extremely rare," answered Ted.

"What in God's name took place here, doc?" asked the sheriff.

"I don't know for sure, but it appears that the boy may have died from some type of heart problem. He's awfully young for that, but it happens more often than you think. The thing that perplexes me, though, is the rigidity—the firmness of the body...I've *never* seen rigor mortis set in that fast before... he was like that when we found him...hard as a brick."

"Any witnesses?"

Ted pointed over to Henry Pickridge.

Sheriff Evans walked over to the old carnie. "Hi, Mr. Pickridge, can you tell me what you saw here tonight?"

"Reckon I can, sheriff...never seen anything quite like it before—except for that *monster* what tried to kidnap me by Fletcher's Pond!" Henry wasn't overly fond of the sheriff, since he had always felt that Buck didn't believe a word of his alien abduction story.

Buck, after hearing Henry's statement, stifled a grin and

kept a concerned look on his face, not wanting to offend the old alcoholic.

Henry continued, "I was running the Doctor Blood's Castle ride, when this red-headed boy shows up and gives me his ticket. The kid was a real smart-aleck...very disrespectin to me...a royal diaper stain, if you get my drift. When I put the boy on the ride, he was alive...when he finished the ride, he were dead — a *smartass* when he went in, and a *deadass* when he came out. It's as simple as that...you do the math!"

"Did you see anything suspicious?" asked the lawman.

Henry scratched the back of his neck and reflected, "We had a power outage at the carnival tonight, when the kid was inside the attraction — but it only lasted for about five minutes, and I didn't see or hear a thing — the ride started right up again when the electricity came back on."

"Was the boy acting strangely, like he was on drugs?"

"Nope, the kid finished the ride and then fell out of the buggy — deader than a doornail — it was pretty *fugly!*" remarked Henry, utilizing his contraction for "fricking ugly."

"Anything else you can remember, Mr. Pickridge?"

"Not a damn thing. Sorry about what happened to the kid, but you know the old saying, 'What comes around goes around!'"

"Mr. Pickridge, I'll need you to come down to the sheriff's office tomorrow and fill out a witness report for me," said Buck. "Joshua, where were you when all this happened?"

"I don't know exactly," stammered Joshua. "I guess...I think I was in the bathroom, but..."

Ted quickly interrupted, "Niles started an argument with Joshua and then hit him when he wasn't looking. Joshua was dazed, so Tara left him sitting against the concession stand and went to get me. When Tara and I returned, we heard Henry's screams for help, and found Niles dead. Joshua was either sitting up against the concession stand, or in the bathroom...I can vouch for that!"

"I'm not accusing anyone of anything," said sheriff Evans. "I'm just doing my job. If there's any foul play suspected in the death of this young man, then I have to interrogate everyone involved."

"I understand," said Ted. "But I think that Niles died from natural causes...the autopsy findings should verify that."

"I hope you're right," replied Buck. "You all can leave now, but I'll need Tara and Joshua to stop by my office tomorrow and write out a statement for me."

"We'll see you in the morning, sheriff," said Ted.

"Goodnight...and thanks for your cooperation." The lawman took out a blue ballpoint pen and small pad of white paper that were tucked inside his shirt pocket, and scribbled down some notes.

After Buck was done writing, he said to Henry, "I want you to shut this ride down and lock all the doors, except for the entrance. Then, you and I are going to do some investigating inside this attraction."

Sheriff Evans directed his voice to the remaining group of looky-lou's still gathered around. "Okay, people...show's over...ride's closed...please clear the area...thank you."

Henry eyed the noisy bunch of diehard's and then bellowed, "Yeah, shut your damn pie-holes and cart your butts outtahere. You heard the sheriff...get the hell outta Dodge!"

The paramedics placed the frozen-faced, hardened body

of Niles Slovinsky into the ambulance, and drove off slowly toward the hospital, this time without any flashing lights or blasting sirens. Buck and Henry thoroughly searched the inside of Doctor Blood's Castle, but found nothing out of the ordinary—except for Niles's car keys and penlight, which were still attached to his key ring—lying next to the track just beyond the location of the giant rubber spider. Sheriff Evans thought that the key ring might have accidentally fallen out of the boy's pocket, but that didn't make any sense because the penlight was still on. Niles must have turned on the tiny light during the power outage—obviously in order to see in the dark. But why was it still on...and even more importantly, what did the teenager see?

#

The county coroner, Elroy Dobbs, M.D., a board-certified pathologist, was the one who would perform the autopsy on Niles Slovinsky. He had completed his pathology residency at Harvard Medical School, and was then hired on as a staff pathologist. A man of few words, Elroy had spent most of his past twenty-five years either looking through a microscope or dissecting dead bodies. The art of conversation was definitely not the physician's forte, since most of the patients he had contact with were already dead—in those cases, you don't have to worry much about your bedside manner. Desiring to live and work in a rural area, Dr. Dobbs had recently accepted the Chief of Pathology position at Tranquil Community Hospital. And being the only pathologist in the area, Elroy serviced all of the small hospitals located within a twenty-mile radius of Tranquil.

Niles Slovinsky died on Friday night, and the autopsy

had been scheduled for sometime the following day. Sheriff Buck Evans, keenly interested in finding out the cause of the teen's untimely death, requested a copy of the autopsy report from the pathology department, as soon as it was completed. Being the well-organized officer of the law that he was, Buck went down to the sheriff's office early Saturday morning, to go over his notes and set up a case file on the Slovinsky boy's death. Sipping down a cup of hot coffee while perusing his paperwork, the lawman was distracted by the clanging chime of his workplace telephone. It was a call from the hospital—a Dr. Elroy Dobbs. Not one to mingle words, the non-conversationalist pathologist got right to the point. "Sheriff, this is Elroy Dobbs...come by the morgue, I've got something to show you." Before Buck had a chance to reply, the caller hung up the phone. The pathologist's monotone voice was high-pitched and whiny, which is probably one of the reasons why he didn't talk too much.

Sheriff Evans jumped in the patrol car—the *only* patrol car—a 1999, two-door, 4x4, K1500 Chevrolet Tahoe Sports Utility Vehicle. He placed the silver key in the ignition switch and cranked over the motor. The two-toned truck was champagne-and-silver colored, boasting a 5.7 Liter, fuel-injected, V-8 engine that Buck had turbocharged. The rumbling sounds of the aftermarket, stainless steel muffler and true dual exhausts were music to his ears, especially when he revved up the engine. An intimidating black grill-guard, made up of a strong interconnection of thick, rough-textured bars, wrapped around the front of the vehicle, protecting it like a rhino's body armor. Four oversized, all-terrain tires, centered with custom chrome rims, balanced each axle. The rest of the SUV was dollied-up with nerfbars, taillight covers, and strategically placed, colored pin-striping. On the sides of the vehicle, painted in rubeola red, were the words *Juniper County Sheriff's Department.* Positioned below the wording was a rendition of a cool-looking, five-pointed gold star, reminiscent of the badge that Wyatt Earp wore when he was the sheriff of Tombstone. It was truly an awesome-looking vehicle, and Buck was very proud of it, especially since he had used his own money to pay for all of the add-ons.

Sheriff Evans drove over to the hospital, and carefully ambulated down the long flight of stairs that led to the basement where the morgue was located. He knocked three times on the entrance door, and then waited. Hearing no response, the law officer opened the door and stepped inside. Sitting behind a big wooden desk with his head buried in a pathology book was Dr. Elroy Dobbs. The coroner had on a pair of green rubber surgical gloves, which extended onto his forearms. Buck had only glimpsed Elroy a couple of times before at the hospital, when he had to bring in drunks for blood alcohol tests. The reclusive pathologist usually restricted himself to the confines of the morgue — referred to as the *dungeon of death* by most of the hospital employees — and he rarely ventured out from its dankness. If Dr. Dobbs wasn't there, then most likely he could be found lurking in one of the cold, dark corridors that connected the maze of underground tunnels located beneath the hospital. The sheriff had never officially met Elroy before, so he took this opportunity to formally introduce himself. "Hi, Dr. Dobbs, I'm Buck Evans. How are you doing today?"

Dr. Dobbs looked up from the medical book he was studying, and nodded his head once, as if to say, "Fine." The

151

pathologist was wearing wire-rimmed trifocal glasses that sat high up on the bridge of his long, thin nose. The lenses of his ocular prisms were coke bottle thick, making his eyes appear like little narrow slits, giving him the appearance of being Chinese. A fleshy shine radiated from his cleanly-shaven head, and two symmetrically pork-chop-shaped sideburns extended down from the front of each big ear. The two preauricular shaggy growths connected to a big bushy, untrimmed, handlebar mustache that hung down over both of his upper and lower lips. Elroy's unshorn facial hair was predominantly black in color, interlaced with streaks of gray and white. The mustachioed medical man looked more like a bartender from the Old West than a trained pathologist. He rose from his chair and held up his gloved right hand, motioning to Buck with a "come here" gesture by flicking his curled forefinger back-and-forth several times. The strange-looking physician abruptly turned and walked through an opened door with a sign posted above it that read, "Postmortem Room – Authorized Personnel Only." The sheriff silently followed behind him.

As Buck entered the room, he immediately observed the naked body of Niles Slovinsky, lying stiffly supine on a hard metal, pewter-colored autopsy table. There was a long, Y-shaped incision that extended downwards in a vertical fashion—originating at the level of the boy's collarbones and ending just below his belly button. Niles's bony breastplate had been longitudinally sectioned with an electric saw, and the hemi-sternum and ribs had been retracted laterally, exposing the heart, lungs, and other viscera. The calvarium—the dome-like superior portion of the teenager's cranium—had been surgically removed with an oscillating saw blade, and lay on the table next to his head. To Buck, it was reminiscent of a scene from the movie, *Raiders of the Lost Ark* — when monkey heads with exposed brains were served to people as a dinner delicacy. Another movie that had come to mind was *Hannibal* — the gory part of the story, where Anthony Hopkins removes Ray Liotta's skullcap, and then feeds him a gray matter hors d'oeuvre from Ray's own frontal lobe. Sheriff Evans also had a vague recollection of an exposed-brain scene from one of the many *Friday the 13th* flicks, in which the immortal antagonist, Jason Voorhees, fillets a teenager's head wide open — but he couldn't remember the specifics. Well, this wasn't the movies, and staring up at Buck was the glistening, worm-covered surface of Niles's naked brain, protruding out like a woman's pregnant belly under a midriff blouse. Later, the curious Dr. Dobbs would completely remove the teenager's brain from its osseous home, in order to examine it more thoroughly. Eerily, Joshua's comment at the carnival about Niles not having a brain would ring true — literally.

Elroy picked up a scalpel, walked over to the head of the table and said, "Lookie here." The eccentric pathologist made a small incision into one of the big epidural vessels that ran along the external surface of the boy's exposed brain. Thousands of tiny red beads flowed out of the cut artery, like dry Kool-Aid poured from a package. The red sand spilled out onto the table, making high-pitched pinging sounds, as the crystallized corpuscles struck the hard metal surface. The medical examiner moved over to the open chest cavity, and made a tiny incision into the superior vena cava, the big vein that drains blood from the head and neck into the right atrium of the heart. "Lookie there," squeaked Elroy, as a gush of the red salt streamed out from the surgical wound, emptying into the dead teenager's chest cavity.

Intrigued by the finding, Buck remarked, "That's strange as hell. The Slovinsky boy's blood...it's all dry and crystallized... what would cause that?

"Don't know," answered Elroy, in his monotone Mickey Mouse voice. "Never seen anything like it."

"Is the heart normal? Dr. Tisdale thought that the boy might have died from some kind of a heart problem."

"Heart's normal," replied the off-key tenor. "But even a normal heart can't pump sand."

"When we found him, his whole body was stiff, like rigor mortis...what do you think about that?" asked the sheriff.

"Don't have the answer," responded Elroy, in his characteristic shrill pitch. "One thing I do know...*the boy died from unnatural causes.*"

"This is a baffling case...I'd like to know what in the hell killed this kid," said Buck, trying to prolong the conversation.

No response was elicited from the reticent pathologist regarding the sheriff's comment about it being an interesting case. The peculiar doctor continued on with Niles's autopsy, fiddling with another organ in the chest cavity, seemingly oblivious to the lawman's presence.

Sheriff Evans stood there for a while in the silence, watching Elroy carry on the meticulous dissection, anxiously awaiting an utterance from the strange spectacled specialist. After a couple of minutes of sustained muteness, Buck began to feel uneasy, not knowing exactly what to do or say. Finally, the lawman awkwardly announced, "Well, I'll be on my way now...thanks for your help, Dr. Dobbs...keep me posted on what you find out."

Without looking up, the Kojak-headed coroner lifted his right hand and formed a circle with his thumb and index finger, then returned back to his work.

"Bye now," smiled Buck, who walked out the door and headed back to the comfort of his patrol car, relieved that the eerie encounter with the eccentric Dr. Dobbs was over. The sheriff drove back to his office and settled into his easy chair, ready to continue the important paperwork that Elroy had so rudely interrupted.

A couple of hours later, a young man walked into the lawman's office and said, "Sheriff Evans, I've got a delivery for you...a report from the hospital."

"Thank you," said Buck. The messenger handed a sealed envelope to the peace officer, and then turned and walked out. Ripping open the flap, Buck pulled out a Xeroxed copy of the typed autopsy report on Niles Slovinsky, courtesy of Dr. Elroy Dobbs. The one-paged narrative was brief and to the point, almost as limited as Elroy's conversational skills. The sheriff skimmed over the body of the findings—the part that contained descriptive information about the color, size, shape, and weight of the heart, lungs, brain, and other internal organs—turning his attention to the bottom area of the page, where an explanation of any abnormal findings and the cause of death would be found.

Under the heading of "abnormal findings," Dr. Dobbs had typed in the following: Anatomy of the nervous, musculoskeletal, digestive, respiratory, urogenital, and endocrine systems, as well as the skin and connective tissues, were all unremarkable. Except for the blood components, the circulatory system was also within normal limits. All blood elements examined — plasma, erythrocytes, leukocytes, and thrombocytes — were found to be in a solidified, micro-crystalline form, which appears to have been responsible for the premature effects of the advanced stage of rigor mortis found in the body. The etiology, or cause, of this unusual crystallization is unknown. I have sent blood samples to the NIH and CDC for evaluation.

Beneath the caption, "cause of death," were the two typed words, Cardiac Failure. *Elroy was right about one thing,* thought Buck, "Even a normal heart can't pump sand." In parenthesis, next to "Cardiac Failure" was Dr. Dobbs's hedging, politically correct, cover-your-ass explanation: {Death Resulted From Undetermined Causes; Cannot Rule Out Homicide.}

Whatever had happened to Niles that night when he was alone inside Doctor Blood's Castle — the ghastly thing that transformed his blood into a crystal coagulant, causing his heart to freeze up like an oil-starved engine — was a gruesome puzzle that Sheriff Buck Evans couldn't solve yet. He needed more pieces.

Chapter X
OUTING

Since it was such a beautiful Sunday, Joshua and Tara decided to have a picnic at Fletcher's Pool, the pond located north of Tranquil, just off old Route 44. Dr. Tisdale wasn't on duty that day at the emergency room, so he drove them there. Upon arriving, Ted noticed a few cars parked alongside the road — evidently, other people had decided to go on an outing, as well. As Joshua opened the car door, he heard the screaming voices of kids having fun at the old swimming hole. Ted lifted the trunk, and pulled out the old patchwork quilt — the one with the different colored square patterns that had been so patiently cross-stitched by his beloved wife, Doreen. The bedcover wore a few punch and mustard stains, but was still in pretty good condition, considering its usage and age.

Ted and Doreen took little Tara on many picnics, always using the same eiderdown-filled comforter to set their food and drinks on. *It's hard to believe that Doreen has been gone for over ten years*, thought the doctor, as he handed the sentimental quilt to Tara. The loneliness was overwhelming. If it weren't for his precious daughter, Ted didn't know if he would have ever made it. For the past ten years, the physician had dedicated his life to Tara, a beautiful child who reminded him of his wife in so many ways. The reincarnation of his soulmate provided Dr. Tisdale with the love and happiness that he so sorely missed after Doreen's tragic death. Ted couldn't thank God enough for Tara's phenomenal recovery from the malignant brain tumor that almost ended her life. She wasn't out of the woods yet, but his daughter was alive and well—and most importantly, Tara was happy, and to Ted, that's what life was all about.

"Okay, Joshua, you grab the food, and I'll bring the drinks," said the physician. Tara spread out the quilt, and then Ted and Joshua laid out the provisions, which consisted of sandwiches, chips, potato salad, and an assortment of soft drinks. After they had all eaten, Ted stretched out on the big, duck-down patchwork, and peered up at the infinity of blue that lay overhead. He sleepily yawned, and then said, "Why don't you kids go swimming with the dolphins while this old duffer takes a nap?"

Tara took off her midriff blouse and cutoffs to reveal a blue bikini that had been constructed from a soft, velvet-like material. The swimsuit conformed to a perfectly proportioned figure that would have even made a *Victoria's Secret* model envious. Joshua smiled as he thought back about the phrase that Patrick had used when referring to the bra part of a girl's bikini — an "over-the-shoulder-boulder-holder," as he would say. And without a doubt, this stunning blond had two of the sexiest boulders that Joshua had ever seen before.

"Come on, Joshua...last one in's a rotten egg," teased the voluptuous Tara.

After he had pulled his eyes back in and wiped the drool from his mouth, Joshua said sheepishly, "I...I never learned how to swim...I've always been afraid of the water." Especially a big bathtub full of holy water that he was about to be submerged in. The boy had never forgotten the frightful aquatic antics that he was forced to endure at his baptism.

"Don't worry about a thing," said Tara, "I'll teach you how to swim."

Joshua hesitated and then said, "I...I don't know."

"Tara is a certified lifeguard and a water safety instructor... she taught swimming at the YMCA last year. If she can't teach you how to swim, nobody can!" boasted Ted. "And I'm a board certified emergency room physician...could you be in any better hands?"

"You've got a good point there," said Joshua. Then the boy took in a deep breath and said, "You know, Tara, I guess it's about time that I learned how to swim!" Joshua left on his blue jean cutoffs, but removed his red-and-white t-shirt, and tennis shoes. Around his neck dangled the silvery sign of peace, the gift from Patrick that he always kept close to his heart. Exposing his naturally chiseled physique, Joshua jokingly flexed his biceps in an Arnold Schwarzenegger pose and said, "Let's do it, Tara!"

This time, Tara was the one in awe, attracted by his

flawless and symmetrical muscular build. Crimson-faced, she smiled and said, "All...all right then, Joshua...let's go!" The two teens scurried off towards the pond, holding hands and laughing loudly.

"Be careful!" yelled out Ted. Dr. Tisdale was extremely elated that his cherished daughter was having so much fun with Joshua—a boy that he thought very highly of. "A pair made in Heaven!" he uttered to himself. The physician then closed his eyes, hoping that he could drift off into a restful sleep.

"Hey, doc...Doc Tisdale, is that you?" the male voice called out. When Ted turned his head around to look, the man said, "Well, suck on a tit and don't ever quit...it sure as hell is you!" The man wearing the Yankees baseball cap and blue jean overalls, holding the rusty fishing pole with one hand and a tackle box in the other, was none other than...

"Henry Pickridge...at your service!" bellowed the old codger.

"Hi, Henry...how are you doing today?" asked Ted.

"I'm doin better'n a three-legged man in an ass-kicking contest!"

"That's nice to hear," answered the sleepy doctor.

The senior citizen set his fishing gear down, pulled a small metal flask from one of his overall's big front pockets, twisted off its cap, and took a long gulp from the silver container. After he had swigged downed a sizable portion of the intoxicating refreshment, the boozer fastened its lid back on, winked at Ted and retorted, "For medicinal purposes, doc!"

Then the amateur fisherman pointed to the other side of the pond and said, "Well, I can't stay and jabber, I'm on my way over yonder...to the deep water, where the whoppers live. Wish me luck, and most important, doc...don't let your meat loaf!"

Ted shook his head and grinned, "I'll try not to, Henry."

Henry inserted the metal container of hooch back into his pocket, picked up his pole and tackle box, and then headed off towards the pond. Having a conversation with old man Pickridge was akin to engaging in a wild adventure in linguistics. The old rummy's mouth was like a box of Cracker Jack — until it was opened, you had no idea what the surprise would be!

Ted laid his head back down on the soft quilt, allowing the warmth of the afternoon sun to caress his handsome face. He closed his tired eyes and quickly floated off into the land of dreams. Having worked in the emergency room for so many years, the physician had adapted his sleeping habits to conform to virtually any type of haphazard schedule, allowing him the ability to either drift off into a deep sleep, or awaken from one, all in the proverbial blink of an eye.

#

Tara and Joshua walked up to the edge of Fletcher's Pool, and looked out over the triangular-shaped body of turquoise water. The area where they would swim was a shallow point that was only about three or four feet deep, gradually increasing to a depth of twenty feet or more in the direction of the other two points. As the pair of romancers stood on the grassy bank, they heard a ruckus coming from a cove located on the other side of the pond. Two men, swinging on a tree-rope that dangled out over the deep end of water, had eyed the blond bombshell and were yelling out lewd comments. Both of the catcallers had long black hair, and their upper bodies appeared to be heavily tattooed. One of the males cupped his hands around his mouth and shouted, "Hey, baby, why don't you come on over here and swim with us?"

Then the other one hollered, "Yeah, princess, don't be shy, we'll show you a really good time!"

"Just ignore them, they're idiots," said Tara.

"Do you know who they are?" Joshua asked.

"I've never seen them before, and I hope to never see them again!" replied Tara.

Getting no response to their unsavory invitations, the two men continued with their splashing horseplay across the water's way.

Tara and Joshua sat on the bank's edge next to each other, dangling their feet in the refreshingly cool water. Beneath the shimmering sapphire surface, they observed small schools of fish swimming leisurely along the pond's sandy bottom. Only a stone's throw away, a white-plumed egret posed with one foot in the water, patiently awaiting the opportunity to spear an unsuspecting fish. A golden eagle, with wings outstretched, soared resplendently above them, screeching out a warning signal to its hiding prey below. In a nearby cove, a green box turtle surfaced like a submarine, gulped in a big breath of fresh air, and then dove back down into the watery depths.

"Would you look at that!" said Tara, pointing to the water around her feet. As Joshua leaned forward to observe the object, Tara teasingly slapped the water with the bottom of her foot, catapulting a splash of the wet stuff directly onto Joshua's face. She giggled and then flirtatiously flung her head back, sending her sleek golden locks into undulating waves of silky motion.

"That's pretty funny!" grinned Joshua. The handsome teen mock-tackled her around the waist, sending her backwards onto the grassy bank, and then began tickling her stomach with both hands. Tara erupted into shrieks of laughter.

Barely able to catch her breath, she begged, "Okay, I give up, Joshua...please, no more...I'll be good...I promise!"

"Promise?" he asked.

"Yes, yes, I promise!" she giggled.

As Tara lay on her back, a light breeze caressed her blond hair, flittering it sensuously around her seraphic face. Joshua gently brushed the velvety strands of gold aside with his hand, then looked into her eyes and embraced her welcoming lips with his. The pair of lovers' rapture was short-lived, though— rudely interrupted as the two hooligans on the other side of the pond began shouting out their unwelcomed remarks again.

"Whee, momma, come on over here to daddy!" said one of the men.

His buddy joined in on the harassment, "Yeah, sweet thing, let me show you how a real man does it!"

"Them again," sighed Tara.

"Why don't they get a life," frowned Joshua.

Tara sat up and chirped, "Oh, well...I guess it's time for your first swimming lesson now, Joshua!"

"Whatever you say, teach!"

Tara went through her usual spiel about the basic mechanics of swimming—the proper, coordinated way of moving the arms, kicking the legs, and breathing. After some dry land practicing, Joshua felt like he was ready to give it a try. The couple slid into the pool's shallows, where the flustered boy instinctively began to dog paddle.

"Swim, silly," said Tara.

Joshua stood up in the waist-high water and began to chuckle, "Oh, yeah...what the heck was I doing? I just lost my head there for a second!" He started over again, this time initiating the technique that Tara had taught him—slowly crawling over the water, while stroking his arms and kicking his feet in synchrony. The teenage boy wasn't any Michael Phelps, but he was, nonetheless, getting the job done.

"Very good...now, you're getting the hang of it!" said Tara.

"I'm a fast learner," replied Joshua, while swimming back and forth across the shallow part of the pond. He continued to gracefully glide over the water, as Tara observed him from the shoals, happily admiring her pupil's new aquatic skills.

"Tara...thanks to you, I'm swimming...I'm really swimming!" Excited by his recently acquired talent, Joshua headed towards the deep end of the pool.

"Wait a second, Joshua," warned Tara. "Let me catch up with you."

"I'm okay, Tara...catch me if you can!" At that moment, he was the old Joshua—the Trisomy XXI boy who was joyfully racing his bike with his blood-brother friend, Patrick. The beginning swimmer had a lengthy head start on Tara, who quickly stroked out after him.

Joshua enjoyed the ripples of coolness splashing over his face, as he paddled furiously in the direction of the opposite bank, dangerously entering into deeper water. The teen's forward progress was abruptly halted, when his head was forced downward by a pair of strong hands—someone had grabbed the back of his neck and was submerging him underwater. Startled, the boy frantically struggled to get away, but the two-handed grip securely held his head in a dunked position below the water's surface. Flashbacks to his baptism, and the terror that he experienced when his father immersed him in the holy water—all in the name of God— raced menacingly through Joshua's mind. Panicked from a rapidly diminishing air supply, Joshua maneuvered his body and kicked his legs forcefully, finally breaking free from the drowning hold. Choking and gasping for air, the teenage boy surfaced the watery tomb, coming face to face with two men—the same pair of tattooed tormentors that had harassed them earlier.

"Hey, homeboy, you don't swim too good," grunted the man with the big cobra tattoo on his neck.

"Yeah, I think we need to give you another lesson," said his buddy, who wore a silver nose ring, and had a trail of tears tattooed below the corner of each eye.

"Leave him alone!" shouted Tara, who had finally caught up with Joshua.

"We're just dickin with him," said the nose-ringed troublemaker. "Hey, pretty lady, why don't you leave this wimp here and come with us? We'll be gentle."

"In your dreams," said Tara, sarcastically.

Joshua coughed a few more times, and then said, "Why don't you two guys just go away and leave us alone?"

"How about if I come over there and kick your ass, tough guy?" sneered cobra-neck.

Tara's boyfriend hesitated for a second, and then cocked

his head to the side, like he was listening to something. The boy's stationary eyes reflected a look of intense concentration. He focused directly on the two inked aggressors and then said, "That's right, men, you *don't* want to start anything with us, because if you *do*, you *will* violate your parole, and they *will* send you both back to prison!"

"How the hell did you know that? We were just released today," said the parolee with the serpent tattoo. "This kid is too damned weird!"

The two men definitely didn't feel comfortable with the teenager's apparent telepathic powers, so the one with the indelible blue tears motioned to his felon friend and said, "Screw'em...we'll get'em later...let's just get the hell outta here!"

"Yeah, we'll catch ya later, kids," growled the other man. The pair of parolees gave out a sick laugh, and then turned and swam away from the two teens, headed back to the deep-watered cove they had just come from.

Tara floated over to her boyfriend, placed her hand on his shoulder, and asked, "Are you all right, Joshua?"

"Yes, I'll be okay. I just wasn't expecting those two scumbags to try and drown me."

"How did you know they were just paroled from prison?"

"It's all very strange," said Joshua, "I *heard* the thoughts of the one with the tattoo on his neck...not his voice, but what he was thinking...relayed to me in some weird form of telepathy!"

"Let's swim over to the bank so you can rest and catch your breath," smiled Tara. Her boyfriend shook his head in the affirmative. Then the two teens began slowly paddling back towards the water's edge, located only about thirty yards away from them.

Suddenly, and out of nowhere, an ominous sign appeared to Joshua, as he was traversing the swimming hole with Tara. It started out as a partial loss of vision, followed by a series of multicolored lights, flashing wildly before his eyes. A high-pitched humming sound followed, rapidly progressing to a decibel level that rocked the boy's ears. The veins of Joshua's face and neck began dilating into ugly varicosities, powerfully pulsating with his every heartbeat. Like a huge drum, the teenager's head started to bang continuously, quickly escalating into an excruciatingly painful migraine. The rancid smell of decaying meat permeated Joshua's olfactory glands, while his taste buds were assaulted with a blend of unsavory flavors. It was an aura—similar to the episodes he had experienced at Patrick's funeral and the carnival—only this one was much more intense.

Joshua immediately ceased to swim, and began treading water, hoping the terrible pain in his skull would soon subside. Beads of dark red blood suddenly started to pour out from the teen's nose. The flow of crimson turned into a coral pink, as his plasma rapidly dissolved into the blue waters of Fletcher's Pool.

"Oh, my God, Joshua, what's wrong?" cried Tara.

"Another...black...out...spell," he garbled, delirious from the pain.

The apprehensive girlfriend looked into Joshua's eyes and observed the vessels of his sclera enlarging—dilating with bright red blood—like the bulging, distended abdomen of a mosquito engorging itself on a fresh capillary. The whites of his eyes blushed fiery red, and Joshua's round, black pupils

167

elongated into vertical slits, giving him a macabre reptilian appearance. The bizarre snake eyes rolled back into Joshua's head, as his entire body twitched several times, and then went noodle limp.

"Joshua...Joshua!" screamed Tara. But there was no response from her boyfriend. Utilizing her lifesaving skills, Tara kept Joshua's head above the water, while carefully positioning him on his back. Then, employing the cross-chest carry, she placed her left arm over his upper body, and towed him to shore. As soon as Tara reached the bank, she pulled the unconscious boy up on dry land, and attempted to revive him. With his head in her lap, Tara gently patted his face while calling out, "Joshua...wake up...come on Joshua...open your eyes!"

Aroused by her soft touch and soothing voice, the dazed teenager opened his eyes and blinked several times to focus. Joshua looked up at Tara, and said groggily, "Hi, beautiful."

"Hi there yourself...how do you feel?"

"I'm coming out of it now...it was just like the others... preceded by those horrible auras. I just hope that your father can figure out what's causing these spells."

"Do you feel well enough for me to go get Daddy?"

"Yes, I'm okay now...give me a little more time and I'll swim back with you."

"No way, Jose!" said Tara. "You stay put until we come back, understand?"

"Yes, ma'am, I understand," replied Joshua, forcing a half-smile.

Tara leaned over and kissed her boyfriend, then carefully placed his head on a cushiony clump of green grass. The bikini-clad girl stood up and quickly walked over to the edge of the bank. "Be back in a little while, sweetie!" Tara dove gracefully into the water and began swimming towards the opposite end of the pool — to the picnic site where her father lay sound asleep on Doreen's patchwork quilt.

#

As they swam towards the bank, Tara and Ted observed Joshua lying on the ground, with his head resting on the small mound of grass. The pair pulled themselves out of the water and hurried over to where the boy lay. "How are you feeling, Joshua?" asked the physician.

The teenager opened his eyes and replied, "Much better, now, Dr. Tisdale...thanks." Ted performed a cursory examination on Joshua to determine whether he was medically sound, or if the boy had suffered from any physical injuries.

"It looks like you'll be fine, but I want to run some more tests over at the hospital, just to make sure. The results of your previous tests were negative, so I don't have any answers yet as to why you're having these strange spells."

"I know you're doing everything that you can for me, Dr. Tisdale, and I really appreciate it," said Joshua.

"You're more than welcome, son."

"Guess what, Daddy?" chirped Tara, "I taught Joshua how to swim!"

"Congratulations! By the way, Joshua, Tara told me about the two men released from prison and the telepathic encounter that you had with them. It really doesn't surprise me, given the other amazing talents you have acquired since the accident."

"It was a very bizarre sensation, Dr. Tisdale," said Joshua.

"I'll let you know if I have any other extrasensory experiences."

"Please do. Well, kids, I think we've had enough excitement for today. Let's say we make like a banana and split!" crowed Ted, attempting a little humor.

"That is sooo corny," moaned Tara.

"Okay, then, we'll make like a tree and leave!" said her father.

"Please, Daddy," she squealed, "no more puns!"

"You're right, Tara, those were only two-thirds of a pun... *PU*," teased Ted.

"Yes, *PU* is right, Daddy...they really stunk...and they weren't very *punny* either...so make like a fly and buzz off!"

"Okay, I can take a hint, no more puns...for now!"

"Thank you, dear Father!" replied a melodramatic Tara.

Joshua thoroughly enjoyed watching the two of them bantering back and forth, teasing one another. Ted and Tara had a unique father and daughter relationship, and they loved each other dearly. The prodigious teenager only wished that he and his father, Luke, could form such a close relationship, but deep down, he knew that would never happen.

Ted helped Joshua to his feet, and said, "I think we've had enough swimming for today, son...we'll take the dirt path back to the car this time." Tara and Joshua held hands, closely following the physician along the narrow trail that flanked the east side of Fletcher's Pool. The three of them meandered down the grassy footpath for a while, until it led to the exact location where their automobile was parked. The tired trio picked up their picnic gear, and piled into Ted's car, taking old Route 44 back to Tranquil. In no time, they would be home...safe and sound for the time being.

Chapter XI
EVIDENCE

It was late Sunday night, and Ted was relaxing in bed, settling down to a scary Stephen King book, when the phone rang. "Hi, Dr. Tisdale, this is Sheriff Evans...sorry to bother you at this late hour, but I understand that you, Tara, and Joshua Allen were at Fletcher's Pool earlier today."

"That's correct, Buck, we had a picnic and did some swimming there...why the interest?" questioned Ted.

"Well, I'm at the morgue right now, and we've got a pair of dead bodies down here. Two males...one Hispanic, by the name of Hector Lopez, and a Caucasian named Karl Singer—both released this morning on parole from the state prison—each man was serving time on sexual assault charges. A camper reported seeing their bodies floating in Fletcher's

Pool this evening. We fished them out just a little while ago... looks like they drowned, but we won't know for sure until the autopsy. I'm interviewing everyone who was at Fletcher's Pool today — Henry Pickridge was still there fishing, and told me that he saw you and the kids at the pond earlier."

"That's right, Buck. I spoke briefly with Henry today at the old water hole. Tara and Joshua did have a run-in with those men from the prison — the two thugs tried to drown Joshua, and were verbally harassing Tara, but they finally swam off and left the kids alone. We came home shortly thereafter. Those two convicts were probably poor swimmers who got drunk and drowned in the deep end...I don't think they have any swimming pools in prison."

"I'll bet that's what happened too, Ted. If you or the kids remember anything else, you know where to find me. Sorry to have bothered you, have a good night."

"Anytime, Buck...you too." The doctor clicked off his phone, and then turned his attention back to the King of horror.

After speaking with Dr. Tisdale, the sheriff took out his pen and made a check mark next to "Tisdale," the last name on the list that he had scrawled down on his little notepad earlier. "Well, that's everyone who was at Fletcher's Pool today," he sighed, "and nobody reported seeing anything unusual, much less two men drowning...I hope that's all there is to it!"

#

It was Monday morning — Buck Evans had finished his preliminary report on the two men's deaths, and was about to leave the sheriff's office and walk over to the local café for some coffee and donuts. Just as the lawman opened the front door, sure enough, the phone rang. *Par for the course, that damn phone hasn't rung all morning until now.*

Buck closed the door, walked back to his desk, and picked up the receiver. "Sheriff Evans here." He instantly recognized the caller from the first shrill syllable that was voiced from the other end of the line. It was none other than Dr. Elroy Dobbs, pathologist extraordinaire.

"Sheriff...Dobbs here...come on over...you'll want to see this." The officer of the law then heard a click, followed by a dial tone.

Upset by the medical examiner's rudeness, Buck continued to hold the phone up to his ear, quipping into the receiver, "Yes, Dr. Dobbs, I'm doing just fine, thanks for asking. I'll drop everything and be right over. It was very nice talking to you again, as well...I *so* enjoy our lengthy conversations!" The sheriff abruptly hung up the phone and said, "There...now, I feel much better!" He walked briskly out the front door, headed for his patrol car that would take him to the morgue to find out God knows what.

Sheriff Evans walked through the open door with the "Postmortem Room – Authorized Personnel Only" sign above it, and observed the peculiar pathologist's shiny head hovering over one of the ex-prisoners' dissected bodies. Both corpses of the dissolute men exhibited gory evidence of having been totally disemboweled, and lay face up on adjacent metal examining tables. Elroy was attired in a long white coat, and wore a surgical glove on each hand—a green one on the right, and a yellow one on the left. Buck advanced further into the room and said, "I came over as soon as I could...what's up, Dr. Dobbs?" Even though the lawman was curious as hell, there was no way that he was going to inquire about the different-colored gloves thing.

Elroy peered up at Buck with his wire-rimmed, thickened-lens spectacles, and motioned to the sheriff with a green-gloved hand. Buck had been through this drill before, so he walked over next to where the medical pantomime was standing, and patiently waited, hoping that he could decipher the pathologist's next charade. The lawman readily observed that the cadaver he was situated over belonged to none other than Hector Lopez, the Hispanic parolee with a cobra tattooed on his neck. Like his prison buddy, Hector's skullcap had been removed with an electric bone-saw, exposing the top part of his brain—Dr. Dobbs had been a busy little beaver that morning. The medical examiner moved around to the head of the table, and to Buck's amazement, nonchalantly reached in with both hands, and in one fluid motion, removed the man's entire brain from its bony housing. As he removed the organ of intellect, it made a sloshing-suction noise, like the sound heard from jellied cranberries being dumped from a can. "Lookie here," said Elroy, holding the human melon of charred cranial nerve tissue in his hands. "The other man's brain is just like this one...fried to a crisp."

"What do you mean, fried to a crisp?" asked the sheriff.

"Didn't die from drowning," piped Elroy. "No water in their lungs to speak of. Died from CNS assault...brain and spinal cord were cooked...barbecued."

"CNS?"

"Central nervous system—the brain and spinal cord," asserted the coroner.

"You mean they were electrocuted?"

"More like *microwaved*," peeped the pathologist. "Haven't done the microscopic yet, but grossly, every cranial nerve has been burnt up. Only affected the nervous system."

Buck stroked his chin, and then inquired, "If they weren't electrocuted or drowned, then what else could have killed them?"

"Don't know," chirped the specialist. "Never seen the likes of it before!"

Great, thought Buck, *I've got three unsolved deaths that have occurred within the past three days, and Dr. Magoo doesn't know what in the hell killed them! Stuff like this isn't supposed to happen... especially in my town!*

"Thanks for your help, Dr. Dobbs. Please send me a copy of the final autopsy report."

"Will do, sheriff," squeaked the doctor of dissection, who continued to examine the Hispanic parolee's over-grilled brain.

Buck exited the morgue, then jumped back into his truck and returned to his office, with more unanswered questions than he had before. His detective mind, like his fancy truck, was in overdrive on the ride back. *Did the three deaths result from natural causes, or were any or all of them homicides? Joshua Allen, Ted and Tara Tisdale, and Henry Pickridge were present at the scene of all three deaths. Out of these four suspects, Joshua was the only one who was personally involved in conflicts with all three of the victims, so he definitely had a motive. And don't forget the fact that Joshua underwent a miraculous transformation after his accident...from mental retard to boy genius. Yet, there is absolutely no concrete evidence to support any foul play involved in the deaths of these three people. There is no smoking gun...hell, we don't even know how they died yet!* The pieces just didn't fit, and Buck knew it.

Later that day, a messenger from the hospital delivered Dr. Dobbs's autopsy report on the two dead, convicted felons to Sheriff Evans' office. Buck eagerly opened the envelope and read the results, hoping that the good doctor had been able to find more evidence regarding how the men had died. The cause of death in both of the deceased was listed as *Central Nervous System Collapse*. Like the autopsy report on Niles Slovinsky, Dr. Dobbs had no concrete answers, and couldn't rule out homicide as the reason for death. The etiology of the incinerated nervous tissue was unknown, and samples of the brain and spinal cord had been sent off to the National Institutes of Health and the Centers for Disease Control, for further evaluation. Unless the NIH and CDC could provide some answers, it was back to square one again. Buck continued reading the autopsy document, and noticed that the medical examiner had found two small strands of a straw-like material under the nail of Hector Lopez's right index finger, consistent with the type of woven material used in making string or rope. *Not much help*, thought the sheriff, *probably just came from the tree rope he was swinging on at the pond, or...*

Sheriff Evans mused for a while, and then said aloud, "Wait a second...wait just one damned second!" Buck flashed back to the meeting he had with Joshua Allen at the Murdock boy's funeral. Prior to shaking hands, he had remembered seeing Joshua take a shiny symbol and place it in his suit pocket...it looked like a silver peace sign...a silver peace sign that was attached to a *woven straw* necklace!

"It's a long shot, and for Joshua's sake I hope it doesn't

gel, but I've got to check it out," said the sheriff to himself. There was an old saying that Buck's dad, a thirty-year veteran of the Phoenix Police Department, had told him long ago. *If you hear the sound of hoof beats, think of a horse, not a zebra.* That was his father's way of telling him to investigate the most common suspect first—the horse—before going off on a wild goose chase after an obtuse party, namely the zebra. And Joshua was that horse—the most logical suspect in the three apparent homicides.

#

Joshua was surprised to see Sheriff Evans at his door that day, and even more baffled that the lawman wanted to borrow his necklace, but nonetheless took off the twine-attached emblem and handed it over. Necklace in hand, Buck made a quick trip over to his favorite conversationalist, the oddball pathologist, Dr. Elroy Dobbs.

"It's consistent," said Elroy, glancing up from the microscope, glasses propped up on his bald head. "The strands of this necklace are comparable to the fibers found under Hector Lopez's fingernail." The longest sentence that Buck had ever heard uttered from the mustache-covered lips of Dr. Dobbs could lead to the death penalty for young Joshua. This was the lucky break that the sheriff had been waiting for... tangible evidence needed to crack the case.

"That's all I needed to know," said Buck. "Thanks, and don't lose those fibers...they're my only evidence!" The lawman picked up Joshua's necklace and rushed out of the morgue.

Sheriff Evans drove back over to Joshua's house and tapped on the front door. After a second round of repeated knockings, the door slowly creaked open, revealing a darkened figure standing at the entryway. It was the boy's father, Luke, the pitiful pastor dressed in rumpled black clothes, wearing disheveled hair and an unshaven face, with mascara-black circles surrounding each eye. "Hey, sheriff," slurred Luke, "what do I owe this blessed event to?" The offensive malodors of breath and body, along with the stench of stale alcohol, permeated the air, overwhelming the peace officer's sense of smell.

"Hello, Mr. Allen, I was looking for your son, Joshua."

"He's not here right now...left with that uppity doctor's daughter...went over to her house. What you want Joshua for?"

"I just needed to ask him a few questions about the Slovinsky boy's death, and the two men found dead out at Fletcher's Pool."

"Did Joshua have something to do with those people's deaths, sheriff?"

"He may have, Luke...that's why I need to talk to him."

The minister's body began to sway back and forth, so he grabbed the edge of the door to keep his balance. "It's all the doctor's fault...that Dr. Tisdale. He's the one responsible for the demonic possession of Joshua's soul—when he brought the boy back from the dead. Joshua should have died with Mary, during childbirth. It was God's will...hallelujah, praise Jesus!"

Tears began streaming from both of Luke's raccoon eyes. "And after Joshua's accident, Tisdale saved him *again*, allowing the evil spirit to grow even stronger inside my boy, interfering with the divine wishes of God...praise the Lord! You yourself, sheriff, are a witness to this demon's power. Look how Satan has physically changed Joshua, and now the fallen angel of sin has turned the boy into a murderer. I no longer have a son, sheriff...Joshua died at birth...now *he's* the Devil, sent straight from Hell!" Luke abruptly slammed the door closed, and then staggered off into the asylum of his bedroom.

Buck, realizing he would receive no help from Luke, hopped in his truck and drove over to the Tisdale house. The lawman walked along the decorative stone walkway that bordered a perfectly manicured lawn, then marched up the marble steps of the front porch and rang the doorbell. Ted opened the door, and said, "Hi, sheriff, what brings you here?"

"Hi, Dr. Tisdale, I'm trying to find Joshua Allen."

"He's in the living room, studying with Tara for a test. What goes?"

"I need to ask him some questions regarding the three recent deaths we've had here in Tranquil."

"Sure, come on in, sheriff."

The lawman walked into the house and followed Ted into the living room, where the two teenagers were sitting on the sofa, looking over some papers. "Joshua...Sheriff Evans is here to ask you a few questions about Niles and the two men at the pond," said Dr. Tisdale.

Joshua stood up from the couch. "What can I tell you, sheriff?"

"The medical examiner found strands of hemp embedded under a fingernail of one of the ex-prisoners that matches the hemp in your necklace...how can you account for that?"

The boy thought for a second and then replied, "Well, sheriff, when the one man held my head under the water, he

179

must have grabbed my necklace, shredding off some of its fibers with his fingernail."

"Joshua, isn't it true that you got into a fight with Niles at the carnival, then suffered a blackout spell and were left alone, with no alibi or witness corroboration when the Slovinsky boy was found dead?"

"Yes, but—"

"And didn't you have an altercation at Fletcher's Pool with the two parolees, Hector Lopez and Karl Singer, later suffering *another* blackout spell—again left alone with no alibi or witness during the approximate time of their deaths?"

"I was there with him during that time," interjected Tara. "I'm a witness, aren't I?"

"If I remember correctly, Tara," said the sheriff, "you had to swim across Fletcher's Pool to retrieve your father, and then the both of you had to swim back to where Joshua was— that would have taken *at least* fifteen minutes—giving Joshua enough time to kill the two men and then return back to the place where you had left him."

"Listen, sheriff, these three deaths haven't even been ruled as homicides yet," said Ted. "And besides, I can personally vouch for Joshua...he would never do anything like this...these fatalities are most likely the result of some type of natural phenomena."

"Sorry, Dr. Tisdale, but there *is* enough physiologic and anatomical information to warrant that these three fatalities resulted from acts of homicide—circumstantial and forensic evidence point to Joshua Allen as the primary suspect. The boy had the motive and the window of time to commit these murders...I just don't know how he perpetrated them yet. I'm truly sorry, but I took an oath to do my job, no matter what the outcome. I have no other choice...I'll have to arrest Joshua and charge him with three counts of murder."

Tara stood up and screamed, "No! You can't do this, sheriff...Joshua is innocent...he had absolutely nothing to do with those deaths...it was me...I was the one who killed them."

Buck smiled and said, "Look, Tara, I know how you feel about Joshua...and I see what you're doing...but I know that you had nothing to do with these deaths."

"You're making a big mistake, sheriff," said Ted.

"Please don't make this any harder than it already is," said Buck. "Come on, son...don't make me use handcuffs... let's go down to the station."

"Sheriff Evans, I honestly can't remember everything that happened during my blackout spells. But I know that I wouldn't...I couldn't...take the life of another fellow human being," explained Joshua.

Buck, showing concern, stated, "Joshua, if you *really* are innocent, you have my word that I will do everything in my power to see that you are set free."

"Thank you, sheriff," said Joshua. "I *am* innocent!"

Ted walked over to the lawman and asked, "Can I bail him out of jail, sheriff?"

"We'll have to wait and see what the judge says," replied Buck, "but in my experience, anyone charged with three counts of murder would be denied bail." The sheriff then looked over at Joshua and said, "It's time to go now, son."

Tara hugged her boyfriend and said, "Don't you worry, Joshua, we'll get you out of jail...we know you're innocent!" The arrested teen embraced Tara tightly, then lowered his head and solemnly followed the law officer towards the front door.

Ted gave the boy a fatherly pat on the shoulder. "Tara's right, Joshua, we'll have you out of there in no time...don't let this get to you!"

With a tear trickling down the corner of one blue eye, Joshua proclaimed, "I want you both to know that you are the only family that I have, and I love you very much."

"We love you too," wept Tara, wiping the tears from her cheeks.

As Buck and the boy were leaving the house, the sheriff shot Ted a sincere look and said, "I'm really sorry about all of this, Dr. Tisdale...I *really* am!"

The lawman escorted Joshua into the back seat of his Tahoe, then entered the driver's side, started the engine, and drove off towards the sheriff's office. Ted and Tara stood at the doorway, motionless and mesmerized, with an expression of disbelief stamped on their faces. Tara turned to her father and said, "Daddy, we've *got* to get him out of there...we have to protect Joshua...*at all costs!*"

Chapter XII
PARASITE

The white minivan slowly turned off of Route 44 and cautiously crept over the bumpy grass trail for about a mile, stopping alongside the row of evergreen trees located just west of Fletcher's Pool. The van's doors swung open, and out scrambled four little girls, all completely dressed in brown — shorts, shirts, socks, belts, and caps — the entire membership of Tranquil's Brownie Troop 12. It was spring break, and they were going on a camping trip, a prerequisite needed to earn their Girl Scout "campfire" badge. The youngsters excitedly flittered around the car, screeching and squawking, like chickens in a henhouse being chased by a fox.

"Okay, children, quiet down and pay attention now... we're going to set up camp over by that opening," voiced the driver of the minivan, who then pointed at a group of towering growths of timber, "next to those trees." Mrs. Laura Renshaw closed her car door, and walked back to the trunk, where all of the camping equipment had been stored. Laura was the Brownies' troop leader and mother of Amber, the cute ten-year-old with her red hair parted down the middle, wearing the braided pigtails. The other Brownies were Jenny, Latisha, and Rachel—all from the same fourth grade class at Tranquil Elementary School.

"Everyone carry their share of camping equipment and follow me," requested Laura, grabbing the big canvas bag that held the tent, metal stakes, and rope. Each girl patiently awaited their turn to snatch something out of the opened trunk of the van, then followed the troop leader mom single file to the flat, grassy opening that would be home to them for that weekend.

"Mrs. Renshaw, where do you want us to put our sleeping bags?" asked Rachel.

"Just lay them down for now," answered Laura. "After we get the tent set up, we'll stick them inside."

"Miss Renshaw, where do you want the food?" Latisha inquired.

"How about the water containers...what do we do with them?" questioned Jenny.

Amber wrinkled up her little minikin nose and moaned, "Mom, I don't know where this stuff is supposed to go!"

Speaking in a patient voice, the troop leader announced to the bothersome children, "Just hold your horses, kids...set your stuff down on the ground and we'll take care of it later. Jenny, would you please check the car and make sure that we've unloaded everything?"

Laura stooped over and began unpacking the tent bag. She eyed the other Brownies and said, "The rest of you can help me set this up, okay?" The little girls gathered around her while she handed out the stakes and rope. Working diligently together, the group had the tent pitched before sunset. Since there was only enough room inside for three sleeping bags, Amber and her mother volunteered to sleep out in the open. Laura actually preferred it that way—she wasn't looking forward to spending the night in a cramped enclosure with giggling ten-year-old girls—and besides, Amber thought it would be exciting to sleep out under the stars.

A cool evening breeze whispered through the trees, as the evening sun leisurely evaporated into the distant horizon. Feeling the dusky chill, Mrs. Renshaw and the girls built a warm fire, using the abundant fallen timber they had gathered from the adjacent forested area. Utilizing the open flames of the crackling campfire, the troop leader and her unit of Girl Scouts cooked hot dogs and roasted marshmallows. After dinner, the Brownies animated their excitement about what had been planned for the following day—a one-mile hike down to Fletcher's Pool for a picnic and some swimming. The rest of the night would be spent singing songs, and telling scary stories.

It was Amber's turn, and everyone sat silently around the blazing fire. She opened her turquoise eyes widely, and spoke in a creepy voice. "Like, not too far from here is where old man Pickridge saw the space ship, and was captured by the space aliens. The aliens were like, really, really scary...ten feet tall and ugly and stuff...they like, took him back to their planet and then brought him back to Earth. Our teacher, Mrs. Prather, said that he's totally never been the same since the aliens got hold of him...all those experiments and stuff they did on him."

Suddenly, the flickering fire popped loudly, hurling a red-orange glitter of sparks into the air. The swarm of twinkling cinders floated gracefully back down to earth, as if suspended by tiny parachutes. Amber pointed to an area behind where Latisha was sitting and shrieked, "Oh, no, Latisha, watch out... there's an alien...creeping up behind you!"

The frightened Brownies screamed and howled in uncontrollable horror, directing their sight to the place in back of the mortified Latisha. Seeing nothing there, they all began giggling hysterically — what all normal ten-year-old girls do when they get the heebie-jeebies scared out of them.

"I *gotcha* Latisha," squealed Amber.

Latisha cupped one of her hands over her mouth, but a rush of nervous laughter could still be heard emerging from her covered lips. "I'm gonna get you back, girlfriend!" she shouted to Amber.

"Okay, kids, I think we've had enough fun for tonight," smiled Laura. "We have to rise and shine early tomorrow, so it's time we hit the hay. Amber and I are sleeping out here tonight, and Jenny, Latisha, Rachel...you guys are sleeping in the tent."

"How come we have to sleep in there?" asked Rachel.

"Yeah, we want to sleep out here with you guys," whined Jenny.

"We can't all sleep out here tonight, kids...that's why we brought a tent," said Laura. "I'll tell you what, tomorrow we'll

186

switch places, and two of you can sleep out here."

"But that means that one of us will have to sleep in the tent both nights," whimpered Jenny.

"Look, girls...we'll work this all out tomorrow...everyone just go to bed and get a good night's sleep, okay?" groaned Mrs. Renshaw.

"Okay," chimed the uniformed group of girls, almost in unison.

After exchanging several rounds of goodnights, the threesome squeezed through the teepee's tiny pyramid-shaped opening, zipped it closed, and crawled into their down-filled sleeping bags. Laura gave her daughter a goodnight kiss, squirmed into the cozy warmth of her bag, and like a human cocoon, secured the fabric around her body and head. Amber snuggled into her sleep-sack, leaving her pigtailed-noggin totally exposed to the refreshing, cool night breeze. Weary from the day's tiring events, they all rapidly slipped into a deep, sound slumber.

In the depth of the night, Amber was abruptly aroused from her dreams by a brilliant flash of light, flickering across her thickly-lashed eyelids. Upon opening her eyes, the Brownie observed what appeared to be a shooting star, or maybe even a meteor, streaming across the overhead, darkened sky. "Cooool," she whispered. The excited youngster looked over at her mother, Laura, who lay motionless in her sleeping bag, like an encased giant caterpillar. Then, Amber glanced over at the green teepee that housed her fellow classmates, and could hear no sounds emitted from her friends snoozing inside the ground-hugging, canvas dwelling. Amber gazed upward again, and viewed the mysterious flying object, silently zigzagging across the starry heavens above. The cute Brownie breathlessly watched as it dipped closer, hovering next to an assemblage of stately ponderosa pines that overlooked their campsite. Then, in the blink of an eye, it suddenly dove out of sight, disappearing into a large grassy meadow neighboring the cluster of evergreens that stood alongside the pitched tent. Amber reached out with her hand and gently shook her deep-sleeping mother. "Mom...mom...wake up," she whispered. "I just saw a flying saucer."

Interrupted from a sound snooze, Laura, half-awake, turned over and grumbled, "Go back to sleep, honey...you were just dreaming." Then Amber's mother yawned widely, smacked her lips a couple of times, and quickly dozed back off into the land of nod.

"I *wasn't* dreaming," pouted the pigtailed Brownie. "I saw it...there in the sky!"

Amber lay motionless for about a minute, thinking about what she had observed. Then, she quietly wriggled out of the sleeping bag, and put her tennis shoes back on. She picked up the flashlight that her mother had placed between their makeshift beds, and tiptoed over to the hushed tent. Rachel, Jenny, and Latisha were all fast asleep, and the entrance was zipped tightly closed. Amber knew that she would get into big trouble from her mom if she woke up the other girls, so she silently stood alongside the snoozing Brownies' wigwam, and nervously shined the flashlight into the tree line—looking for any sign of the thing that fell from the sky. A wispy fog had crept in during the night, spreading a weightless sheet of white haze over the campsite and surrounding areas, thus limiting the little girl's visibility. The beam from Amber's light illuminated a collection of heavily branched trees, casting a host of spooky, shadowy figures on the murky, woodland floor. Still not sighting anything out of the ordinary, the pigtailed Brownie crept a few steps closer to the edge of the woods, all the while sweeping her curious beam of white light back and forth across the chain of evergreens. It was eerily quiet. Amber stood there for several minutes, hoping to catch a glimpse of something...anything.

Nothing.

No mysterious light, except hers...no spaceship, no alien, no unearthly sounds...absolutely nothing.

"Maybe it *was* a dream," she muttered to herself. This wouldn't be the first time that her imagination got the best of her, and after all, it was Amber who told the whopper story about the scary aliens earlier that night.

It was probably just a shooting star, she thought. As the little girl was about to retreat to the comfort and safety of her warm nap sack, she heard a sound.

Crackle.

A distant sound. It started out as a faint crackling noise, emanating from within the heavily wooded area that lay directly before her. One of her auburn pigtails flipped as she cocked her head and turned her right ear toward its direction. She listened intently. The softened sound caught her attention again.

Crickle.

What's that? Amber wondered.

The redheaded Brownie wrinkled up her forehead, pressed her lips firmly together, and concentrated on what she had heard. After a few seconds, an expression of complacency

189

filled her face—the same self-assuring look that Amber gave in class, when she knew the right answer to the question asked by the teacher. *The rustling of leaves – that's what it sounded like, the rustling of leaves*, she concluded.

The noise occurred again, only slightly louder.

Crackle.

Amber flashed her light furiously through the trees, but could see nothing but the early morning mist. Her head froze, and she strained both ears, but all the girl heard was silence. She waited.

Crickle...crackle.

There it was again. A cold shiver flew down the frightened Brownie's spine, making the hairs on her neck stand at attention.

Crickle...crackle...crickle.

The sounds occurred closer together, and were growing louder—getting nearer.

Crackle. crickle. crackle. crickle.

It sounded like...footsteps. Someone or *something* walking in her direction—getting closer with each stride. Amber frantically whipped the beam of her flashlight toward the sound, but still couldn't see what was making the noise. The young girl stopped breathing and stood statuesque, petrified from fear.

Crickle-crackle-crickle-crackle-crickle-crackle.

Those were definitely footsteps—whatever it was, it was moving faster—and it was headed straight towards Amber. The Brownie's heart began to thump faster, and she couldn't move a muscle—her entire body was paralyzed with terror. Opening her mouth widely, the diminutive child was only seconds away from letting out the most blood-curdling scream she could muster up. Suddenly, the thing that Amber had heard walking in her direction ambled directly out of the fog, and into the path of her flashlight beam. The creature had gleaming red eyes, and froze in its tracks when it encountered the Brownie's light.

The thing that had made the noise in the woods, the organism that was walking straight towards Amber, the entity that had so horrified the girl, was nothing more than a tiny mammal. It was a baby deer! The pigtailed Girl Scout gave off a sigh of relief—it was only Bambi.

"You are so precious!" she whispered to the adorable animal.

The tiny fawn cautiously took a few wobbly steps towards the Brownie, and then stopped. Amber slowly inched closer to the young doe. "I won't hurt you," she said softly. "I just want to pet you." Not wishing to scare the helpless waif away, Amber slowly crept deeper into the woods, with her one hand extended, all the while speaking in a reassuring, high-pitched voice.

"Come to Amber, you pretty little baby...come to Amber" she crooned.

Having come to within a foot of the petite deer, the cute Brownie crouched down and extended her hand to pet its beautiful fur—a soft tawny color, dappled in snowy white velvet. The little girl was surprised that the wild animal continued to stand motionless, and hadn't bounded off into the woods from fear—the stationary yearling appeared to be tame and unafraid. As her fingers made contact with its plush fur coat, Amber's sweet cherub face lit up with a jubilant smile, her mouth accenting a melodious purr of excitement.

Suddenly, the Girl Scout felt a shocking sensation — as if an electric current was traveling up her hand. The jolt continued to spread, reaching into her extended arm. Amber tried to pull her hand away, but the glue of electricity refused to let go. The fawn looked up at the petrified Brownie, its brown eyes now streaked with blood-engorged vessels that pulsed in rhythm with the girl's every heartbeat. This *wasn't* a dream — it was a horrible nightmare that was really happening. Some type of bizarre energy source was exiting the tiny doe and entering Amber, taking full control of her body!

The paralyzing grip of the unknown force pushed its way into the Brownie's torso, and then crawled down inside both of her legs. She tried to scream, but the signals from her brain had been short circuited by the overpowering invader. Amber, well aware of what was happening, was unable to do anything about it. The entity acted like a skeletal muscle relaxant — paralyzing the upper and lower extremities first, then the torso, and lastly, the brain. It was as if someone had injected poor Amber with a massive dose of succinylcholine. The girl's disarrayed, panicked thoughts gradually faded into oblivion, replaced by the superior intellect of the malevolent thing that had callously stolen her body. In no time, the alien life form completely disseminated into the unsuspecting Brownie, consuming both her mind and body — like water being absorbed into a dry sponge.

After the completion of the ghastly transference, the innocent fawn's legs buckled, and its lifeless carcass slumped to the leaf-laden soil below — as if some red-necked poacher named Bubba dressed in a green camouflage outfit had blasted a thirty–ot–six slug between its big beautiful, brown eyes.

The monstrous parasite that now controlled Amber's body stood up, and using the little girl's eyes, peered down at the limp deer sprawled out on the foliage-covered ground. The set of eyes staring at the dead doe were *physically* Amber's — white sclera, blue iris, black pupil — but there was no trace of emotion in them at all. These eyes were blank and cold, expressionless and uncaring — like the vacant gaze of an animal mounted in a taxidermist's office. The Brownie's body began to twitch uncontrollably, as if her nervous system had been afflicted with Parkinson's, or overcome with a grand mal seizure. She turned her palsied head, and instead of a smooth fluid motion, her neck jerked in a chaotic, arrhythmic fashion — similar to a lizard's head tweaks during its mating ritual. In an effort to speak, the thing hideously contorted Amber's tongue and lips, then spastically pumped the muscles in her throat. A serpentine tongue convulsively writhed around the inside of her distorted, opened mouth, and her neck grotesquely sucked in and bulged out in paroxysms of spasm. Thick strings of ropey saliva drooled down from the girl's bottom lip and chin. The parasitic-possessed child looked more like she was trying to vomit, than verbalize. Finally, after a few moments of gruesome muscular manipulation, Amber's gullet loudly heaved out several weird guttural sounds, followed by a sequence of eerie, high-pitched squeals.

The bizarre noises emitted from the transformed Girl Scout resonated through the trees, abruptly awakening the troop leader from her deep sleep. Laura drowsily glanced over at the sleeping bag beside her, and seeing that Amber was missing, quickly sat up and scanned the area for her daughter. Out of the filmy darkness, a glowing beam of light unexpectedly appeared from the wooded area behind the tent. The white radiance wandered around the campsite, dancing about like a giant firefly, finally focusing itself on the troop leader's puzzled face. Mrs. Renshaw saluted her right hand over both eyebrows and squinted into the blinding brilliance, quickly ascertaining that the illumination had originated from a handheld flashlight. Tilting her head out of the path of brightness, Laura could barely distinguish the outline of a shadowy figure—standing motionless in the dark—rigidly frozen behind the glinting shaft of light.

"Who's there...is that you, Amber?" she called out. There was no response, and the silent silhouette remained fixed in its upright, stationary stance.

A huge outpouring of goose bumps began migrating down Laura's neck, flowing over her shoulders and onto her arms. The troop leader shuttered uncontrollably as the fear navigated over her spine. "Amber, if that's you, this isn't one bit funny, young lady!"

Without warning, the dark shape began moving, one step at a time, in the troop leader's direction. The being displayed an unsteady gait, staggering and tottering with each step. As it slowly and deliberately walked, the gleam from the flashlight bobbed and jolted in the cool night air. Laura watched in horror as the thing tenaciously bounded towards her, ambulating like a drunken Doctor Frankenstein's monster. The threatening creature was only about ten feet away when it tripped and almost fell, accidentally directing the shining flashlight at its pigtailed head. The illuminated face was as featureless as an old statue, with vacant eyes generating an empty stare, but

Laura could still recognize the features—it was her only baby, her beloved ten-year-old daughter, Amber.

Believing that her child was suffering from another episode of somnambulism, the mother asked, "Are you sleepwalking again, sweetie?"

The animated object elicited no response.

Stunned by what was happening, Laura rose up on her knees and said, "Amber, darling, come over here and talk to Mommy...what's going on, baby?"

The alien Brownie strode over to Laura, then gaped open her mouth and articulated slowly, "WH-WH-WHERE IS THE BE-ING...THE ONE W-WITH THE EX-TRA CHROM-O-SOME? The words that emerged from Amber's lips weren't human—they were sounds that were harsh and raspy—belched out like a laryngectomee using an artificial voice box. The thing's gloomy black eyes stared at the troop leader coldly, showing no emotion at all. Laura couldn't believe what she was seeing—her Amber had soft, beautiful blue-green eyes—this clone, this look-alike, it possessed the eyes of a raven. Devil eyes, that were dark and dead.

Mrs. Renshaw, now speechless and immobilized from shock, continued to kneel before the celestial stranger who was masquerading as her daughter, Amber. Deadpan, the distraught mother stared out blankly at Amber—like she was under the influence of some weird, hypnotic spell.

"THE TRI-SOM-Y HU-MAN...W-WITH THE AD-DIT-ION-AL GE-NE-TIC MA-TER-I-AL...TELL ME W-WHERE TO FIND HIM!" it burped out impatiently, only louder this time. A seepage of gooey saliva oozed down from the corner of Amber's mouth as she spoke.

The chilling sound of the unearthly voice temporarily fetched Laura out of her incapacitating trance. "I don't know what you're talking about!" she blurted out, almost in a frenzy. "What have you done with my Amber?"

The little girl's doppelganger took a step closer and threw Laura a menacing look. "TELL ME W-WHERE HE IS...NOW!" it squalled.

Still not believing, or *understanding*, for that matter, what was happening, Amber's mother, Laura, who was on the verge of having a nervous breakdown, screeched hysterically, "*I don't know!*"

A zipping sound emerged from the opening to the girls' tent, and Rachel's head popped out. She rubbed at her tired eyes and sleepily inquired, "What's going on, Mrs. Renshaw?"

"Rachel, get back in there...now!" screamed the troop leader. Even though she was numb from shock, Laura still had enough sense to realize that the life form that stood before her — the being with the uncanny resemblance to her daughter — posed a serious threat to all of them.

Dissatisfied with the Earth woman's "I don't know" answer, the stone-faced creature with the red pigtails pushed Amber's face next to Laura's and bellowed, "YOU ARE EX-PEND-A-BLE, HU-MAN!"

The loud commotion had awakened Jenny and Latisha, who now, along with Rachel, peered out from the unzipped triangular aperture. The blackness of the night had faded into early dawn, so Laura and Amber were now more clearly visible. "Mrs. Renshaw, like, what's happening?" asked Jenny.

In the blink of an eye, Amber's thin arms transformed into monstrous green extremities, each ending in a hand-like appendage of six fingers, all armed with jagged, razor-sharp claws. The alien animal's arm shot out and grabbed the front of Laura's blouse with its left hand, holding her quivering body steadfastly in place with its compressive grip. Amber's head then mechanically twisted around and stared back at her alarmed Girl Scout sisters. It stretched the child's lips into a hideous smile, and growled, "LIKE, I AM GO-ING TO KILL THE BITCH!"

Laura, dazed and overwhelmed with fear, continued kneeling on the sleeping bag, offering up no resistance against the clutch of her hostile assailant. Amber jerked her head back around and glared at her mother's face. On the brink of a psychotic meltdown, Laura looked into her child's odious black eyes and whimpered, "Honey, Mommy loves you... Mommy loves you very, very mu..."

At that exact moment, the embodiment of Laura's daughter thrust its saurian right hand into the troop leader's neck, and in one smooth motion of its scalpel-sharp claws, ripped out the contents of the woman's throat. An expression of horrified disbelief coursed over Laura's face as the beast's talons ravaged the structures in her neck. She opened her mouth and attempted to scream, but her vocal cords could produce no sound. Both of the troop leader's carotid arteries and jugular veins had been severed, and her trachea and esophagus had been torn in half by the sinister swipe. Gushes of bright red blood spurted out of her neck, arching into the air like streams of colored water from a fountain. Exsanguination occurred quickly — virtually all of the woman's blood had spilled out of her body and onto the ground — in only a matter of seconds. The merciless matricide was violent and quick.

Rachel, Jenny, and Latisha were initially silenced by the grisly, horrific act of violence — literally too scared to scream. After they had snapped out of the stupor and collected their thoughts, all three of them began "yelling their fool heads off," as the old saying goes. The girls could yell and scream "til the cows came home," but there was no one around to hear them — "as the crow flies," their campsite was at least a mile away from Fletcher's Pool, too far away for their shrieks of terror to travel.

From the wigwam's opening, the trio of petrified Girl Scouts observed that the monster had not relinquished its left-handed grasp on the troop leader's blood-soaked blouse. Laura's eyes were still open, but only the white part could be seen — the rest had rolled back into her head. Mrs. Renshaw's neck, slashed-open like a freshly gutted fish, drooped over to one side, exposing a deep, blood clot-filled crater that extended from just beneath her chin to a trifle above the sternum. The avulsed tissues of her neck left a gaping, stellate defect, bordered by raised, skin margins that were jagged and rough. The giant, star-shaped gouge was flooded with a mixture of dark blue venous, and bright red arterial blood, which had spilled over the edges of the wound. A gushing overflow of purple plasma splashed down on Laura's sleeping bag and streamed onto the ground, branching off into a complex of scarlet serpentine tributaries.

The diminutive redheaded murderer turned toward the appalled observers hidden inside the tent, and exhibited the contents of its bloodied right hand — a gnarled mass of human neck meat — comprised of skin, muscle, nerves, and cartilage. The vicious alien held the abhorrent heap of gory anatomy

198

under its borrowed nose and sniffed in deeply, like a lion relishing the scent from a fresh kill. Lifting up one side of Amber's upper lip, the thing bared the little girl's teeth and let out a ferocious snarl. Opening its mouth widely, the ravenous brute then bit forcefully into Laura's raw flesh. It ripped off a big hunk of meat, and quickly swallowed the morsel down whole.

"THIS TASTES DE-LIC-IOUS!" snorted the creature.

Amber's red pigtails bounced and flopped, as she savagely chomped off huge chunks of her mother's red gore from the alien, clawed hand. Like an eagle devouring its prey, the vile cannibal voraciously gulped down the remaining handful of the woman's soft tissue. The thing gave out a loud, croaky belch, regurgitating a thick gobble of macerated human flesh into its mouth, but then quickly swallowed the partially processed food back down its throat—like a hungry wolf. Rachel, Latisha, and Jenny watched in horror as Amber's squirming tongue eagerly lapped up the blobs of coagulated blood from its grotesque, green fingers. A thick rope of mucous slithered out from one of the clone's tiny nostrils and dangled precariously from her upper lip. Then, the alien Brownie smacked her clot-stained lips together several times, and groaned in ecstasy. Incapacitated by fear, the frightened triad of observing Girl Scouts remained frozenly crouched inside their pitched tent, intermittently crying out in anguish.

Having temporarily satisfied its hunger, the satiated carnivore—still holding the dead troop leader with its clawed left hand—nonchalantly flung the slaughtered corpse to one side. Laura's lifeless body flopped awkwardly onto her daughter's sleeping bag, landing like an old rag doll. The deadly entity ungainly shuffled Amber's feet to turn her body, then headed in the direction of the Girl Scout tent. Crying hysterically, the panicked bevy of Brownies hastily zipped up the entry, and crowded to the center of the makeshift bedroom. They hugged each other tightly, oblivious to their surroundings, and unmindful of what would happen next. The three trapped girls could hear the sound of the monster's approaching feet — one slow, clumsy, purposeful step at a time. Stopping at the triangular-shaped entryway, the homicidal extraterrestrial stood in silence. After a few seconds, it began pawing at the zipper, apparently unaware of how to open the sealed canvas flap. The metal fastener jingled and bounced as the creature's clawed hand attempted to unzip it. Suddenly, the clinking sounds stopped, and there was dead silence. Latisha, Rachel, and Jenny sat motionless in the darkened space, eyelids squeezed tightly together, a symphony of thumping hearts with each shallow breath taken. Rachel felt like she was going to faint, Jenny was nauseous, and Latisha had already vomited up her dinner from last night.

A throaty voice grunted out, "W-WHERE IS THE ONE WITH THE EX-TRA CHROM-O-SOME...HE IS CALLED JOSH-U-A?"

The three terrified Brownies knew that they would suffer a horrible death at the hands of the human flesh-eater inhabiting Amber's body, if they didn't answer its question — fast. Jenny, whose family used to attend Luke Allen's church, recognized the name of *Joshua*, rumbled out by the thing standing just outside their flimsy abode. With trembling lips barely able to form the words, she nervously called out, "You mean...Joshua Allen...the preacher's son?"

"WHERE IS HE?"

Not knowing the Allen's home address, and hoping to appease the murderous alien and possibly save their lives, Jenny provided the next best answer. "He's at the church... The Chapel of God...in the city of Tranquil." The being's mind searched Amber's memory banks and could find no information about The Chapel of God, but there *was* some data about Tranquil—the small town the human child in the enclosure had just mentioned. A distorted expression of accomplishment filled Amber's face, and she gave off a hoarse grunt of satisfaction.

The brutal predator then directed its attention to the girls hiding in the tent. Since killing the three life forms would really serve no purpose—the heinous creature had already consumed a hearty breakfast—it decided to conserve its energy and let them live. Amber's ghastly inhabitant turned to face the just rising sun, and like a human compass, directed the girl's body roughly fifteen degrees to the right, in the direction of Route 44. Standing perfectly still, a grimace appeared on Amber's face, and she let out a painful groan as the monster's unsightly upper limbs instantly melted away, exposing the recognizable human form of a child's pink arms. Loud ripples of borborygmi—rumbling noises caused by the propulsion of gas through the intestines—emanated from Amber as her bowels attempted to digest the unchewed slabs of swallowed meat. The extraterrestrial's host was having a hard time processing the food it needed—the next time it fed, it would have to masticate the human flesh more efficiently. Walking like a drunken sailor on stilts, the alien-parasitized girl, wearing the bloodstained Brownie uniform with the shredded sleeves, stumbled off toward Route 44—Amber's red pigtails jangling with each uncoordinated step—headed south for its six-mile hike back to the town of Tranquil.

Chapter XIII
INCARCERATION

Sheriff Evans clanked the jail door closed, and said to Joshua, "I'm really sorry about this, son, but I don't have any other choice." Buck had already advised the teen of his legal rights, "Mirandized him," as the law liked to say, and now the boy was incarcerated, or in layman's terms "put behind bars." Joshua examined the tiny cubicle he had been confined to—a dinky, eight-foot square box that contained a generic sink and commode, each controlled with a push of a round, metallic button. A flat, narrow bunk holding a thin foam mattress, covered with a gray army blanket, extended from the wall. Adjoining the adolescent's small breathing space were two other miniature lockup rooms of identical size and shape. Tranquil only had three jail cells, and they were empty most of the time, given the town's tiny population and low crime rate.

Joshua could see no one occupying the cell at the far end, but the compartment adjacent to him housed another male prisoner. The teenager was unable to determine the neighbor's identity, because the inmate was facing the opposite direction and was fast asleep on his bed, snoring like a steam engine driving a chugging train. Even though a blanket concealed most of the jailbird's body, the boy could still see that the man was wearing a pair of tattered overalls. The head of the person in the next cell was covered with a dark blue baseball cap, cocked forward so its brim would shade the fellow's eyes from the light. Long uneven tufts of grizzled hair projected out from under the back of the lawbreaker's hat, and extended down the nape of the gentleman's wrinkled and tanned neck. There was something very familiar about this noisy-sleeping, gray-haired inmate, but Joshua couldn't quite put his finger on it.

Flopping himself down on the uncomfortably hard prison bed, Joshua took in a deep breath and sighed heavily. The incarcerated teen folded his arms behind his head and stared up at the sterile white ceiling. *What did I do to deserve this...how could I have killed three people and not be aware of it?* he pondered. *I'm not some cold blooded murd...*

The boy's thoughts were suddenly interrupted by the voice of the imprisoned man in the next cell, who restlessly wriggled around on his squeaking mattress. "Who the hell you think you're talking to?" mumbled the resident. "Don't make me bitch-slap you!"

"I beg your pardon?" half-questioned Joshua, wondering

if the character in the adjacent cell was also telepathic.

The neighboring jailbird snorted loudly, then opened his eyes and sleepily said, "Who's there?"

Relieved that the fellow inmate was only talking in his sleep, the adolescent answered, "I'm in the next cell, sir...my name is Joshua Allen."

"Well, hell's bells, I must have been dreaming out loud again!" exclaimed the locked up man. The prisoner kicked off his blanket, turned his head towards the teenager, and lifted the brim of his baseball cap. Joshua instantly recognized the haggard face that matched the ratty clothes and the foul mouth. It was Henry Pickridge.

"What in the name of Jupiter's balls are you doing here?" queried the old geezer.

Joshua hung his head down and said, "Sheriff Evans arrested me for the murders of Niles Slovinsky...and the two men at Fletcher's Pool."

"Why in the hell would Buck want to do that...it don't make no freakin sense!" said Henry. "For all that flatfoot knows, I could be the murderer. I was there too, ya know... at the scene of all three crimes. Maybe I should crap in his ear and give him a new set of brains!"

"It's not Sheriff Evans' fault," said Joshua. "He's just doing his job...my arrest was based on circumstantial evidence...the sheriff is doing what he thinks is right."

"Maybe so, but it doesn't sound one damn bit fair to me," replied Henry, shaking his head from side-to-side.

"Unfortunately, as we all know, Mr. Pickridge, *life* isn't fair," said Joshua.

"You sure as hell got that one right, sonny...and since

we're going to be roommates for a spell, you can call me Henry...all my other friends do." The old alcoholic took off his Yankees baseball cap, stroked back his wavy gray hair with one hand, and then repositioned it back on his head. He raised his stubbled upper lip and formed his mouth into a mischievous smile. "Do you have a *liar*...I mean a lawyer yet?"

"Not yet. Dr. Ted Tisdale, who has been like a father to me, and his daughter, Tara, will be helping me out with legal counsel. They both know that I didn't commit these murders. It might take some time, but I'll be proven innocent."

"Well, if there's anything I can do, just let me know."

"Thanks, Henry, I truly appreciate your support."

"I know how it feels when no one believes what you're saying. Nearly everyone in town thinks that the flying saucer and alien thing I saw back yonder by Fletcher's Pool was just pigments of my imagination...hallucinatories. Well, I know what I seen was real, and if them turd-hoppers don't believe my story...they can all just kiss my rosy red ass, if you know what I mean!"

Sheriff Evans opened the heavy door that connected the front of the sheriff's office to the back room that contained the three jail cells. The lawman carried in two trays of food, and set them down on the small table that stood in the corner of the room, opposite Joshua's cubicle. "I thought that you guys may be getting hungry, so I brought you some dinner." He slid the first tray through the narrow horizontal opening located between the bars of Joshua's cell, and then, in a similar fashion, provided Henry with his platter of food through the middle cell's slot.

"Thank you," replied Joshua.

Henry grabbed his tray and said, "Yeah...ditto, sheriff."

The hungry septuagenarian placed the salver of food on his lap and began wolfing down its contents. "Pretty damn good grub," he muttered, with his mouth full of chow.

"It's good to see that you slept off your drunk, Henry... any idea of why you're in jail?" asked the lawman.

"Not a friggin clue," answered Henry, as he gulped down a huge fork-load of mashed potatoes.

"You were arrested for drunk and disorderly conduct... at The Fireside Bar," said the sheriff. Buck pulled the notepad from his uniform's shirt pocket, thumbed through several pages and said, "Okay, here it is. Last night, according to several witnesses, it seems that you were sitting at the bar next to Trudi Mae Tanaka, Bip Ferguson's Japanese-American girlfriend, and tried to flirt with her...using some of your famous sexually offensive language in her presence. First, it was reported that you asked her if she would like to hold your *trouser snake*. Then you said something about dancing with her...*doing the horizontal mambo* were your exact words, I believe. There were several other obscenities that flowed from your inebriated mouth last night, which I can't mention in front of the boy, but the topper was when you said to her, *'let's play Pearl Harbor...I'll lay down and you blow the hell out of me.'* Having a Japanese ancestry, Trudi Mae felt that your comment was racially prejudiced."

"Shucks, sheriff, I'm not prejudiced against Orientals," said Henry. "When it comes to poontang, I like it no matter which way it slants!"

"Anyway," continued Buck, "that was the comment that made Ferguson confront you about your behavior towards his girlfriend. And, in his defense, all he did was politely request that you quit bothering Trudi Mae. Instead of leaving it alone, like any normal person would have done...you, Henry...you chose to deliver the *coup de grace*. You snuck his beer mug while he wasn't looking, urinated into it under the counter, and then put it back in front of him. Thank God someone saw you do that...if Bip had taken a swig of that drink, there's no telling what would have happened to you, Henry...the guy is over six feet tall and weighs almost three hundred pounds!"

"Sounds like I had a great ole time...wish I had been there to enjoy it!" exclaimed the gaffer.

"You may think it's funny, Pickridge, but that booze is going to be the death of you someday," warned the sheriff.

Henry, who always lived every day as if it were his last, because at some point in time it would be, laughed and said, "Sheriff, I can't think of any better way to leave this screwed-up world!"

Buck frowned and said, "Whatever, Henry. I'll come back in a little while to pick up your trays. And by the way, Joshua, Dr. Tisdale and Tara called earlier and said to tell you 'hello.' I'll be finished with your arrest report tonight, so I told them that they could come by and visit you first thing tomorrow morning."

"Thanks for the update, sheriff," said Joshua. "I appreciate it."

The two jail-mates finished supper, and spent the rest of the evening talking—mostly Henry discussing his encounter with the alien spacecraft and its extraterrestrial inhabitant. At different times during their conversations, the adolescent's telepathic ability returned, and he was temporarily able to read Henry's mind. The more the teen concentrated on the old duffer's thoughts, the stronger his psychic energy became. Joshua determined that for now, his gift of clairvoyance only acted on the feeble-minded, but as his power increased, he was hopeful that his paranormal talents would work on anyone.

Chapter XIV
PURSUIT

The parasite puppeteer maladroitly maneuvered its host's legs over the mile of rolling hills and deep valleys of landscape that lay between the Girl Scouts' campsite and Route 44. Amber steadfastly continued in a southerly direction, reaching the old highway in less than two hours. She had actually made good time, considering the fact that the being inside of her was responsible for awkwardly ambulating her short legs and limited stride. Basically, in order to walk, the creature would flex one of Amber's knees and lift the leg, then extend the knee and fall forward until the sole of the foot touched the ground; the same procedure would then be accomplished with the other lower extremity. In essence, the thing at Amber's controls was attempting to execute a balancing act with every step the little girl took.

This uncoordinated style of spastic walking produced some adverse consequences on the Brownie's frail body—she had tripped and fallen numerous times, bloodying both shins and sustaining a plethora of bruises and scrapes all over her entire body. But those were only the minor injuries. One treacherous tumble not only seriously broke Amber's left wrist, but also fractured her thumb and three fingers. The accident grossly disfigured her four digits, causing her hand to flop flaccidly in all directions. Another disabling mishap occurred when the little girl stepped into a gopher hole, resulting in a compound fracture of her right ankle—a jagged chunk of bone with bloodied flesh attached to it, jutted out through her knee-high, brown sock. Sadly, the damage had produced a horribly deformed foot that pigeon-toed grotesquely inward, pitching the Brownie's body into a left tilt.

The macabre organism hidden inside of the small child didn't want its carrier damaged to the point of being unusable—Amber would be worthless to the invader if her body couldn't function properly. Besides, the parasitic life form would now be traveling over a desolate country road on a distant planet, and if its transporter died, then its human disguise would be lost. For now, the entity would have to repair the female unit, or at least keep it healthy until another host could be found. The abominable alien had come too far for anything to get in its way—it had an important mission to accomplish, and would do whatever it took to carry out the plan. Even though the thing required a substantial amount of energy, its camouflaged mode of transportation had to be preserved at all costs.

Amber's crippled body hobbled over to the side of the seldom-traveled road, and stopped behind a small clump of aspens. A gusty breeze of wind wafted through the row of skinny poplars, launching their brightly colored leaves into a quivering flutter of spasms. The physically impaired girl carefully looked in all directions, making certain that there were no vehicles or people in sight. Standing perfectly still, the alien clone closed her black eyes and took in a deep breath. The animated force within Amber stretched the Brownie's mouth widely open, emitting a deep growling sound that slowly escalated into a deafening, spine-chilling howl—like the cry from a wounded animal. The loud, strident off-key yowls echoed throughout the surrounding countryside, sounding like a pack of moonstruck wolves.

Suddenly, the alien-inhabited child began to shake violently, as if a thousand volts of electricity had been shot throughout her entire body. During this "electrocution" period, all of the little Brownie's injuries were inexplicably renovated by an accelerated phase of advanced wound healing. The girl's multiple areas of bruising and abrasion vanished. Like time-lapse photography, the floppy left wrist remodeled its broken bones, and snapped back into its normal anatomical position. Amber's contorted thumb and fingers autogenously repaired their deformities, quickly returning her digits to a natural configuration. The bulging lump of bone extruding from her brown stocking melted away, and the girl's misshapen foot rearranged its anatomy—magically restoring the hard and soft tissues to their proper location. Using its phenomenal powers of healing, the extraordinary extraterrestrial within Amber had repaired all of her wounds.

The creature spent a great deal of energy restoring the child's maimed body, and was in desperate need of more fuel. Using several unsteady steps, the little girl reeled back to Route 44 and faced due south. Amber then proceeded directly towards Tranquil, increasing the length of her footsteps until she was at full stride. The town was only five miles away, but the beast had to preserve its supply of energy, as it was running dangerously low. After about twenty minutes of inept ambulation, Amber heard the sound of an automobile engine, approaching her from behind. An antique, purple-colored Packard pulled up alongside of the faltering Girl Scout, and came to a quick stop.

The old lady driving the car leaned over her seat, and gawked out the open passenger side window at Amber. After a few seconds of staring, the elderly woman opened her mouth, and in a gravelly-toned southern accent, called out, "Land sakes, little girl...what in heaven's name are y'all doing out here...all by yourself on this God-awful road?"

The unearthly being was well aware that the voice it produced from Amber's larynx was not normal, so it didn't vocally respond to the gray-haired woman. Instead, it attempted to produce a smile by forcefully spreading the Brownie's lips apart—but the final outcome was more of a grimace than a grin. Several shredded morsels of ragged, red meat could be seen extruding from between Amber's baby teeth, as she displayed a pseudo-smile from her blood-splattered face.

"Where are your parents, sweetheart? My goodness, what is that smeared all over your uniform...is that blood?"

Amber was silent.

Oh, you poor little thing...you're probably in shock, and here I am jabbering away like some old ninny. Hop right in, honey, you can come with me to Tranquil!"

Amber nodded affirmatively, and then took a few rickety steps over to the early model sedan. She swung open the passenger door, and clumsily climbed in. The little girl extended out her hand to close the door, but her arm was too short to reach the handle.

"Just stay right where you are, darling, and let Hattie get that door for you."

The aged matron put the idling car in park, then lifted the inside faded chrome lever and pushed her door wide open. Taking her time, the widow swung out her legs, then rocked back once and forcibly thrust her body forward, propelling herself to her feet. Hattie was probably pushing eighty, with a disproportionate body that was short in stature and stout in shape. She wore bifocals, the kind that darken when exposed to the sunlight, and her heavily wrinkled face, neck, and arms were ashen white—similar to an albino's skin. The geriatric lady's gaudy purple dress, with its swirled patterns of garish pink flowers, extended all the way down to her black, orthopedic shoes. In no apparent rush, the stooped-over granny walked around the front of the car, hobbling in an unstable gait not too dissimilar to Amber's. Hattie grabbed the opened passenger door's silver handle and looked over at the seated child. "Watch your fingers, youngin," she warned. Then the ashen-skinned woman creaked the old door shut, and shuffled her feet back to the driver's side of her vintage auto. Catching her breath, she slowly reseated her body behind the large white, circular steering wheel. The elder closed

215

the driver's door, and then squinted through her glasses at Amber. "I'll drive you over to the hospital...they'll know what to do." The old biddy clanked the transmission into drive, and rambled off towards Tranquil, unaware of the morbid dangers posed to her by the innocent-appearing, young passenger.

The redheaded Brownie's consumer had approximately five mile's worth of time to decide what to do next. Either the thing could leave the small girl it was living in now, and enter the old woman called Hattie, or it could stay put where it was, and gather more strength later. It would have to make a decision soon—the parasitic ghoul had used up a substantial amount of power repairing its young host's wounds, and sorely needed to replenish its stamina. If the creature waited too long, its dwindling energy source could force it to unmask itself prematurely—it would not only lose the element of surprise, but also be more vulnerable—besides, that wasn't a part of the plan anyway.

Traveling at the top speed of fifty, the odd couple continued south on Route 44, heading towards the little mountain town of Tranquil—Hattie in control of the purple Packard, and the life force in control of Amber. The Brownie's body sat silently in the car, pretending to listen to the blabbing, one-way conversation of the granny's gossip. If Amber had known how to drive an automobile, the bloodthirsty alien would have killed the old busybody a long time ago. The parasite searched the Girl Scout's mind for instructions on how to operate a motor vehicle—even a simple driving manual would have sufficed—but it was only able to find information on the modus operandi of riding a bicycle. Amber's invading organism needed the driving skills of the old lady to get it to Tranquil, the town where Joshua Allen — the boy with the extra chromosome — could be found.

"We made it, hun!" drawled Hattie, turning her vehicle into the Tranquil Community Hospital parking lot. She pulled the old Packard up to one of the slots marked *Visitors Only*, and applied the brakes, stopping the car abruptly. Then, the elderly woman shifted the lever to park, applied the emergency brake, and twisted the ignition key, killing the automobile's engine.

Hattie turned to her blood-soaked rider and said, "Sweetie, I don't know what happened to you out there, but you don't have to be afraid anymore. We're at the hospital now, and the people here will help and protect you." The graying granny gave Amber a warm smile and said, "You're safe now, baby girl."

"YOU ARE NOT!" belched back the evil animal.

The cunning creature had made its decision. It instantaneously transmuted Amber's right arm into a horrendous green extremity and thrust its sharp claws into the old lady's abdomen. The reptilian hand made a repulsive gushing noise, as it sliced into her plump tummy. Dark red blood exploded from the gaping slash, splashing all over the dashboard and front window, as the woman's inferior vena cava was instantly transected. The vicious attack happened so quickly that Hattie didn't know what had hit her — there wasn't even enough time to scream. Totally incapacitated by the savage blow, the elderly widow could only sit helplessly by and witness her own slaughter. The monster withdrew its Komodo Dragon-like appendage from the helpless granny's belly, holding a conglomeration of bloody guts in its huge hand. Included in the hodgepodge of hemorrhaging flesh were muscles, fat, and entrails. The snatched mass of gore looked like a soft tissue taco—a shell of abdominal muscles wrapped around lumps of liver and transverse colon, with a smidgen of gall bladder thrown in. All the entree needed was a grated-cheese topping and some seasoning sauce!

The last thing that Hattie saw before her heart gave out was the cruel, cataleptic stare from the little girl's coal-black eyes. Amber held the butchered pile of innards close to her face and whiffed in a snoot full of its pungent odor.

"MMMMM...THERE IS NOTH-ING LIKE THE SMELL OF FRESH KILL!" it croaked.

Remembering that the teeth of its female transporter were poorly adapted to adequately macerate its human victim's flesh—it required animal protein for sustenance—the extraterrestrial transformed Amber's mixture of primary and permanent teeth into its own alien dentition. The oversized, serrated canine teeth of the beast protruded grotesquely out from Amber's mouth, causing the girl's features to distort freakishly, thereby giving her face the gruesome appearance of a hideous Halloween mask.

In preparation for its nourishment, the ghoulish inhabitant spastically contorted Amber's lips widely apart, abnormally stretching the child's mouth open beyond its anatomical limits. Unable to gain sufficient clearance to chew, the being dislocated Amber's lower jaw from its hinges, and manipulated the girl's oral opening even wider, brutally ripping the corners of her mouth apart. Viscous globs of saliva dripped profusely from its famished fangs, as the predator prepared to dine. The monster's enameled daggers effortlessly cut through Hattie's detached organs like a sharp knife, slicing off tasty fillets of Homo sapiens. Famished, the alien vigorously munched away at the raw meat, this time chewing the flesh thoroughly before swallowing it down. By properly masticating its meal, the gluttonous carnivore could derive its energy more efficiently, since Amber's stomach and intestines would be able to absorb the nutrients in a shorter period of time. Besides, there was no one else in the hospital parking lot, so it had plenty of time to enjoy the buffet. After gulping down the last bite of delicacy, which was mostly made up of liver, the homicidal maniac licked the red gore off its hand, and then kissed Amber's lips together several times. *THESE EARTH PEOPLE...THEY TASTE MUCH BETTER THAN NALURIANS...MORE TENDER,* the cannibal thought. It was still hungry, and could have continued to feed on the old lady's corpse, but the girl's petite stomach could only hold so much food. To conserve its energy, the sadistic slayer dematerialized its muscular appendage and razored fangs, returning a normal right arm and set of child's teeth to Amber.

The uncaring killer left Hattie's gutted body where it was, propped up behind the bloodied steering wheel of her old, parked Packard. She and her husband Ralph had purchased the automobile in Biloxi, Mississippi, when it was brand spanking new—to celebrate their first wedding anniversary. The two of them had worked hard their entire lives, saving up enough money to retire to the state of Arizona. Ralph had died of a heart attack only two years ago, so his widow continued to drive the pristine Packard—the vehicle that she and her husband had shared together for over fifty years. That car had meant everything to Hattie, so it would have been impossible to put a price on the sentimental value or the memories associated with the classic sedan. Over the past couple of years, she had spent a lot of money restoring the antique auto, keeping it stylish and in good running condition. Now, Hattie wouldn't have to worry about that anymore—they probably don't drive cars where she was going anyway.

After feasting on the old woman, the refueled parasite had enough strength now to continue on with its assigned mission. It would have to find the church the young girl at the campsite spoke about—"The Chapel of God," she had said. On hindsight, the creature should have asked the wrinkled woman where this "church" was located, but at that particular time it was starving, and its energy reserves were too drained for it to think logically. From the interior of the sanguinary auto, Amber scanned the surrounding area to make sure that nobody was around. Seeing no one, she depressed the shiny inside handle, swung open the squeaky passenger door, and clumsily climbed down out of the old purple car. Then, the Brownie stumbled away from the hospital parking lot, steadfastly determined to track down the location of the religious structure called "The Chapel of God,"—the place where the trisomy human could be found.

Amber walked over to the phone booth located across from the hospital, and folded in its accordion-like door. The telephone receiver had been ripped from its cord, but a phone book was still present, stuck between the two metal covers that held it in place. She swung up the hanging carrier, and spread the book of information open. The publication was worn and tattered, with its edges badly frayed, and numerous pages of the directory had been partially ripped or completely torn out.

Quickly searching Amber's mind, the creature found the data that it needed. Thumbing through the damaged guide to the yellow pages, the Girl Scout flipped the pages to the heading of **Churches**, and fingered down the listing to:

The Chapel of God
43 West Elm Street,
Tranquil, Arizona... 928-555-0123

The intelligent humanoid knew that this "church" was in Tranquil, but had no idea of the whereabouts of Elm Street. It scanned the girl's stored knowledge again, and identified where the passageway called Elm Street was located. From the phone booth, it would have to walk two blocks east, turn south, and then travel one block to reach Elm Street. From there it would head west, to the address called 43, where it would uncover Joshua — the special Earth-being it had traveled light years to find.

Chapter XV
VISITATION

The sheriff was sipping his morning coffee while reading the Tranquil Gazette, when Ted and Tara walked through the front door of his office. Buck peeked over the town's weekly rag and greeted both visitors with a "Good morning, folks."

"Good morning, Buck," said Ted.

Tara smiled at the lawman and replied, "Hi, sheriff."

Buck set his half-filled cup of black java back on the desk, and laid the ruffled newspaper down. Then, he skated his wooden easy chair back, and slowly got up. "I know that you're both chomping at the bit to see Joshua. The boy probably didn't sleep too well last night, but he's doing just fine. At least he had someone to talk to—Henry Pickridge is locked in the cell next to him."

"That's one conversation I would've enjoyed hearing," said Ted.

"I trust both of you completely, but I have to uphold the procedures set up by the state of Arizona for visitation of prisoners," Buck explained. "Please empty out your pockets and place everything in this bowl."

The doctor placed his wallet, keys, penlight, change, and cell phone into the container. "That's all I have on me, sheriff."

"Here's my purse," said Tara, handing it over to him.

Normal protocol called for the searching, or "frisking" of anyone visiting a prisoner in jail, but since Buck personally knew Ted and Tara, and had no doubts as to their integrity, he waived making them undergo the embarrassing examination.

"Okay, you both can come with me now," announced the lawman.

Ted and Tara followed the sheriff through the swinging wooden gate and big steel door, which led to the back of the building where the prisoners were housed. When they entered the jail room, Joshua, elated to see his surrogate family again, jumped up from his bunk, and with a joyful smile excitedly said, "Hi, Tara...hello, Dr. Tisdale...it's so good to see you... thanks so much for coming!"

"We would've been here sooner, Joshua, but we had to wait until the sheriff completed your paperwork," said Ted.

Buck slid up two chairs next to Joshua's jail cell. "You two can sit here and chat with the boy." Tara and Ted seated themselves down next to the confining bars of the claustrophobic cell, while Joshua took his place on the edge of the prison's hard bed.

"If you need anything, just let me know...I'll be at my

desk," said the peacekeeper. The sheriff gave Tara a tender pat on the back of her blond head, and then walked through the strong metal door that connected the front office with the holding cells. A loud "clunk" sound rang out as he shut the heavily fortified entryway behind him.

"Joshua, I've contacted an attorney, and we're going to do everything that we can to get you out of here," said Ted.

Tara reached her fingers between the bars and affectionately squeezed her boyfriend's extended hand. "Keep your spirits up, Joshua...remember that I love you!"

Joshua greatly appreciated his girlfriend's caring words. With a heartfelt expression on his face, he replied back, "I love you too, Tara."

"Well, hell, while you're spreading all that lovin around, don't forget about old Henry!" laughed the outspoken jailbird in the next cell.

"Henry *has* been a big help...I probably would have gone crazy in here by myself if I didn't have anyone to talk to," said Joshua. "He *also* believes that I'm innocent!"

"Thanks, Henry, we appreciate your support...we know that Joshua didn't kill those people," said Tara.

"Aw crap, it were nothing...that's the least I can do. I ain't book-learned like everyone else, but I do know an innocent face when I seen one, and besides, I was right there, running the carnival ride when that Slovinsky boy died. I was also around when those two men turned up dead at Fletcher's Pool. It just don't add up...Joshua just couldn't have killed them people!" opined the boozer.

"I don't think they have enough proof to get a conviction... every bit of evidence the sheriff has is circumstantial," reasoned Ted. "But unfortunately, nowadays, with the news media frenzy and circus hype, a person is guilty until proven innocent!"

"If it goes to trial, I'll just have to hope that the jury believes in my innocence," sighed Joshua.

"Sonny, I know what it's like when folks don't believe what you're sayin'," asserted Henry. "I've been branded a liar by most of the townspeople here in Tranquil...a drunken liar to boot! Old man Pickridge looked over at Ted and Tara. "Just like you both know that the boy is innocent, I *know* what I seen in that pasture out by Fletcher's Pool that night. It was a flying saucer, flown by somethin green...and it wasn't a little green man...it was a huge, guacamole-skinned, pig-fornicatin monster!"

Henry took off his cap, scratched his head, and continued his ramblings. "I knowed I put a bullet in that thing with my .357, but it must have survived the hit, because when I come to, I were back at my camp. When I went back to where the spaceship had landed, it were gone...and so was the goddam alien. I just hope that while I was knocked out, that bastard didn't do no anal probing or weird stuff like that...I don't fancy some rump-ranger from another planet shoving something up my butt, if you get my drift!"

Even though Mr. Pickridge's story was somewhat humorous, Joshua decided to change the subject, because the old man was going off on another one of his tangents—and the boy knew that if Henry's narrative continued, the vulgar expressions would only escalate. Anyway, the young genius had already heard the alien abduction story so many times before, that he had the entire account memorized, word for

226

word. Also, Tara was present, and she didn't need to hear that kind of language. Joshua cleared his throat loudly to get Ted's attention, and then asked, "Dr. Tisdale, what did the attorney have to say about my case?"

"I called Adam Goodman...he's one of the best lawyers in the state, and an old friend of mine," said Ted. "He'll be driving up from Phoenix tomorrow to personally speak with the district attorney. After he finds out exactly what the charges are, and what evidence they've collected, he'll meet with us. Adam's won most of the cases he's taken on, and he's saved a lot of falsely accused, innocent people from spending time in prison. You'll like him, Joshua...he's a straight shooter, and a really good man. From what I told Adam on the phone, he's not too impressed with their so-called incriminating evidence."

"Dr. Tisdale, I can't thank you and Tara enough. I promise that I'll pay you back every penny," said Joshua. "You've saved my life twice already now...I just hope that I can return the favor someday."

"You will," said Tara, "you will."

Sheriff Evans squeaked open the heavy door, and brought in a large serving tray that held two platters of scrambled eggs and bacon strips, along with a couple of miniature cartons of two-percent milk. "Breakfast time, boys!" he announced. Ted and Tara quickly stood up, then moved away from the jail cells to give Buck more room.

The old geezer rubbed his hands together and exclaimed, "My favorite meal...cooked hen embryos and fried hog's ass!"

Sheriff Evans took the pair of hot food plates and slid one through each of the prisoner's jail slots. Henry greedily grabbed his allocation of rations and plopped himself down on his messy bunk. The old codger held the steaming dish up to his bulbous nose and sniffed in its appetizing aroma. Then, like a starving animal, he took his plastic fork and began voraciously wolfing it down. "Mmmm...mmmm...mmmm... good!" he babbled. Joshua took his serving of food, and set it down next to him on the bed.

"Ted, you and Tara don't have to leave," said the lawman. "You both can stay and visit them while they eat their breakfast."

"Thanks, sheriff," replied the physician, as he and his daughter resumed their same seating arrangement.

Suddenly, Buck's office telephone rang. "Excuse me," said the sheriff, as he briskly walked to the front of the building to take the call. In less than a minute, the elected official rushed back into the room of visitors and announced, "That was Huey Spencer...he was out checking on his cattle, when he saw three little girls wandering around his field. He said they appeared to be in shock, mumbling something about their troop leader being attacked by some animal. I sure could use the help, Dr. Tisdale, if you'd like to come with me."

"Let's go, sheriff...Tara, you stay here with Joshua."

Buck eyed Tara and said, "You three continue on with your visit here...we should be back shortly." The lawman locked the front office entry, and then the two men slipped out the back door to where the sheriff's custom-tailored Tahoe was parked. They both jumped into the officer's souped-up truck, and sped quickly away towards Route 44, having no idea of the horrors they were about to discover.

Chapter XVI
LUKE

Amber's body, still occupied by the cannibalistic extraterrestrial from another galaxy, walked west on Elm Street, past the long span of quaint old houses and staggered line of stately trees, until the creature finally found the sign that it was looking for:

CHAPEL OF GOD
Luke Allen, Pastor
43 West Elm Street

This was the place the young girl hiding in the tent told the alien about—the church where it would find the human called Joshua—the Earth creature that it had been sent to destroy. The arrogant being was confident that its important mission would soon be over, so it twitched the Brownie's mouth into a misshapen grin.

Amber faltered towards the front door of the church, nearly toppling when she tripped over one of the steps in the stone pathway. Arriving at the locked entryway of the tiny house of worship, the visitor from another planet took Amber's fist and banged on the front door several times. The diabolical creature inside the Girl Scout could hear the distinctive sound of shuffling feet coming from within the building, slowly advancing towards the bolted door. Unfastening the lock, Luke swung open the church door and laid his sleep-deprived, bloodshot eyes on the brown uniformed little girl standing before him. The clergyman was recuperating from another hangover, and had been preparing his sermon for the following Sunday service.

"What do you want?" the minister requested curtly. "I don't need any Girl Scout cookies."

"I WANT JOSH-U-A," it burped out from Amber's lips.

"What do you want Joshua for?"

"IT IS VE-RY IM-POR-TANT!" barked the entity.

"Joshua's in jail," the preacher replied. "What's wrong with your voice...and what happened to your uniform, little girl?"

"WHERE IS JAIL?"

"Why are you asking me that?"

"I HAVE TO KNOW!" it said hoarsely.

"Why...what's going on?" asked Luke.

"IT IS A MAT-TER OF LIFE AND DEATH!"

"It's none of your business, but Joshua's been arrested. He's in jail—down at the sheriff's office," Luke told the Brownie. "A matter of life and death...for who?"

"FOR YOU!" growled the monster.

The thing transfigured one of Amber's arms, and pushed the religious zealot back into the church with its enormous, lizard-shaped hand. Then the alien intruder walked in and slammed the door closed behind it. Luke stared down in amazement at the pigtailed child attired in the bloody Brownie outfit. The bewildered holy man couldn't believe his reddened eyes. Instead of possessing the normal-shaped arm of a young girl her age, she had a thick, hypertrophied green appendage bulging out from her right shirtsleeve.

Was this a hallucination...a case of delirium tremens...from the excessive alcohol that he had imbibed last night? wondered Luke. The preacher rubbed both of his eyes and looked again—the image of the repulsive extremity was still there, indelibly stamped on each lens of Luke's two inflamed eyeballs. Horrified, the reverend stepped back and shrieked, "What, in the name of God, *are* you?"

The extraterrestrial glared at the cleric with its cold, dark eyes and belched out, "I AM *YOUR* GOD NOW!"

"You're not *my* God...you're the prince of darkness... Beelzebub himself, disguised as an innocent child!" screamed the outraged evangelist. Luke stepped over to Amber and laid his right hand on her shoulder, in an attempt to exorcise the malevolent spirit from the little girl. "I command you to leave this unblemished body...I summon the power of God to damn your evil soul back to the fires of Hell!"

Unfazed by the religious purging, the smiling Brownie let out a hideous giggle, and then gave the pious pastor a flirtatious wink. The poor man had no earthly idea of what was about to happen next. All of a sudden, the fingers of his positioned hand began to tremble uncontrollably. A gripping bolt of energy surged through his arm, and squirmed up his shoulder. Luke strained to pull his hand loose, but like Brer Rabbit and the Tar-Baby, he was stuck fast to the girl's body.

The vile invader continued to assimilate into its new host, rapidly flowing through the alarmed preacher's chest and legs. Amber's shark eyes turned back into their original aquamarine color, as the dissipating parasite abandoned her tiny body and entered into the servant of God. It was quite ironic that the parson had spent most of his adult life performing exorcisms — delivering people from evil, as he used to say — but now, *he* was the one in dire need of the religious ritual. After the macabre transference, the Brownie's energy-depleted body went totally flaccid, crashing to the floor of the church like a marionette whose strings had just been cut. The alien within Luke felt its new set of arms and chest, marveling at the increased muscle tone and size of its recently hijacked body.

"THIS HUMAN IS MUCH BETTER...MUCH STRONGER!" it said, in a well-articulated tone that was very deep, even for a male's voice. Indeed, this body would be *much* better suited for the celestial organism — Luke had more stored knowledge and strength than Amber, he was a trusted man of the cloth, *and* he could drive a car. Except for the damaged liver from the alcohol toxins the human had consumed over the years, the body was in relatively good condition. The newly-possessed preacher picked up Amber's lifeless corpse and placed it behind the pulpit, then marched out of the tiny chapel, locking the door behind him.

Excited with his new vessel, the otherworldly clergyman

spastically strode out to his car. Luke's alien copy opened the door, and then climbed in. On the dashboard was a pair of dark sunglasses. He put them on, then pulled down the visor and looked in the mirror. No telltale black eyes could be seen now. "THIS IS GOOD!" the thing said with a crooked smile. Quickly inspecting the files of information stored in Luke's brain, the clever beast inserted the key into the ignition and started the vehicle's engine. It engaged the transmission, and rolled off towards the sheriff's office, where it would find the prize that it had been hunting for all this time — the human with the extra chromosome — the boy they called Joshua.

Chapter XVII
WITNESS

The chrome-rimmed, oversized tires of the 4-wheel drive, Chevy Tahoe bounced over the bumpy terrain leading up to the Girl Scouts' campsite. As Sheriff Evans and Dr. Tisdale continued down the rarely traveled grass trail, Buck could see Huey Spencer in the distance, waving his arms back and forth to get their attention. The rancher was standing in front of a green tent, next to three small figures seated on the ground, closely huddled together with red blankets draped around them. Pulling up next to Laura's white minivan, Buck and Ted jumped out of the sheriff's truck and hurried over to the man.

"Thanks for getting here so quickly," said Huey. "I had to call you from Ned Walker's place...my mobile phone wouldn't work way out here...I just couldn't get a signal."

"Where's the troop leader—the one who was attacked?" inquired Buck.

"It was more than an attack," said the rancher. "The lady's been brutally murdered. I covered the poor woman up. She's over there...under the sleeping bag."

Buck and the physician walked over to Laura's blanketed body, and squatted down beside it. Ted, noticing a small swarm of flies buzzing over the concealed corpse, waved his hand to shoo the annoyance away. The sheriff lifted up the part of the down-filled sleeper that shrouded the dead woman's head, revealing the gruesomely ripped out neck of the massacred mom. Crawling around the inside of the massive wound was a teeming horde of white wriggling maggots, expeditiously nibbling away at the troop leader's bloodied subcutaneous tissues.

The sickening sight of gore was even repugnant to Dr. Tisdale, who, over the years of working in hospital emergency rooms, had been a witness to just about every type of trauma under the sun inflicted upon a human being. Buck started to gag, but averted his eyes away from the disgustingly foul image of the dead woman, thereby preventing himself from heaving up his breakfast. The nauseated sheriff threw the cloth covering back over the face of the mutilated mother, quickly stood up, then turned and took a few steps away from her dead body. Buck breathed in several deep gulps of fresh air to keep from puking, and then swiveled his head around to face Huey.

"Any ideas on how this happened?" asked the lawman.

"When I first found the little girls, they were all in a state of shock...they couldn't provide me with much information.

The only thing I could get out of them was that their troop leader had been attacked...what I told you on the phone," reported the rancher. "On the way back to the campsite, one of the Brownies...I think her name is Jenny...she told me that Amber was the one who killed their troop leader. But get this, sheriff, Amber is the dead woman's ten-year-old daughter...a classmate of theirs. I found the murdered woman's purse over by her body, full of credit cards and money...her name is Laura Renshaw. Doesn't look like a robbery to me, sheriff...I sure as hell can't make any sense out of it!"

"Neither can I," said Buck. "I just hope we're not dealing with a serial killer here." The law enforcer walked over to the huddled trio of Girl Scouts, and knelt down in front of them. If the three little girls were witnesses to the ghastly slaying of their troop leader, Buck had no idea how traumatized they might be, or how his questions would affect them. The sheriff couldn't even begin to imagine the horrors the little Brownies must have encountered during their horrible ordeal.

A series of loud bleeping sounds from the ambulance siren could be heard off in the distance, getting closer.

"Hi, girls, my name is Buck Evans, and I'm the sheriff of Tranquil. I know that all of you have been through a frightening experience, but I need to ask you some questions...did anyone see what happened?"

The three Brownies all sat quietly. Latisha, with tears streaming down both cheeks, mechanically rocked back and forth, while clutching at the blanket that was draped around her back and shoulders. Rachel softly hummed an unrecognizable tune, as she stared listlessly out into space. Jenny was the only one to make eye contact with Buck.

The silence continued on for a few more seconds until Jenny finally opened her mouth and said softly, "I sort of did."

"What did you see, Jenny?" asked the sheriff.

"It was terrible...it was a monster that looked like Amber... and it killed Mrs. Renshaw with its bare hands...then it...it..." Beads of tears rolled down Jenny's eyes, as the frightened and psychologically overwhelmed young Brownie began to cry. Dr. Tisdale reached over and put his hand on the frightened girl's shoulder.

"It's okay, honey," said Ted, in a soothing tone of voice. "You're safe with us now...no one's going to hurt you, I promise. Take your time and tell us what you saw."

Jenny used the blanket wrapped around her to wipe away the drops of sorrow sliding down her cheeks. She cleared her throat and shuttered in a deep breath. "We hid inside the tent...it wanted to know where to find Joshua Allen...I told it that Joshua was at the church...then it left."

"Do you know where Amber is?" Buck asked the grieving Brownie.

Jenny's lower lip and chin began to quiver. "I think that thing *was* Amber!" she cried.

"That's okay," said Ted, who gently stroked her hair. "You've been a big help to us."

"Yes, thank you very much, Jenny," smiled the sheriff.

The ambulance finally pulled up, and two paramedics dressed in blue uniforms scrambled out of its doors. Dr. Tisdale directed them to take the three distressed Brownies to the emergency room for psychological evaluation and sedative treatment, as indicated by the physician on call. After the anguished girls had been loaded onto the white hospital vehicle, the paramedics drove off, headed back down the undulating green trail towards Route 44.

Sheriff Evans recognized that the area would have to be cordoned off and treated as if it were a crime scene—he anticipated several more hours of work ahead of him—to secure the campsite and examine the surrounding grounds for any clues or physical evidence.

After the ambulance departed, Ted walked back over to the tent where Buck stood and commented, "Sheriff, I was just thinking...there's something that really bothers me about what Jenny said. If whoever, or *whatever* killed the troop leader is looking for Joshua, then..."

"You're right, Ted...I read you loud and clear!" interrupted the lawman. "Joshua, Henry, and Tara...they're all over there at the jail by themselves...defenseless...like sitting ducks. Dammit, we've got to get back to the jail, before the killer finds them first!"

Buck pulled out his wireless and punched in his office number...nothing. "What the hell is wrong with this cell phone?" he said, banging on the buttons again. "We're not that far out...we should be able to get service out here!"

"Same thing happened to me," said Huey. "It's like something is blocking the signal."

The officer handed his cell phone over to Dr. Tisdale, "Keep trying the number, Ted...we've got to get through to them!"

"I'll do my best, sheriff," answered the doctor.

"Huey, do me a favor and stay here with the body. We've got to get to town, fast...we'll be back as soon as possible... thanks," said Buck.

239

"Sure, sheriff...whatever you say," replied the rancher.

"Let's high-tail it, doc!" directed the lawman.

Ted shook his head and forewarned, "I've got a bad feeling about this, Buck...if what Jenny said is true, they won't have a chance against that butcher!"

"All I know is that something very strange is going on around here," said the sheriff, "and I intend to get to the bottom of it!"

The two men hustled over to the parked SUV and hopped in the cab. Buck kicked over the turbocharged engine, yanked the lever into the drive position, and stomped on the gas pedal. The two-toned truck lurched forward, its rear wheels spinning up a dark gray cloud of dirt and dust. Quickly overtaking the meandering ambulance in front of them, they raced down the crude meadow byway, hurriedly heading towards Route 44. In only a matter of minutes, the sheriff's speeding patrol car had traversed the mile stretch of verdant trail and reached the main road. Buck gunned the V-8 and squealed south on the old highway, his truck's rear end fishtailing like a hooked trout dancing on the water's surface. The Tranquil jail was only five miles away, but the killer had gotten a hefty head start. If Ted's dark premonition was correct, it was imperative that they reach the sheriff's office in time.

Chapter XVIII
QUARRY

Ted continued to dial the number to the sheriff's office on the cell phone, as they sped back on Route 44 towards the jail. About two miles out of town, the wireless finally picked up a signal and transmitted the call. "It's ringing, sheriff!" exclaimed the doctor, who was anxiously awaiting an answer from the other end of the line.

The telephone in Buck's office jingled. Once, twice, three times. No answer. "Someone pick up the damn phone!" demanded the physician.

"Hello...sheriff's office," the sweet voice answered.

"Tara!"

"Hi, Daddy, what's up?"

"Listen, angel, and pay close attention to what I'm about to say. Keep the front door locked and *do not*, I repeat, *do not* open it for anyone. The sheriff and I are on our way back to the jail, and should be there in a couple of minutes. There's a murderer loose, and we have reason to believe that, for some reason, he's after Joshua. I'll explain later...hang up the phone now, and make sure the doors are all locked!"

With a tone of urgency in her voice, Tara said, "Okay Daddy, I'll do it right now!" Then, she hastily slammed the receiver back down on its cradle, and scurried over to the front entrance—it was locked. Next, she dashed through the office to the back door—also locked.

"What's going on, young lady? You're running around like a squirrel on speed!" quipped Henry.

"That was my father on the phone...he said that we might be in danger...a murderer is loose and, for some unknown reason, is after Joshua," relayed Tara. "Daddy and the sheriff are on their way back, and should arrive here at any moment now!"

"Listen!" whispered Joshua. A jiggling sound was heard at the rear entrance, like someone was trying to turn the knob to get in. Suddenly, the door flew open and in rushed Buck and Ted. The sheriff looked at Tara and asked, "Is the front door locked?"

"Yes, I just checked it," replied Tara. Ted slammed the back entryway closed, laid Sheriff Evans' cell phone down on the table next to the exit, and then engaged the dead bolt lock.

"We're all safe now," said Buck. "Dr. Tisdale and I just returned from a murder scene...a group of Girl Scouts and their troop leader, Laura Renshaw, were camping out west of Fletcher's Pool last night, when the woman was savagely attacked and killed by someone. One of the Brownies told us that it was the troop leader's daughter, Amber, who had taken the life of her mother...but the little girl said that Amber had turned into some sort of a monster, and had killed the woman with her bare hands! This so-called monster wanted to know where it could find Joshua...so that's why we called, and rushed back over here. We thought that all of you could be in danger from the killer...especially Joshua. I know how this must sound, but that's the story we got—it doesn't make any sense to me either, but it's all we had to go on."

From inside his cell, Joshua's rapidly developing psychic powers were sending him a message. It was hard to decipher, but he knew that it meant trouble. "I can't explain it, sheriff," said the boy savant, "but I'm sensing that something bad is about to happen...please be *very* careful!"

Suddenly, there was a loud knock on the front door. "You all stay back here!" said Buck, partially closing the reinforced metal door behind him. The law enforcement officer walked into the front office and over to the locked entryway. He adjusted the holstered revolver that sat on his right hip, and then looked through the door's dime-shaped peephole. A man dressed in black was standing outside. Even though the fellow was wearing dark sunglasses, Buck quickly recognized him as Luke Allen.

"False alarm, guys. No little girl or monster named Amber out there. It's only Luke...Joshua's Dad," Sheriff Evans called out. The lawman twisted the metal latch counter-clockwise, disengaging the dead bolt lock, and pulled open the door.

"Hi, Mr. Allen...how are you today?" the officer asked.

"SUPERIOR," answered the clergyman, in a raucous voice. "IS JOSHUA HERE?"

"Yeah, he's in the back...sounds like you have a bad cold."

The alien hesitated for a few seconds, searching Luke's mind for the definition of "cold." Finding the answer, it cleverly responded, "I DO."

"Police policy, Luke, you'll have to empty out your pockets into this bowl." The creature fumbled around with the preacher's pants, finally withdrawing a wallet, car keys, and a chained crucifix, which he shakily placed into the container.

"Now, I'll have to frisk you before I can let you go back... please hold both of your arms out to the side." Luke, sunglasses still on, gauchely lifted both arms up and held them out at different levels. The armed officer quickly patted the pastor down, and as expected, found nothing.

"I'm sorry, but unless you wear those to correct your vision, you'll also have to hand over the dark glasses," Buck explained.

"I NEED THEM," it replied, in a throaty tone.

"Now Luke, I *know* that you have perfect vision...unless you can give me a good reason, I must insist that you give me those sunglasses...rules are rules!"

"THE GLASSES STAY ON!" the thing roared.

"Mr. Allen, I'm sorry, but you can't visit Joshua until you remove those dark glasses!"

"SCREW YOU...THEY STAY ON!" it bellowed.

The sheriff couldn't believe his ears. "What did you say to me, Luke...are you drunk?"

The pompous being, lacking any hint of self-control or patience, began to move toward the jail cells. Buck quickly stepped in front of the reverend, reached his hand out, and jerked the sunglasses off of Luke's face, uncovering a pair of sinister black eyes that coldly stared down at him.

"GET OUT OF MY WAY, MORTAL!" shouted the entity from another world.

The puzzled peace officer stood in front of the minister and exclaimed, "What in God's name happened to your eyes, Luke?"

In less than a second, the intolerant life form had transmuted the cleric's right hand into a horrendous, green paw. It grabbed Sheriff Evans' left forearm, and squeezed down on his flesh with its huge scaly claws, instantly crushing the lawman's radius and ulna with its clamp-like grip. Buck screamed out in agony as the alien appendage crunched the sheriff's limb bones together — generating a disgusting grating sound. The pain was so excruciating that the uniformed officer buckled to his knees and fell to the floor. Believing that it had effectively incapacitated the interfering human, the alien invader released its constricting grip on Buck's left arm.

"DO NOT MESS WITH ME, HUMAN!" it snarled.

The sheriff tried to move the fingers of his left hand, but the debilitating injury prevented him from doing so. That upper limb was useless now. Using his right hand, Buck drew the nine-millimeter automatic from his side holster, and from a kneeled position fired three bullets into Luke's chest. The projectiles made a thwacking sound as they ripped through the cleric's black shirt, their impact thrusting the wounded man's body backwards, and onto the floor.

Hearing the gunshots, Ted and Tara pulled open the heavily constructed, connecting door, and rushed into the front office. "Are you okay?" the physician voiced loudly.

Buck rose to his feet, glanced back at them and said, "Both of you stay where you are. I don't know what the hell's going on...I just had to shoot Luke Allen...but it *wasn't* him! I think that something has taken over his body...maybe the thing that killed the troop leader."

The injured law enforcement officer crept cautiously over to where the evangelist had landed, all the while using his right hand to continuously aim his 9mm at the downed man of God. Luke was lying on his back—sprawled out on the floor, with dark, red blood gushing profusely from the three bullet holes in his unmoving chest. Sheriff Evans stood over the parson's motionless body and looked for any overt signs of life.

He saw none.

As Buck was observing the torrent of red discharge spilling from the holy man's torso, the trio of bloodstreams suddenly stopped, then eerily reversed direction and began flowing back into the entry wounds. The three tributaries of burgundy-colored liquid appeared to have a mind of their own, purposefully navigating their way back uphill, only to be sucked back into the dime-sized openings in Luke's flesh. Stunned, the lawman slowly moved back from the supernatural-healing body, not knowing what to expect next.

All of a sudden, the enduring parasite lifted Luke's head up and glared at the sheriff with its daunting ink-black eyes. "YOU CANNOT KILL ME...I AM GOD!" it clamored. Then, the narcissistic humanoid sprung to its feet, extended its huge chameleon hand outward, and lumbered towards Buck. Not taking any chances this time, the trained law professional instinctively aimed the revolver, and emptied the remainder of the clip into the attacking entity.

The ensuing shots rang out like a string of firecrackers

going off. In only a matter of seconds, the marksman had accurately hit his intended target—five bullets had plowed through the chest cavity, and four slugs had slammed into the pastor's head. Luke's body reeled backwards with every thumping hit, finally flopping spastically onto the hardwood floor of the sheriff's office.

"Now stay the hell down this time, goddam you!" Buck shouted. Unable to move his left hand, he called out, "Doc, come over here and help me reload!"

The alarmed physician hurried over to the sheriff's side to help him with the empty weapon. Buck deftly flipped the notched lever with his good thumb, releasing the spent ammunition clip from the bottom of the revolver's handle. It clanked loudly as it bounced across the floorboards, coming to rest under Sheriff Evan's wooden desk. "Grab the extra clip out of my belt and insert it into the handle!" instructed the injured official. Ted snatched the loaded metal ammo receptacle from its leather pouch located on the lawman's black belt, and speedily jammed it into the handle until it clicked.

"Thanks," said Buck. He gripped the gun tightly and aimed it at the partially metamorphosed body he had just blasted. Shuffling his feet backwards, the sheriff called out, "Ted...Tara...head on back to the cells, now! I don't know if this thing can be stopped or not!" Tara and her father quickly scrambled through the sturdy metal door that separated the jail cells from the front office.

"What the frick is going on?" questioned Henry. "Sounds like a damn shooting gallery out there!"

"*Not now*, Henry...I'll tell you later," replied Ted.

Just as the sheriff reached the impenetrable steel door,

Luke's head popped up like a gopher emerging from its hole. The immortal alien rumbled, "YOU ARE MAKING ME VERY ANGRY, EARTHLING!" Then, it clambered to its feet, and stormed towards the flabbergasted law officer.

"The damned thing won't die!" Buck announced loudly.

Without delay, Ted and the sheriff slammed the armored door closed and secured its lock before the irate extraterrestrial could reach them. The maleficent monster walked up to the bolted barricade and banged its clawed hand on the solid surface several times, producing a series of sizable dents in the exterior of the impervious metal door.

"He's strong, but he won't be getting through *that*," said the sheriff. "Three inches of reinforced steel!"

Then the banging suddenly stopped.

Silence.

That's what they heard coming from the other side of the protective barrier now. Dead silence.

The intelligent being was busy examining the fortified obstacle, closely investigating the damage it had inflicted on the blocked entryway. After carefully analyzing the situation, the being took its hand, and raked its sharp claws over the metal surface of the impediment, producing a chilling, squealing sound, similar to fingernails scratching on a chalkboard. Then, it slowly turned around and lumbered back through the front door of the sheriff's office.

Hearing the fading sounds of the thing's footsteps, Tara stated, "Maybe it's leaving now."

Ted took in a deep breath and said, "I sure as hell hope so."

Buck set his semi-automatic weapon down, and using his

good hand, unhooked the big shiny ring of keys from his belt. "Ted, take these two keys here and let Joshua and Henry out... then take this one and open up that cabinet...you'll find my 12-gauge and Henry's .357 in there." The emergency room doctor hastened over to the jail cells and freed both of its prisoners. Then, he unlocked the repository door and quickly removed Buck's shotgun and Henry's magnum revolver.

"Listen up, everyone...there's something out there... something not human...something that's taken over Luke's body," explained the lawman. "I emptied a full clip of 9mm shells into the beast, and it didn't even phase it!"

"I'll bet you dollars to dumplings that the thing in Luke's body is the same frickin green alien that tried to kill me," Henry claimed. "And I only got to shoot at the dickzilla one time!"

The injured lawman looked over at Dr. Tisdale and said, "Ted, give Henry back his snub nose, and you take the scattergun...I'm going to need all the help I can get!" The physician handed over the ivory handled revolver to Henry, then released the safety from the 12-gauge pump and lowered its barrel.

Ted and his daughter made eye contact for several seconds, and then bobbed their heads in the affirmative at each other. "We have something extremely important to tell all of you... an incredible story that will seem unbelievable at first, but it is absolutely true," said Tara. "And now is as good a time as any to explain it. First of all, inside of me is..."

Tara's beginning narrative was suddenly interrupted by the noisy scream of an automobile engine, followed by the explosion of glass, along with the sounds of splintering wood.

The roar of the car's motor escalated to a deafening pitch, as Luke's vehicle crashed through the sheriff's front door. It traveled through the office, and then slammed into the steel barrier like a motorized, medieval battering ram. The startled spectators made a mad dash for the back of the room, as the speeding car buckled in the heavy steel door—kicking it open and knocking it partly off its jamb. Its heavy duty lock was instantly snapped in two, as the thunderous collision flung debris everywhere. After the smoke cleared and the dust had settled, the assaulted onlookers were able to observe the outcome of the devastating crash.

The front of Luke's automobile was severely smashed in—rippled like an old accordion—immediately disabling its engine from the high-speed impact. As a result of the crash, the dashboard had been catapulted back into the reverend, compressing his chest between the steering wheel and the car's front seat. Both of the clergyman's legs were badly fractured, and his throat had been impaled by a jagged piece of glass from the broken windshield. Virtually all of the bones in Luke's face had been shattered by the collision, giving him the appearance of a bizarre-looking, cabbage patch doll. The preacher lay motionless in the decimated vehicle, with his bloodied head facing downwards, both eyes closed.

"He sure as hell's gotta be dead now!" proclaimed Henry, in a nervous voice. "Nothing coulda lived through that!"

Without warning, the malevolent minister propped up his bashed-in face, then widely opened both of his sunken, pitch-black eyes. The horrified group watched in awe, as the grisly ghoul took its lizard hand and nonchalantly ripped out the sizable chunk of serrated glass that was embedded in Luke's neck. When the creature dislodged the shard, a fountain of bright red blood squirted out from the gaping gash, which almost stretched from ear to ear. The entrapped alien animal easily bent the steering wheel aside, and then moved the dashboard out of its way. Next, the creature used its massive strength to force open the vehicle's demolished door, steadily maneuvering the cleric's mangled body out of the wreckage.

The powerful parasite grimaced threateningly at its quarry, and then delivered an inhuman polyphony from Luke's mouth that sounded like an exotic mixture of yelps, roars, and howls — while simultaneously healing the evangelist's damaged legs, slashed open neck, and flattened face. As the thing stood next to the crashed car, the organism's devilish eyes glowered at its astounded prey. "YOU CANNOT ESCAPE ME!" it squalled.

After witnessing the disfigured minister's fantastic resurrection, Henry stared at the metamorphosed man in disbelief and exclaimed, "It's Howdy friggin Doody time, people!"

Buck pointed his gun at the pastor. "Luke, it's Sheriff Evans...you know me, I'm your friend...if you're still in there, you have to fight whatever it is that's taken over your body...I know you don't want to hurt anyone."

The vengeful extraterrestrial glared at the sheriff, then replied in a guttural tone of voice, "OH, BUT I DO!"

Joshua suddenly began receiving a mental imprint of something alien — something dark and evil that had taken over his father — but he refused to believe it. The teen studied the black figure that resembled Luke and said, "Don't you recognize me, Father...it's Joshua, your son!"

The thing twisted Luke's lips into an evil smile and

251

sneered, "*YOU* ARE THE ONE THAT I WANT!" Then it menacingly advanced towards the teenaged boy.

"Out the back, quick!" shouted Buck. Dr. Tisdale released the dead bolt lock and jerked open the door. Tara, Joshua, Henry, and Buck rushed out in single file, followed by Ted, who glanced back over his right shoulder before trying to close the rear entryway. Immediately behind the fleeing doctor was the preacher in black, reaching out with a monstrous green hand, trying to grab him with its ripping claws. The horrified physician frantically yanked the door shut behind him, and then scrambled to follow the others.

"We'll take my Tahoe!" yelled the lawman, as he punched the remote to unlock the doors. Tara, Joshua, and Henry jumped in the passenger's side and scrambled to the back, while Buck hopped into the driver's seat and kicked over the engine. Just as Ted reached the side of the truck, the rear door of the sheriff's office jettisoned outward, thrust off its hinges by the supernatural strength of the pursuing predator. It staggered through the opening, and quickly headed straight towards the Tahoe. Ted ran a few steps alongside the moving vehicle, then jumped into the passenger seat and slammed the door shut. Buck clomped his foot down hard on the accelerator pedal, propelling his beefed-up SUV towards Main Street, away from the trailing monster.

The outraged alien invader, limited by the walking speed of its human host, screamed out at the departing truck, "NO MATTER WHERE YOU GO, HUMANS, I WILL FIND YOU!"

Chapter XIX
TEIRKEN

Sheriff Evans used his good hand to steer the speeding Tahoe, as he swerved its squealing tires onto Main Street. Joshua peered through the rear window of the truck and observed the darkened figure of his possessed father, angrily waving his arms about, reminiscent of the animated sermons the evangelist used to deliver to his congregation at church. As the distance between the truck and the creature grew, Ted looked back and said, "Thank God that thing can't fly...I think we're out of harm's way now!"

#

The irritated entity quickly calmed down, and relied on its superior intelligence and the power of logical reasoning to determine *where* the vehicle carrying Joshua was headed.

Since these human beings were extremely fragile, with no self-healing capabilities to speak of, the intelligent life form deduced that the individual it injured would have to go somewhere for treatment of the limb it had fractured. The parasite scrutinized the life experiences stored in Luke's mental files, and found that when the parson was a child, he had broken his arm falling out of a tree. The boy's injury was treated in a place called a *hospital* — and the closest hospital around was located in Tranquil. It searched further, and quickly found the saved information in Luke's mind regarding how to get there. The vehicle that held the human with the broken arm, *and most importantly Joshua*, were headed for the structure that would repair the man's injury...a place called Tranquil Community Hospital. In order to preserve its dwindling energy, the alien restored normal anatomy to its human host's arm, and then mentally mapped the shortest route of travel to the hospital. Luke, his shirt ripped and tattered from the full clip of 9mm ammunition that Buck had emptied into his chest, starting walking towards Main Street.

#

Still somewhat dazed from his terrifying encounter with the unearthly creature, Buck slowed his truck down and turned south onto Lincoln Avenue.

"What in the diddly-crap happened back there?" asked Henry.

"All I know is, I've got to contact the sheriff over in Pinetop County...I'll be needing some backup," stated the concerned lawman. "Ted, do you have my cell phone?"

The doctor reflected for a moment and then said, "Dammit, sheriff, I set it down when I locked the back door. It's still on the table by the rear exit...with all the commotion going on, I forgot to grab it...I'm so sorry."

"Don't apologize for that," said the lawman. "We're all lucky to be alive...that cell phone is the least of my worries...I can make the call later."

As the sheriff tried to lift his left hand up to the steering wheel, he let out an agonizing groan, having felt the intense pang from the loose bones jostling around in his arm. The harrowing events experienced back at his office had distracted him enough to momentarily forget about the throbbing pain in his forearm. Ted, hearing the utterance, looked over and observed a grimaced expression on the officer's face, as he tried to move his damaged upper limb into a more comfortable position.

"Buck, why don't you pull over and let me drive?" asked the physician. "We need to get you to the hospital so I can take a look at that arm." Sheriff Evans nodded affirmatively, and then veered the truck over to the side of the road, so that he and the doctor could exchange positions. After they stopped, the wounded officer scooted over to the passenger seat, using his good hand to cradle the injured left arm. Ted jumped into the driver's seat and took over the controls, heading the truck straight towards the emergency room.

Feeling some relief from the persistent pain, Buck turned his head towards the shaken passengers in the rear and said, "Okay, everyone...mums the word for now...we don't want to cause a panic in town, and that's exactly what will happen if any information about what just occurred gets around. If the citizens of Tranquil knew that there was a murdering monster in our midst, parading around as one of us, they would shoot first and ask questions later...no one would be safe." Everyone, even Henry, would have to agree with that line of reasoning.

Joshua, who was sitting next to Tara in the back seat, looked over at her and said solemnly, "Tara...that wasn't my father back there."

"I know it wasn't," consoled Tara. "When we get to the hospital, Daddy and I have something we need to tell all of you."

Dr. Tisdale drove over to the hospital and parked the sheriff's truck in one of the "Reserved for Physician" spaces. Buck thought for a brief moment, and then barked out a few more requests. "Henry, conceal that weapon under your shirt. Ted, wrap my coat around the 12-gauge...that should hide it well enough for you to sneak it into your office. Listen, everyone, we don't want to arouse any suspicions, so try to act as normal as possible!"

They all piled out of the Chevy Tahoe and accompanied Sheriff Evans to the emergency room. There, Ted X-rayed the lawman's injured forearm, and then quickly applied a fiberglass cast to immobilize the fractured bones. Next, the doctor placed Buck's wounded limb in an arm sling that extended upwards, around his neck. Except for the three traumatized Brownies, who were treated earlier and released into the care of their parents, the emergency room had been essentially quiet for the entire day.

"Later, you may need a surgical procedure to realign those broken and crushed bones, but this will hold you for now, Buck," explained Ted to the lawman.

"Thanks, doc," smiled Sheriff Evans. "It feels much better already."

After his treatment, Buck called Spence Taylor, the sheriff of Pinetop County, requesting that his colleague come and assist him in tracking down a murderer who was loose in Tranquil. If Buck mentioned anything about an alien monster during the phone conversation, he was afraid he wouldn't be taken seriously. The lawman planned to brief Sheriff Taylor after he arrived — hopefully, *before* they had another dangerous encounter with Luke's doppelganger.

Ted gathered everyone into his office — an isolated room located around the back of the hospital — and then pulled the shades down and locked the door. The physician unwrapped the shotgun and laid it across the table. Henry pulled the veiled magnum from under his belt, and held it at his side. They all felt safe, at least for now.

"Please sit down and make yourself comfortable," said Ted. "I'm sure that psychotic thing has figured out where we are by now, and will be coming after us soon, so we don't have much time left. Tara and I have something of the utmost importance to tell all of you."

Buck, Henry, and Joshua settled themselves down on the three-cushioned couch that faced the entrance to Ted's private office. Tara sat in the easy chair that was located next to the door, and the emergency room physician rested himself on the edge of his big mahogany desk. Ted, wearing a serious expression on his face, looked at the three men on the couch and stated, "If you hadn't seen the creature with your own eyes, you probably wouldn't believe what I'm about to tell you. I'll start at the beginning. As you all may or may not know, last year Tara was diagnosed with a glioblastoma — a malignant brain tumor — and it was inoperable. Her medical oncologist had given her less than a year to live. She underwent a weekly combination of chemotherapy and radiation treatments, which were only available in Phoenix. The medications made her extremely ill, and her symptoms were getting worse—Tara and I both knew that she didn't have much time left to live. One night, about six months ago, we were driving back home after one of her therapy sessions. We usually traveled on the old Route 44—Tara liked it because of the mountain scenery, and there were always deer or other wildlife running around for us to see. Besides, we weren't in a big rush anyway. It was cool that night, so we had the car windows down. Traveling just north of Fletcher's Pool, we heard a loud *bang*, like the sound of a gunshot. I spotted a lone campfire adjacent to the pond, so I pulled off the highway and drove over to investigate. There was an old Chevy pickup parked next to the fire, so I stopped the car near the campsite and got out to see if anyone was around. I called out, but no one answered. I decided to look around, so I instructed Tara to wait for me inside the car. I explored the area west of the campsite and observed something glowing through the trees. When I entered the open field, I could clearly see what was producing the blinking lights—it was a spacecraft—a flying saucer. As I approached the alien ship, I saw Henry. He appeared to be unconscious, suspended in the air by some type of tractor beam that was composed of colored lights radiating from the UFO. I could see a gun on the ground below him."

"Yee-ha! Kiss my royal red ass and pork me sidesaddle! See, sheriff...I *was* tellin the truth!" Henry interjected haughtily.

"Apparently so," agreed Buck.

Ted continued, "I walked closer to the alien ship, and

258

observed something lying down on the inside of an opened panel of the craft. It was green...reptilian-looking...with an oversized head...and it appeared to have been wounded. My heart was pounding, and, to be honest, I was scared to death. But as a physician, I took an oath to try and save all human life, and even though this thing didn't look too human, it was still a life—and one worth saving, I felt. The creature had suffered a bullet wound to its heart from Henry's gun, and would have surely bled to death if I hadn't found it. I applied pressure to the area to temporarily stop the flow of blood, and in a matter of seconds, the alien opened its eyes and looked up at me. Its eyes were diamond-shaped and had no pupils, and they fluoresced a golden-yellow color...this creature was definitely not from our world. Even though it had an ugly outward appearance, its luminous eyes generated an inner kindness. Communicating by some form of mental telepathy, it directed me to go into the saucer and retrieve a blue-colored vial that contained a medication which would halt the bleeding. I entered the spacecraft, found the medicine, and applied it to the alien's chest wound—and sure enough, the bleeding stopped immediately. The creature told me that his name was Teirken. He was a member of the Nalurians, a peaceful race of aliens from Chimea—a planet located in a solar system light years away from ours. Teirken meant no harm to Henry, but was only trying to disarm him of the weapon he was carrying."

"Sure coulda fooled me!" quipped the old boozer.

Ted smiled at Henry, and then continued on with his fascinating story. "The Nalurians possess many supernatural powers—one being the capacity to read the human mind.

Teirken was able to ascertain from my thoughts that Tara was dying from brain cancer. Since I had saved his life, he offered to help my daughter, as a token of his appreciation. The benevolent alien professed to me that he had the ability to physically enter Tara's bodily structure and form a symbiotic bond with her—a mutual healing—thereby allowing him to cure her of the brain tumor. Teirken would use the strength of Tara's healthy heart to heal his bullet-damaged organ, and he would use the power of his superior mind to repair her cancer-ridden brain. The alien explained that in order for him to mend her brain, he would need to be hidden inside of her—Tara's mind would be in full control of her body, and he would only emerge if she were in danger. I knew that Tara was going to die no matter what, so I thought this would be an opportunity to save my precious daughter's life."

Joshua glanced over at his girlfriend, Tara, with a puzzled expression, and then quickly turned his attention back to Dr. Tisdale.

"Teirken removed Henry from the paralyzing beam of light, while I picked up his revolver, which was lying on the ground. Even though the alien was weakened from his heart wound, he was endowed with unbelievable strength—Teirken carried Henry back to the campsite under his arm, as if he were as light as a pillow. Then he laid Henry down on his sleeping bag, and I placed the firearm next to him," explained Ted.

The emergency room physician looked directly at the elderly Pickridge and confessed, "I had never seen you before, Henry, so I looked through your wallet to find out who you were."

"I'll be a lesbian's lover! That's how you knowed me at the carnival that night...when I found the Slovinsky boy dead," said Henry. "We'd never ever met before that!"

"Correct," answered Ted. "And I'm sure that you and Sheriff Evans are wondering what the hell happened to the saucer."

"As a matter of fact, I *would* like to know," said Buck. "Henry and I searched that whole field and didn't find a damn thing!"

The doctor smiled. "Believe it or not, Teirken concealed the entire UFO with a small hand-held cloaking device... something to do with dimensional isomerism. It's way too complicated for me to understand, but basically it has to do with changing the molecular makeup of an object so that it is not a part of our dimension anymore, and therefore invisible."

"Yeah, I understand...like on *Star Trek*," said Henry.

"Uh...right, Henry...right!" smiled Ted.

"How do *I* fit into all of this?" inquired Joshua.

"In a *huge* way," responded Tara, who then winked at her boyfriend. "Please be patient, Joshua...you'll find out!"

Dr. Tisdale returned to his lengthy narration. "I returned to the car and explained everything to my daughter about Teirken's compassionate offer. Tara immediately broke down into tears, overwhelmed with happiness over the kind alien's gift. She had already prepared herself for death, so this was like getting a new lease on life. Tara and I had to swear to Teirken that we would *never* disclose this important secret to anyone, unless he gave us permission to do so. We both happily took an oath of silence—Tara would get her life back, and I would have my wonderful daughter returned to me. The transference—Teirken referred to it as a mosaic molecularization process, or an intermingling of his molecules to coexist with hers—was accomplished that night, and was totally painless for Tara."

"So you mean that green alien that I put a bullet in... Teirken...he's inside of her right now?" Henry asked.

"That's right," answered Tara. "Teirken's presently dormant, because he has to conserve his energy to fight my cancer, which according to him, will be completely gone soon. But when Teirken's turn comes to talk, you'll know it."

"Please tell Mr. Teirken that I'm sorry as hell I shot him. I didn't mean him no harm...honest," apologized Henry. "I was just horrificated that night...scareder than a worm trapped in a coop full of starving chickens!"

"He knows that and accepts your apology," smiled Tara.

Ted looked over at his daughter and said, "Why don't we let Teirken speak now?"

Tara nodded, and then shut both of her blue-green eyes for a moment. When she reopened them, they had changed into a brilliant fluorescent, gold color. The pupil-less organs of sight eerily examined everyone in the room as Teirken opened his host's mouth and used the girl's soothing voice to speak. *"I AM TEIRKEN. YOU HUMANS — MAMMALS AS YOU CALL YOURSELVES — HAVE EVOLVED TO BECOME THE SUPERIOR SPECIES OF YOUR EARTH. ON OUR PLANET, CHIMEA, WE REPTILES ARE THE DOMINANT LIFE FORM. MANY CENTURIES AGO, ALL LIVING THINGS INHABITING OUR WORLD WERE NEARLY DESTROYED IN A GLOBAL NUCLEAR WAR. SOME OF OUR ANCESTORS WERE ABLE TO SEEK REFUGE FROM*

THE FALLOUT IN THE BARRIERS CONSTRUCTED BELOW GROUND – THE OTHERS WERE CAUGHT OUTSIDE AND HAD TO ENDURE THE BOMBARDMENT OF GAMMA RADIATION. AS A RESULT, TWO DIFFERENT RACES EVOLVED: THE NALURIANS AND THE EBOR. I AM A NALURIAN. MY RACE LIVES UNDERGROUND AND IS PEACEFUL. WE ARE SYMBIONTS – OUR SPECIES POSSESSES THE SPECIAL ABILITY TO COEXIST INSIDE ANOTHER LIVING ORGANISM – RESULTING IN A MUTUAL BENEFIT FOR BOTH ENTITIES. AFTER YEARS OF SUFFERING THE MUTATING EFFECTS OF RADIATION POISONING, THE EBOR HAVE DEGENERATED INTO PARASITES, DESTROYING THEIR HOSTS BY DRAINING THEM OF THEIR ENERGY. THEY ARE ALSO STRICTLY CARNIVOROUS – EVEN CANNIBALIZING THEIR OWN KIND. ON OUR PLANET, THE PROCESS OF EVOLUTION IS NOT ORDERED, BUT ONLY HAPHAZARD AT BEST. THE EBOR HAVE BEEN AT WAR WITH THE NALURIANS FOR GENERATIONS, BUT HAVE BEEN UNABLE TO DESTROY US BECAUSE OUR TECHNOLOGY IS SUPERIOR TO THEIRS. RECENTLY, THEY WERE ABLE TO INFECT OUR ENTIRE RACE WITH A SYNTHETIC MICROBE THAT PRODUCES ONE EXTRA CHROMOSOME IN EACH CELL OF OUR BODIES, DRASTICALLY SHORTENING OUR LIFE SPAN, LIMITING OUR PHYSICAL POWERS, AND RENDERING US STERILE – TOTALLY UNABLE TO REPRODUCE. WE HAVE FOUND NO CURE, AND OUR SPECIES IS DYING BY THE THOUSANDS EACH DAY. IF WE DON'T FIND AN ANTIDOTE SOON, THE NALURIAN RACE WILL RAPIDLY BECOME EXTINCT. IN ALL OUR YEARS OF DEEP

SPACE EXPLORATION, EARTH – LIKE CHIMEA – IS THE ONLY OTHER PLANET WE KNOW OF THAT HARBORS INTELLIGENT LIFE FORMS. I PILOTED A SCOUT SHIP ACROSS THE OCEANS OF THE COSMOS TO YOUR WORLD TO FIND A SUITABLE HUMAN SPECIMEN."

"Teirken asked me to work with him on finding a cure," interposed Ted. "The Nalurian scientists discovered a vaccine, made-up of biochemically-mediated enzymes that had the ability to alter the genetic sequence of the extra chromosome, thereby destroying it, but it was unstable in living tissue... ineffective when administered to an infected Nalurian. They sent Teirken to Earth to find an experimental model to test the drug on. When Joshua, who suffered from Down Syndrome – caused by Trisomy XX1, or an extra chromosome located at the twenty first level – came to the emergency room in a coma, I felt that he would be an ideal candidate to try the experimental solution on. The night of Joshua's hospital admission, I slipped into his room and injected the alien serum into his IV line."

Ted looked directly at Joshua, and then said, "I wasn't trying to play God, Joshua...you were either going to die or be a vegetable, so I did what I thought was best for you. This was an opportunity to not only save your life, but to prevent the extinction of the Nalurian race. Initially, Tara and I served as your guardians – our function was to be your protector. But since we've gotten to know you better, you have become an integral part of our lives. We now consider you as part of our family."

"If I were in your shoes, Dr. Tisdale, I would have followed your footsteps...you did the right thing and I thank you for it," acknowledged Joshua. "And I definitely feel the same way about you and Tara."

Ted smiled at Joshua. "Teirken and I have been evaluating the results of the drug on your body. It has destroyed the extra chromosome in all of your cells, and that is why the mental and physical symptoms of your Down Syndrome have completely disappeared. The only adverse side effects you have had are the episodes of syncope—those terrible fainting spells—and those should subside as your body adapts to the serum."

"THE BIZARRE SENSATIONS AND TEMPORARY PHYSICAL CHANGES YOU ENCOUNTERED IN THE BLACKOUT SPELLS APPEAR TO HAVE COME FROM YOUR BODY'S REACTION TO THE NALURIAN HORMONES," added Teirken.

"That's correct," said Ted. "The extra benefit of Joshua's increased intelligence, rapid self-healing, and paranormal gifts resulted from the fact that the drug I injected into him contains extracts of Nalurian hormones—alien biochemicals that are responsible for their superhuman powers. The Nalurian brain is much more advanced than ours, allowing them the ability to read minds and to communicate telepathically. Nalurians are like super salamanders...possessing extraordinary powers for self-healing, even to the point of replacing lost or damaged body parts. I collected an extract from Joshua's blood serum that contained the antibody specific for the alien microbe, combined it with the Nalurian drug, and introduced it into a test tube containing Teirken's infected protoplasm. After performing a crude karyotype on the alien sample that was infected with the Ebor microorganism, I found that the extra trisomy chromosome had disappeared from all of Teirken's cells—the blood tests showed no sign of a triple chromosome anywhere. Initially, I couldn't figure out why the alien drug was unstable and ineffective when given to the Nalurians, yet worked when administered to Joshua, a human. The answer finally dawned on me—so simple, that I could kick myself for not figuring it out sooner. The genetic building block of the Nalurian cell is RNA, or ribonucleic acid, whereas in humans, the carrier of genetic information is DNA, or deoxyribonucleic acid. RNA is made up of four base pairs: two purines—adenine and guanine, and two pyrimidines—uracil and cytosine. Adenine pairs up with uracil, and guanine pairs up with cytosine. The double helix of DNA is also made up of four base pairs: like RNA, it has adenine, guanine, and cytosine. But instead of uracil, it substitutes the pyrimidine *thymine*, which pairs up with adenine. The basic difference between the structure of RNA and DNA is that DNA has thymine instead of uracil. So the reason that the alien drug was stable in Joshua, but unstable in the Nalurians is clear-cut and predictable: thymine, along with Joshua's antibody to the unearthly microbe, is the key ingredient needed to prevent the biochemical enzymes from breaking down in an infected Nalurian. I haven't had time to try it out on Teirken, but all we have to do is clone Joshua's antibody, add it along with thymine to the Nalurian drug, and bingo, we've got a cure that will save millions of lives. But we must have Joshua to accomplish this."

"I RECEIVED A TRANSMISSION TODAY FROM MY SUPERIORS. THE BEING THAT IS AFTER JOSHUA IS AN EBOR. ONE OF THEIR SPIES INTERCEPTED MY COMMUNICATION TO CHIMEA ABOUT THE VACCINE AND OUR EXPERIMENT ON THE TRISOMY BOY. THIS

EBOR IS A SKILLED ASSASSIN – A MURDERER ASSIGNED TO KILL JOSHUA AT ALL COSTS. HE WAS ABLE TO BYPASS THE SPACE BARRIERS THAT WE SET UP AROUND OUR PLANET, AND LANDED HERE ONE EARTH DAY AGO. THIS EXECUTIONER IS ABLE TO PARASITIZE YOUR SPECIES, ASSUME THEIR IDENTITY, AND TAKE ON THEIR HUMAN FORM. HE WILL LITERALLY SUCK THE LIFE OUT OF ANY BODY THAT HE INHABITS, USING THE HOST'S ENERGY SUPPLY UNTIL IT IS ENTIRELY EXHAUSTED. THIS EBOR IS A FORMIDABLE ADVERSARY AND MUST BE STOPPED!"

"Let me make sure that I've got this straight," said Buck. "This Ebor landed near the Girl Scout campsite, took over Amber's body, killed the troop leader, and then went into town and possessed Luke?"

"That's what I would say," said Ted. "It probably has killed others as well."

"Am I to presume that this thing also killed the Slovinsky boy and the two men at Fletcher's Pool?" the sheriff inquired.

"I WAS THE ONE WHO KILLED THE BOY AT THE CARNIVAL AND THE TWO MEN AT THE POND," said Teirken. *"BUT IT WAS TO PROTECT JOSHUA AND TARA'S LIFE. PLEASE LET ME EXPLAIN. THE BOY AT THE CARNIVAL CALLED NILES SLOVINSKY...I WAS ABLE TO READ HIS MIND WHEN TARA CONFRONTED HIM ABOUT ATTACKING JOSHUA THAT NIGHT. HE WAS GOING TO KILL JOSHUA TO PREVENT HIM FROM TESTIFYING AT THE GRAND JURY HEARING. I TOOK OVER TARA'S MIND AND BODY, AND USED HER VOICE TO SPEAK – SHE WAS TOTALLY UNAWARE OF WHAT HAPPENED. I CAUSED THE POWER SHORTAGE, AND THEN ENTERED THE*

STRUCTURE THAT CONTAINED THE AMUSEMENT RIDE THAT NILES WAS TRAVELING ON."

Teirken walked over to the sheriff, extended Tara's arm, and said, *"PLEASE TAKE MY HAND."*

Buck hesitantly reached out with his good limb and grasped the young girl's hand. It was soft and warm. Suddenly, a brilliant flash of light blinded his eyes. Miraculously, the lawman's mind was now full of sight and sound — like watching a motion picture shot in color from the front row of a theater — running the events of what had happened that night at the carnival when the Slovinsky boy was found dead. The scene that Buck was viewing showed Niles inside the Doctor Blood's Castle amusement ride, seated in one of the electric-driven carriages. The lights suddenly go out, and the teenager's runabout rolls to a squeaky stop. It is pitch black. "What the hell is going on? I can't see a damn thing...turn the friggin ride back on!" yells Niles. The panicked adolescent grabs his key ring and turns the attached penlight on. Its beam falls on Tara, who is standing next to the boy's stalled buggy.

"What are *you* doing here?" Niles asks.

"I know that you're planning on killing Joshua," says Tara, "To keep him from testifying against you at the grand jury hearing."

"How the hell did you know that? I didn't tell you!"

"I just know."

"Well, I think you know too much, slut," smirks Niles. "Now, not only am I going to kill your retarded boyfriend, but I'm going to have to kill you too!" Then the redhead reaches out and grabs her arm.

"I'm sorry, but I can't allow that," says Tara.

"There's nothing you can do about it, bitch...the sheriff will think the carnies killed both of you!" laughs Niles. He pulls her closer and leans forward, putting both of his hands around her neck in an effort to strangle the poor girl. His penlight falls to the ground, landing with its beam shining upward, delivering enough light to illuminate the vicious attack. She struggles to get away, but Niles is too strong for her to break his death grip. Tara closes her eyes momentarily and then opens her lids to reveal two solid globes of golden light. Suddenly, the boy's hands—the ones that are wrapped around her neck—begin to shake violently.

"Wha...what...are...you...doing...to...me?" Niles stammers out.

Beginning at his fingertips, a flow of energy travels up the sociopath's arm and over the rest of his body, immobilizing the acne-faced teenager in a paralyzing grip. The boy's skin turns from pink to white as the debilitating power surges over his flesh. Niles tries to scream, but his mouth freezes open. He releases his grip and falls back in his seat, petrified, with the look of sheer horror stamped on his ugly face. Tara looks at the dead assailant and then walks out through the exit. The electrical power resumes, and the coach car holding Niles's dead body slowly propels forward.

"I ALSO INTERVENED AT FLETCHER'S POOL, WHEN THE TWO MEN WERE GOING TO RAPE AND KILL TARA," confessed the Nalurian.

The scene immediately shifts to a grassy bank at Fletcher's Pool. Tara is bending over to kiss Joshua, whose head is lying on her lap. She gently positions his neck on a big tuft of grass and stands up. "Be back in a little while," she says. Then she dives into the pond and begins to swim towards the opposite side. As Tara strokes over the water's surface, she rounds the bend and runs into two heavily tattooed men. They had been lying in wait for her, and were purposely blocking the girl's way. Buck instantly recognized them as Hector Lopez and Karl Singer — the two parolees who served prison time on sexual assault charges, and had just been released from the state penitentiary.

"Hey, senorita, it's party time!" says the one with the cobra tattooed on his neck.

The other man grabs her arm and grins, "Yeah, baby, you need to come with us!"

"Please let me go...NOW! I have to get help for my boyfriend!" protests Tara.

"Sorry, sweet thing...you're ours now!" says Hector.

The sheriff hears a male voice, but neither one of the men's lips are moving. *You're not going anywhere, bitch. Me and Hector's planning on porking your brains out...then when we're done playing with you...you're going to drown!* Buck quickly realizes that he is magically able to hear what the men are thinking.

I can't wait to get at her sweet box! says Hector's sick mind. *Too bad that we're going to have to kill her afterwards...she can identify us...and I ain't going back to prison!*

As the sexual predators start dragging Tara to shore, she discharges a deadly current of electrical energy into both of them, throwing their bodies into a suffering torrent of violent convulsions. The two degenerates furiously flop and thrash about, like fish out of water, until their entire nervous systems have been totally frazzled — brutally incinerated by the overload of alien energy discharged into their bodies. Tara puts a halt to her flow of deadly current and swims away from the decimated, floating bodies of the two would-be rapist-murderers. Buck's mental, motion picture scene slowly fades away as Teirken breaks the physical contact by releasing the young girl's grip on the sheriff's hand.

The lawman blinked his eyes several times as his blurry surroundings gradually came into a sharper focus. Buck rattled his head and then said, "Man, that was one hell of a trip!"

"THAT IS EXACTLY HOW IT HAPPENED," explained Teirken. *"I DID NOT WISH TO EXTERMINATE THE THREE HUMANS, BUT THEY GAVE ME NO CHOICE. I HAD TO PROTECT JOSHUA AND TARA."*

"I appreciate you clearing those deaths up for me, Teirken," said Buck. "A picture *is* worth a thousand words, and in this case—literally—I certainly couldn't have gotten a clearer image than what you provided for me. Beyond a shadow of a doubt, you have proven that all three of these deaths resulted from actions of unavoidable self-defense. As sheriff of Juniper County, presiding over the town of Tranquil, I will personally see to it that all three of the murder charges against Joshua Allen be dropped."

Sheriff Evans looked over at the falsely accused boy and said, "Please accept my apologies, Joshua...you are a free man now!"

"Ass-hum...er...ah...awesome!" crowed Joshua.

"Thank you very much, sheriff," Ted exclaimed.

"I knowed he were innocent!" raved Henry.

"THE EBOR THAT INHABITS JOSHUA'S FATHER... HIS PHYSICAL FORM WILL BE VULNERABLE WHEN HE

DEPARTS HIS HOST'S BODY...ONLY THEN CAN HE BE DESTROYED. THE NALURIAN INFECTION HAS SAPPED MY POWERS, RENDERING ME TOO WEAK TO KILL THE EBOR AT THIS TIME. FOR NOW, I MUST RETURN TO MY QUIESCENT STATE TO CONSERVE ENERGY. TARA'S CANCER AND MY HEART ARE ALMOST TOTALLY HEALED...I DON'T THINK IT KNOWS YET THAT I SHARE THE GIRL'S BODY. WE MUST PREVENT THIS KILLER FROM HARMING JOSHUA – THE BOY IS THE KEY TO THE SALVATION OF MY RACE. YOU MUST ALL PREPARE YOURSELVES NOW...THE EBOR ASSASSIN WILL BE HERE SOON!"

Chapter XX
ENCOUNTER

It was late afternoon by the time that Spence Taylor, the sheriff of Pinetop County, parked his patrol car in front of Tranquil Community Hospital. He headed towards the emergency room, walking with a noticeable limp. Spence made his way to the back of the hospital, where Dr. Tisdale's private office was located, and knocked on the closed door. "Hey, Buck, it's Spence Taylor," he called out, "you instructed me to meet you here."

Sheriff Evans opened the door to see his old friend, Spence—all 280 hypertrophied pounds of him, packed onto a six-foot-five inch Herculean frame. The two of them played football together while attending Tranquil High School. When they were seniors, Buck was first-string quarterback, and

Spence was his star fullback. Their team had advanced to the state finals that year, but lost to the Tucson High Tigers by a single point—21 to 20—in the championship game. Buck was too small to play college football, but Spence could have easily received a football scholarship to one of Arizona's universities, if he hadn't blown out his right knee in that state championship game. Tranquil was behind by one point, and had driven the ball down to the Tucson thirty-yard line, too far to kick a field goal. With just ten seconds left in the game, there was time enough for only one more play. The coach sent in a call for a deep pass, but when the ball was snapped, Buck had to dump it off to his fullback, Spence, because both of his split ends had drawn double coverage. Breaking two tackles, the ball carrier bulled his way down the field, headed toward the goal line. Out of nowhere, a defensive back torpedoed his helmet into Spence's right knee, taking his legs out from under him. The fullback was stopped just short of a touchdown—on the two-yard line—when game time expired. Spence, immobilized from the excruciating pain, lay helpless on the field. Unfortunately, the tackle had impacted the boy's joint at just the right angle needed to destroy the ligaments. As a result of the extensive damage, an orthopedic surgeon was needed to rebuild Spence's entire knee, thus ending his football career. Except for a conspicuous limp, the reconstructed knee was, for all practical purposes, totally functional.

Spence had been a dedicated body builder for most of his life, and was as strong as a bull. The powerful policeman could pick up the back end of a Volkswagen Beetle with ease. Buck's friend was exactly the person that he needed to help him subdue the creature masquerading as Luke Allen.

A mountain of a man, Sheriff Taylor stood at the door, his brawny body nearly filling the entire entryway.

"Hey, Buck, long-time-no-see," smiled the Goliath of sheriffs.

"Thanks for coming, Spence, I can really use your help," replied his friend.

Sheriff Taylor looked down at the cumbersome sling that cradled his comrade's arm and remarked, "What the hell have you been up to, Buck?"

"We've got a situation here that I need to fill you in on," the sheriff of Tranquil replied.

Detecting a serious look on his old buddy's face, the peacekeeper of Pinetop County took his hat off and said, "What's up, Buck?"

"YOU ARE!" growled the voice behind him.

As Sheriff Taylor turned around, two behemoth saurian-shaped paws suddenly reached out and seized Spence by the head, lifting his burly frame several inches off the ground. Acting on instinct, the stunned policeman grabbed the green, tree-trunk sized arms of the being, and tried to pry its crushing grip from his head. It happened so quickly that everyone in the office was in a state of shock from the unexpected attack, and could only watch in utter amazement.

Spence, unable to budge the vice-like hands that were compressing his skull, reached down into his holster, pulled out his .45-caliber revolver, and blasted six slugs into Luke's body. The brute's black eyes glared devilishly at the face of the suspended sheriff, while its clawed digits brutally squeezed the helpless officer's head. A squishing sound was heard, as both of Spence's eyeballs herniated out from their sockets and flopped onto each cheek. They grotesquely hung from their muscle attachments, like a pair of dice dangling from a car's rearview mirror. Then a loud crunching noise erupted from the sheriff's cranium, as it ruptured open like a ripened melon, spilling blood and fragments of brain through the dying lawman's rifted scalp. Satisfied that he was no longer a threat, the malicious Ebor casually tossed Spence's hefty body aside, as if it were made of lightweight papier-mâché.

Caught totally off-guard by the ambush, Buck looked down at the mangled head and lifeless body of his old schoolmate, then turned toward the ruthless butcher and yelled, "You son-of-a-bitch...you killed my friend!" He immediately drew his pistol and fired off five deliberately spaced rounds into the vicious murderer. The infuriated sheriff screamed along with each blast from his revolver, "Die... you... alien... bastard... die!"

Seeing that the bullets from Buck's handgun were having no effect on the thing, Ted sprung from his desk and leveled the shotgun at the preacher with the grotesque alien arms. In order to gain the maximum effect from his weapon, he moved nearer to the beast and pulled the trigger.

"Blaam!"

The close-range force behind the blast of pellets sent the minister's body reeling backwards against the hallway wall. Dr. Tisdale quickly maneuvered to the side of Luke and fired the scattergun again.

"Booom!"

The second discharge of lead projectiles viciously blew open Luke's chest, hurling the hideous hybrid body of the parson onto the gray carpeted floor of the physician's office.

"Get the hell out of here…go, NOW!" screamed Ted to the others. Tara grabbed Joshua's hand and headed for the door, followed by Henry. The threesome bolted out of the room and ran down the hall, away from the mutant monster.

"Go with them, Buck…I'll be right there," said the doctor.

"No way! I'm not going to leave you here by yourself!" replied the sheriff.

Ted gave the lawman a confident look, and then said, "Go on, Buck, I know what I'm doing…I promise I'll be right there."

"Okay then, I'm holding you to your word," answered the peace officer, who then exited the room.

As the physician crept closer to the reverend's body, he observed the felled Ebor entity rapidly reabsorbing the blood lost from Luke's gaping chest wounds. Just as before, the phenomenal healing capacity of the pernicious parasite allowed it to completely renovate all of the bullet wound and shotgun injuries. Nearing rejuvenation, the immortal animal lifted up the pastor's pasty face and delivered a ghoulish grin to the astonished doctor. Ted quickly realized that it would take a hell of a lot more than their primitive weapons to stop the onslaught of this persistent predator. Following the others down the long hall, the retreating M.D. called out, "Go to the elevator…we're going up to the second floor…I've got an idea!"

As soon as it had completed the healing process, the callous humanoid climbed to its feet and barked out at its fleeing prey, "YOUR SPECIES IS INFERIOR…YOU WILL ALL DIE!" It walked over to Spence's dead body and reached down with a clawed hand, scooping out a clotted portion of the sheriff's extruded brain. The starving organism popped the veiny piece of cerebrum into Luke's mouth, chewed momentarily, and then swallowed.

"I HAVE ALMOST DEPLETED THE LIFE FORCE FROM THIS BODY," it said, tasting the gore on its host's lips.

Tara reached the closed door of the elevator first and hurriedly pushed the UP button. Ted, who was sprinting down the hallway with his shotgun in hand, caught up with them just as the steel barricade glided open. After the escaping quarry had piled into the mobile metal box, Henry immediately punched the white plastic circle marked "2". As the elevator's iron ingress was sliding shut, they observed the unrelenting extraterrestrial staggering down the hall, drawing dangerously closer with each clumsy step that it took. The terrorized companions gave out a collective sigh of relief when the elevator door completely closed. It then initiated a jerky move upwards, heading towards the second floor.

"After we get off the elevator, everyone follow me to the operating room," said Ted. "I've got an idea, and if it works, we can stop that murdering alien dead in its tracks."

As soon as the elevator door slid open, Dr. Tisdale—shadowed closely by his four comrades—scrambled out and headed towards the nearest operating room. The physician, followed by the others, entered through the swinging doors of the OR and flipped on the lights. Revolvers in hand, Buck and Henry stood guard behind the surgical entryway, while Joshua and Tara moved to the back of the room. The doctor made a beeline to the intimidating machine on wheels used to deliver gaseous general anesthesia, and began rifling through its drawers. Ted searched each one intently until he found what he was looking for. "Here it is!" he exclaimed, holding up the glass vial of clear liquid. "That thing out there needs a wake-up call, and I've got the phone!"

"What is that?" asked Joshua.

"Succinylcholine," replied Ted. "It's a skeletal muscle relaxant...anesthesiologists use it to paralyze the muscles of respiration when they intubate a patient...in order to place the breathing tube into the trachea to ventilate the lungs during general anesthesia."

"I knew that!" smiled Joshua.

Dr. Tisdale grabbed a 20cc syringe out of one of the other drawers, attached an aspirating needle, and then jammed its sharp point through the rubber stopper of the ten-milliliter vial. He held the small glass bottle upside down and drew out all of its liquid contents, quickly filling the hypodermic half-full of succinylcholine. Ted found a second vial and repeated the same sequence, filling the plunger completely full with another ten milliliters of the deadly drug. He carefully slid the blue protective cap over the exposed 16-gauge needle, and laid the loaded syringe on the anesthesia machine's tabletop.

"Here's the game plan," the physician announced to the others. "If I can get close enough to inject Luke with the skeletal muscle relaxant, then not only will he be paralyzed, but the Ebor inhabiting his body should be immobilized by the drug, as well."

"How long does it take to work?" Tara asked.

"Assuming I can empty the entire syringe into him," reasoned Ted, "it should start affecting him in about thirty seconds."

"Where on the body do you need to stick him?" questioned Buck.

"The buttocks would be the best place," answered the

doctor. "It's the easiest and biggest target to hit, with less chance of hitting bone, which could break off the needle... plus, it has plenty of adipose tissue to absorb the drug more quickly."

"Doc, I ain't no rocket scientist or nothing, but I don't think that freakin thing is gonna stand still long enough for you to jam a needle in its ass!" said the old quipster.

"Precisely, Henry. The creature is smart, so we're going to have to set up a trap for it, and I think I have one. By locking one of the adjacent swinging doors to the OR, it should force the monster to enter through the other access. We'll slide an anesthesia machine up against the locked entryway, and I'll hide behind it. The rest of you will stand over in the corner of the room, and draw its attention when it enters through the unlocked door. When the Ebor comes for Joshua, I'll run up behind it and stab it in the butt with the syringe. We'll all need to stay out of its way until the drug takes effect. If anyone has a better plan, or has any suggestions, please let me know now...we don't have much time left."

"Your strategy sounds good to me," said Buck. "I don't have anything to add."

Joshua and Tara nodded in agreement.

"It's time to open up a big ole' can of whoop-ass on that murdering bastard...just don't miss, doc!" advised the old man. Henry thought for a second and then pseudo-intellectually added, "All you can do is all you can do."

"All right then...we all have a purpose...let's get to it!" said Ted, encouragingly.

Tara rushed over to the entryway and flipped the levers to engage the ceiling and floor bolts, firmly locking the one swinging door, while Buck peered out the other's window for any sign of the approaching alien. Then Joshua, Ted, and Henry all worked together to roll the bulky anesthesia machine across the operating room floor and up against the one secured door. The physician handed Joshua the loaded shotgun and said, "It probably won't do any good, but aim for the head."

Without wasting any time, Henry, Tara, and Joshua rushed over and took their places in the corner of the room. The alcoholic old-timer, holding his .357 magnum cocked and ready—along with Joshua, tightly gripping the raised scattergun—stood protectively in front of Tara. Sheriff Evans hid patiently behind the unlocked swinging door with his 9-mm at his side, peering out its small window at the elevator. Ted picked up the drug-filled syringe, twisted off the plastic jacket covering the needle, and then crouched down behind the bulky anesthesia equipment.

Buck clicked off the light, then momentarily averted his eyes from the window and turned his head towards the others in the corner. "If, for some reason, the plan backfires, empty your guns into the alien and get the hell out of here," he emphasized. "Try to make it back to the elevator...if you can't, go and hide somewh..."

The sheriff snapped his head back towards the glass aperture, as the whirring sound from the moving elevator caught his attention. When the solid metal door slipped open, he observed Luke's gloomy image shuffling his way out of the lift, the entity's fiendish eyes panning the area like a hunter searching for game. "He's here...everyone get ready!" whispered Buck, making his way back through the darkness to join the others herded in the room's back corner.

Stone cold silence. Initially, that's all the waylayers heard at their frozen positions inside the darkened surgery room. Then came the clomping sound of footsteps — an erratic staggering gait approaching — stopping abruptly at the entrance to the operating room. The featureless form of the preacher's haunting face filled one of the windows, as it peered in with its widened melanoid eyes. As they all watched in silence, a heavy exhaust of vapor fogged over the glass pane with every exhaled breath the beast expelled out from Luke's energy-depleted lungs. They all remained transfixed, as the humanoid stood quietly at the door, staring vigilantly through the steamy glass. The extraterrestrial being slowly squeaked open the OR door, its black silhouette stepping forward to occlude the entryway. In the darkness, the Ebor's prodigious clawed hands extended threateningly out from each side of the reverend's body. It reached out with one of its black-taloned digits and turned on the lights, instantly spotting the foursome huddled in the back of the room. "I KNEW YOU HUMANS WERE IN HERE...I COULD SMELL YOU. GIVE ME THE TRISOMY BOY AND I WILL SPARE THE OTHERS!"

"Henry extended the middle finger of his left hand, then aimed his .357 at Luke's head and replied, "Come on over here and get him, you toad-faced freak!"

The enraged animal lifted up both of its deadly appendages and bounded towards the poorly armed party. Ted scrambled out from behind the anesthesia machine and, using both hands, stabbed the steel needle deeply through the minister's trousers and into his tail end. Then, he used the strength of his right palm to forcefully depress the plunger, injecting the entire twenty milliliters of anesthetic solution into the fatty tissue of the clergyman's rump, in only a matter of seconds. The surprised Ebor turned and swiped at the ambushing physician with one of its gargantuan paws, but Ted nimbly ducked as the fleshy weapon whizzed over his head.

"I got him!" yelled the physician. "Get out of here!"

The group scattered from their places in the room's corner like a pack of frenzied rats abandoning a sinking ship.

"Head for the door!" screamed Buck.

Joshua grabbed Tara's hand and raced towards the one open operating room door. Attempting to slow the creature down, the sheriff discharged his remaining bullets into the cleric's body and hustled to the other side of the room. With the agility of someone half his age, Henry skillfully maneuvered around the attacking parasite and emptied six magnums into the back of its head. The relentless organism stopped, then reached into the parson's scalp with one of its claws and dug out one of the bloodied, flesh-covered magnum slugs that Henry had fired. It scrutinized the shattered ammunition, then turned and roared, "YOUR WEAPONS ARE USELESS AGAINST ME," and began to march towards them again.

As the alien thing advanced for another assault, Luke's face began to fasciculate and his arms and legs commenced into a torrent of twitching and jerking, as if every muscle in his body were violently convulsing with uncontrollable spasms. Stopped dead in its tracks by the overwhelming seizure, a look of utter disbelief suddenly appeared on its host's face. The Ebor repeatedly attempted to move the evangelist's lungs to take in a breath, but was unable to do so. "THIS CANNOT BE HAPPENING...I AM INDESTRUCTIBLE...YOU PUNY

HUMANS DO NOT POSSESS THE POWER TO DESTROY
ME!" it barked.

"Isn't life a bitch?" Henry called out to the disabled
monster. "And it looks like she's on the rag right now!"

A foamy, white froth erupted from Luke's mouth and
rolled down his chin, as the alien life force inhabiting the
powerless pastor staggered forward and then toppled to
the operating room floor — paralyzed by the massive dose
of succinylcholine that Ted had injected into it. As they all
crept closer to surround the churchman's immobilized body,
its alien appendages — armed with devastating claws of
steel — mysteriously faded away to expose a pair of normal-
appearing, human upper limbs. Upon further observation,
the Ebor's glaring shark eyes uncannily transformed from a
gloomy black into Luke's original blue color. The dying father
looked up at Joshua and mouthed the words, "Please forgive
me, son." Then the life from the holy man's eyes slowly
dimmed away into emptiness, glazed over by the wooden
opaqueness so distinctive of death's soulless stare.

Joshua continued to look at his fallen father, then whispered
in a quavering voice, "Goodbye Father...I *do* forgive you."

Ted kneeled down beside Luke's asphyxiated body and
examined it for any signs of life. The emergency room physician
was unable to observe any breathing, feel any heartbeat, or
palpate any pulse. Dr. Tisdale frowned sympathetically at
Joshua and said, "There's not anything I can do for him now,
son, he's gone."

With his perfect sense of timing, Henry asked, "Hey, doc,
you dumped that thing like it was a turd...is that murdering,
alien butt plug that stole Luke's body dead?"

"Sure looks like it," said Ted. "I see *no* signs of life." He grabbed a blanket from one of the OR cabinets and covered up the cleric's defunct body.

Tara gave her boyfriend a consoling hug and said, "I'm so sorry about your father, Joshua."

Buck walked over and placed his hand on the boy's shoulder. "We had no other choice, son—it was him or us."

"I know," said Joshua. "I had already accepted his death when he was taken over by the Ebor."

Buck patted the physician on the back with his functioning hand and exclaimed, "If it weren't for you, my friend, we'd all be toast."

"Yes, thanks for saving my life again Dr. Tisdale," said Joshua solemnly.

"You did it, Daddy!" beamed Tara.

"I can't take all the credit," answered Ted. "We acted as a team...I couldn't have done it without your help. You all were the ones in danger...I just snuck up and darted it in the butt with a needle."

"One helluva good stab, doc!" exclaimed Henry.

"Now we can focus on saving the Nalurians," said Tara. "I have mind-meshed with Teirken—he is very grateful to all of us for what we have done."

"Ted, we need to go and retrieve Spence's body and take it, along with Luke's, over to the morgue before anyone else discovers what has happened here," said Buck.

"Thank God it's evening time and there's no one in the operating room," declared Ted. "Let's give Dr. Dobbs a call...being the workaholic he is, he's probably still here...his number is 342."

Buck walked over to the telephone that was mounted on one of the OR walls and dialed the pathologist's three-digit extension. The phone rang three times before a man's squeaky voice finally answered, "Dobbs here."

"Dr. Dobbs...it's Sheriff Evans...meet me in fifteen minutes at your office...got something interesting to show you," said Buck, who abruptly hung up the phone. Then, the lawman began to chuckle, which quickly escalated into a hearty laugh.

"What's so funny?" inquired Ted.

"It's a long story," snickered Buck. "Let's just say that paybacks can be *very* satisfying."

Joshua and Ted picked up Luke's parasitized dead body and placed him on one of the gurneys in the operating room, rolling it, along with another wheeled cot, onto the elevator. They traveled down to the first floor, where the corpse of Sheriff Spence Taylor lay. Tara remained on the stopped lift with the deceased man of the cloth while Ted, Henry, Joshua, and Buck took the other mobile hospital bed to retrieve the murdered sheriff of Pinetop County. It took the combined strength of all four men to lift the dead weight of Spence's massively muscular body onto the gurney. The mutilated sheriff was then covered in a blanket, and rolled back into the elevator with Luke, headed down to the basement where the morgue was located. The alien-fighters encountered the eccentric medical examiner, while wheeling the pair of dead bodies into the autopsy room.

"Hi, Dr. Dobbs," said Buck. "We've got two dead men here...Pastor Luke Allen, from Tranquil, and Spence Taylor, the sheriff of Pinetop County. For now, any information relating to either one of these deaths is strictly classified, and

286

is *not* to be disclosed to *anyone* without my permission. Would you please put both of them on ice for me? I'll fill you in on all of the details later."

Elroy peered out over his bifocals and answered, "Sure, sheriff, I'll store them in the deep freeze tonight...just let me know when you want the autopsies done."

The peculiar pathologist walked out of the autopsy room to his desk, sat down in his chair, and pulled out a cabinet drawer full of files. Elroy fingered through the indexes until he came upon a collection of papers, subsequently pulling out one of the printed documents. Handing the form to the sheriff, the doctor of dissection said, "Fill this out while I wheel these boys into the freezer."

"Do you need any help with the bodies?" asked Ted.

"Nope," replied the quirky coroner, as he headed for the autopsy room.

Joshua, disturbed by another one of his extrasensory perceptions, followed Elroy into the room of dissection and pointed to the lifeless corpse of his father. "Excuse me, doctor, but are you sure that this one is dead?"

Dr. Dobbs pulled back the concealing blanket that covered Luke's head, examined the dilated and fixed pupils of the man's eyes, and felt the neck for a carotid pulse. "Yep, he's dead all right...stone cold dead." Then the medical examiner nonchalantly threw the blanket back over the expired preacher's face.

"Thank you," said Joshua, who then walked back out to join the others, shutting the door behind him.

Buck took the official paper and used the ballpoint pen from his shirt pocket to fill in the required information.

While he was busy writing, Tara and Joshua held hands and discussed the day's traumatic events, while Henry and Ted stood in front of the closed door to the autopsy room, deliberating about what plan would work best should another Ebor assassin land.

"Finished," said Buck, putting his pen away. The lawman looked around and asked, "Anybody seen Dr. Dobbs?"

Henry, standing under the sign, "Postmortem Room – Authorized Personnel Only," pressed his back against the shut door of the autopsy room and said, "I'll get him...he's in here, probably *dissectisizing* one of them dead *cadivers*."

The loud, harsh sounds of exploding wood, along with an eerie liquid gushing noise unexpectedly filled the air, as a mammoth dragon-clawed hand punched through the door and exited the front of Henry's sternum—holding in its grip the bloody, pulsating heart that it had ripped from the old man's chest cavity.

"I WOULD RATHER DISSECT *YOU!*" yowled the voice from behind the door.

"Oooh...Jesus!" gasped the shocked senior citizen, as he stared down at his detached organ of life—its ventricles still futilely continuing to pump while sitting in the monstrous palm of the saurian hand.

"LIFE'S A BITCH AND THEN YOU DIE," mocked the raspy voice.

The Ebor's scale-covered digits closed down over the rhythmic mass of cardiac muscle, before withdrawing its alien fist from Henry's perforated upper torso. Completely stunned, the septuagenarian clutched at his ravaged chest, took one step, and then collapsed to the floor, just as dead as the wood he had fallen on. Unfortunately, Henry had suffered the same fate as his older brother, Fred — the victim of a senseless murder — only this time it was by a killer alien from another galaxy instead of a robbing gang of street punks.

The door to the autopsy room swung open, revealing a hideous personification of the individual known as Dr. Elroy Dobbs — only the figure that stood before them did not possess all of the pathologist's exact body parts. At the coroner's sides hung the colossal, clawed appendages of the Ebor assassin. The medical examiner's torso was supported not by human legs, but by a pair of reptilian-shaped lower extremities — reminiscent of a prehistoric Raptor's hind limbs — putting the human-alien hybrid's height at an intimidating seven feet. The being's obsidian eyes glowered out from behind Elroy's wire-rimmed, thick-lensed spectacles, as it scanned his persevering prey.

"I AM BACK!" the thing boasted. The Ebor raised the hand holding Henry's bloody heart to its mouth, and like biting an apple — ripped out a wedge of left ventricle with its exaggerated canine teeth. It chewed the organ a few times, and then swallowed it down. "YOUR SPECIES IS VERY TASTY...I THINK I LIKE YOUR HEARTS THE BEST!"

"I hope that God damns your miserable soul to Hell, you worthless son-of-a-bitch!" screamed Buck.

"YOUR GOD IS NO MATCH FOR AN EBOR," it retorted.

Dr. Tisdale, who had moved away from the door when Henry was attacked, announced to the others, "The damn thing must've laid dormant inside of Luke until the effects of the succinylcholine wore off, and then it reanimated the body!"

"It was just playing possum!" said the sheriff. "Poor Elroy, he didn't even know what hit him."

The baneful beast glared at the physician who had temporarily incapacitated him earlier, and bragged, "PRECISELY, HUMAN...I TOLD YOU I WAS INVINCIBLE!"

"Time for us to leave!" yelled Buck, as they backed away from the giant creature—slowly shuffling their feet towards the entrance to the morgue. If they didn't get the hell out of there fast, the place would literally be a dungeon of death for them all. The only weapon they could use to defend themselves now was the shotgun—and there were only three shells left. Buck had spent both of his clips for the 9mm, Spence's empty gun lay on his gurney in the autopsy room, and Henry had his .357 on him when he was decimated by the Ebor.

"Follow me!" yelled Ted, as he ran through the morgue's front door. "I've got one more trick up my sleeve." Joshua, Tara, and Buck exited closely behind. Not wishing to be trapped on the elevator by the mutant humanoid, the physician led them up two flights of stairs to the hospital pharmacy, located on the second floor. Since it was late in the evening, the drug dispensary was closed, and its entrance had been locked. Ted used the butt-end of the scattergun to break the glass, allowing him to unlock the door and enter. The physician immediately headed to the back of the pharmacy, following the narrow aisle that was surrounded on both sides by shelves stacked with a plethora of pharmaceutical drugs and medicines. Dr. Tisdale perused a multitude of generalized drug categories until he found, in a small cubbyhole, a white label brandishing the typed words "Antiparasitic Agents." Above the marker sat four tiny cardboard containers, all covered in dust—

each one packaging a glass vial of a powerful, powdered parasiticidal drug—a systemic antiprotozoal, antimalarial, anthelmintic, and antifungal agent. Dr. Tisdale, having taken courses in parasitology and pharmacology, was familiar with the indications for each medication. He quickly gathered up the four packaged preparations, and then hurried over to the pharmacy counter where the others were waiting.

"I tried to use the phone here," said Buck, "but it was dead...I couldn't get a dial tone."

"Do you think the Ebor did that?" asked Tara.

"I wouldn't put *anything* past the thing...that damn extraterrestrial is pretty clever," answered the sheriff.

"I think we've been going about this the wrong way," said Ted. "Everything we have used so far against the monster has been ineffective, and the bullets and succinylcholine have only affected its host. What we need is some type of weapon that will be *specific* for the parasite—something that will destroy the Ebor living inside. This may sound simplistic, but what if Dobbs ingested a substantial dose of antiparasitic medication? Maybe that would kill the being inside of him without harming the host."

"Hell, it's worth a try," said the sheriff.

Ted set the four vials containing the parasiticides down on the counter. "I've got enough firepower here to kill any giant ameba, sporozoan, worm, or fungus," said the physician. "I just hope that this alien organism falls into one of those four categories."

"How will we get the drugs into the brute?" Tara inquired. "The creature is too smart to let us inject it again."

"I don't know, but we're going to have to figure out

something fast...that thing will be here soon," answered Ted.

"I have an idea," said Joshua. "The Ebor is a cannibalistic carnivore that requires nourishment constantly in order to maintain its high metabolism while inhabiting its host. As bloodthirsty as that animal is, why don't we offer it some food tainted with the antiparasitic medication?"

"Excellent suggestion!" remarked Ted. "And I know exactly what to offer it...a big bag of human red liquid protein!"

The physician grabbed a 500cc plastic bag of plasma out of the refrigerator that was used to store blood products, and cut its top off. He poured the crimson fluid into a one-liter glass beaker, dumped in all four vials of powder, and then stirred the parasiticides into solution.

"If I were British," smiled the physician, "I'd call this a bloody milkshake!"

"Daddy, I don't think that anyone is up for your puns right now," commented Tara.

"You're right," said Ted. "Just my silly way of handling stress, you know."

"Hey, doc, I hope those drugs you added act like a super enema on that alien piece of crap...now all we have to do is figure out a sure-fire way to get that creature to drink it," reasoned Buck.

"How about reverse psychology?" asserted Joshua. "That narcissistic Ebor has demonstrated a definite anti-social personality disorder, and believes that it is a superior being, incapable of suffering defeat. Let's leave the glass of poisoned blood out in plain sight for it to see...along with written instructions."

"I get your drift," said Ted.

"Another inspiration of genius!" smiled Tara.

"I feel like Henry now—may God rest his poor old soul—what the hell are you all talking about?" asked the sheriff.

Ted looked over at Buck and grinned. "You'll see!"

Chapter XXI
STRATAGEM

The alien assassin made its way up the stairs to the second floor of the hospital, trailing the scent of its escaping prey like a famished tiger. When it reached the entrance to the pharmacy, the hunter-killer walked in and immediately noticed a big glass of red liquid sitting on the white countertop. Lying against the beaker of blood was a card that had the following words printed on it: HUMAN BLOOD – *DO NOT* DRINK IT, EBOR! The ghoulish meat-eater looked around for any sign of the Earthlings it was searching for, and seeing no one, turned its attention back to the note.

The initial puzzled look that enveloped Elroy's face quickly turned into a furrowed frown, as the beast's coal-black eyes glared at the inked instructions. "NOBODY TELLS ME

WHAT I CAN AND CANNOT DO...I AM OMNIPOTENT!" its voice blared out. The extraterrestrial angrily crumpled up the card, threw it on the floor, and then picked up the graduated cylinder of human fluid with its huge, scaly hand. It cautiously raised the blood-filled container up to the pathologist's nose and snorted in the mixture's malodor. A brimming smile quickly emerged from the puppeteered medical examiner's face. "SO FRAGRANT!" it said excitedly. The Ebor placed the glass receptacle to Elroy's lips and took in a gulp of the noxious medical concoction. "SWEET AND TASTY!" the thing announced. Then the parched parasite tilted the full beaker back, and began slurping down the remainder of the poisonous plasma. As the evil organism passionately ingested the human juice, Ted and the others observed quietly from their crouched position of hiding in the back of the pharmacy. They waited patiently for something to happen, but nothing did.

"Damn...it's not working," sighed the sheriff. As he moved his left arm into a more comfortable position, Buck's cast accidentally clanked against a bottle resting on the shelf behind him. The humanoid finished off the last few drops of the bloody brew, and then slammed the glass beaker back down on the counter.

"I HEARD THAT, MORTALS...READY OR NOT, HERE I COME!"

Without making a sound, Joshua quickly crept over and unlocked the back exit to the pharmacy. Then he slowly turned the knob and quietly pushed open the door. The others snuck out of the dispensary behind him, silently scurrying single file into the open hallway. Ted observed a fire axe encased in the corridor's wall, and used the end of his shotgun to break out the glass that shielded the wood-handled weapon. He handed Buck the scattergun, then hurriedly lifted the heavy fireman's tool from its holder. Sounds from the approaching clumsy Ebor were clearly audible, as it knocked several items off of the packed dispensary shelves while stumbling down the tight, winding aisle of the pharmacy.

Pointing to the part of the hallway opposite the hospital dispensary's outlet, Ted whispered to his companions, "You guys are the bait...stand over there to divert its attention, so I can nail the creature with this axe from behind, when it comes through the exit." Then the physician gripped the pickaxe tightly with both hands, and hid behind the pharmacy's open wooden door. All of a sudden, the giant, alien-human crossbreed lumbered towards the opening. Seeing Joshua and the two others, it ducked the coroner's head under the doorway, and entered into the corridor. All seven feet of the majestic, monstrous being stood forebodingly before them. Elroy's spectacled head was positioned on his fragile human torso, which was attached to long, green muscular upper and lower saurian extremities. Displaying a hideously contorted expression on the pathologist's mustachioed face, the creature stared ominously at the motionless trio across the hall.

"YOU EARTHLINGS UNDERESTIMATE ME. I KNOW THAT THE GIRL HARBORS A NALURIAN. WE HAVE INFECTED THEIR ENTIRE RACE, SO IT WILL BE TOO SICK TO HELP — LIKE YOU PUNY HUMANS, IT IS NO MATCH FOR ME. ALL OF YOU WILL DIE A HORRIBLE DEATH. I WILL SAVE THE FEMALE FOR LAST, SINCE I PLAN ON EATING HER ALIVE!" it grunted out hoarsely.

"Not if I can help it!" announced Ted angrily, who quickly emerged from behind the door. Mustering up every ounce of his strength, he forcefully swung the axe high through the air, striking Elroy's neck with the sharpened edge of the steel blade. With one fell swoop, the weapon hatcheted through the pathologist's collar, sending his head tumbling to the floor, as if it had been freshly guillotined. The headless Ebor began wildly slashing both of its green, clawed hands in front of it, as it staggered a few steps towards Buck, Tara, and Joshua. Its scaly, reptilian knees buckled, as the hybrid body materialized back into the embodiment of Dr. Dobbs, flopping onto the floor alongside the profusely hemorrhaging, severed head. Thick streams of blood gushed from the amputated head and decapitated body, forming viscous pools of gore around them.

"*Yes!*" exclaimed Buck. "Maybe the poison didn't work, but that axe sure as hell did!"

They all moved in closer to observe the two dismembered body parts, pleased that the wicked animal was dead, but sad that Elroy had to lose his life in the gruesome exchange. As they stood over the disjoined anatomy, something very strange began to happen. Squirming green cords of fleshy tentacles suddenly snaked out from the bloodied neck of Elroy's separated head, flagellating spastically towards his ravaged upper torso. The serpentine strands of green protoplasm extending from the pathologist's neck latched tightly onto his freshly hacked upper body, slowly dragging the severed head purposefully over the hallway floor, in an attempt to reattach it.

"This can't be happening!" shouted Buck as he witnessed its miraculous regenerative powers. "How do we kill this

Godforsaken thing?"

Hardly believing their eyes, the horrified bystanders watched in total amazement, as the fleshy, parasitic extensions meticulously realigned the medical examiner's lopped-off head to its disconnected torso, magically remodeling the cut ends of Elroy's severely damaged neck.

"Come on, we've got to get out of here!" shouted Buck. "It will be completely healed soon."

"We need to keep it on this floor, away from the patients and hospital staff," said Ted.

The ER physician led them all down the hall to where the radiology department was located. They made their way through a maze of cubicles that housed the various diagnostic X-ray equipment, finally ending up in the CAT scan suite. Ted attempted to open the "Emergency Exit Only" door, but as luck would have it, it was locked from the other side. "Dammit, we're sitting ducks in here," he said. "We've got to find another way out!"

As they began their trek back through the labyrinth of hospital rooms, Buck stopped abruptly, and then said quietly to the others, "Watch out, everyone...there it is!" Through one of the door's glass windows, they observed the stalking beast looming in an adjacent room, cunningly tracking its prey down by following their human scents. The group of vigilant quarry all backed silently into another room, away from their hounding predator.

Ted eyed a potential escape route and said, "Joshua, you and Tara go through that door and get the hell out of this hospital...Buck and I will try to hold it off until you get away."

"No, Daddy, we're not going to leave you!" insisted his

daughter.

"Listen, honey, that alien is after Joshua, not us — he is the key to the existence of the entire Nalurian race," explained Ted. "The important thing is to get both of you to safety until we can figure out how to kill this damn thing. Believe me, Buck and I don't plan on dying at the hands of that mutant parasite...now GO!"

"You two be careful," admonished Joshua, as he grabbed Tara's hand, and then hurriedly exited through the side door of the X-ray room.

Buck rushed over and tried to open an exit located at the back of the room, but it was also locked. "Dammit!" said the frustrated lawman.

Without warning, the large door to the suite they were hiding in was ripped off its hinges by the powerful mutant Ebor and hurled across the hardwood floor. It made a loud crashing sound, as it violently slammed against the wall. Moving to an area in the back of the room, Buck readied his shotgun, and Ted posed the pickaxe, each man bravely preparing to battle against the onslaught of the savage visitor from another planet.

The invading life form from deep space stooped under the opening and thundered out, "WHERE IS THE BOY?"

"He's gone, and you'll never find him, you murdering circus freak!" screamed Buck.

"YOU TWO WILL DIE NOW," it croaked out nonchalantly, in a monotone voice. The evil extraterrestrial snarled at the two men, then lifted up both of its clawed hands and moved aggressively toward its prey. As it approached their defensive positions, the creature reached out with one of its paws, and casually pretzeled over the solid steel arm of an X-ray machine that was blocking its way. Buck used his good arm to aim the scattergun at the attacking medical examiner's head, while Ted planted his feet and gripped the axe firmly with both hands. He cocked it back as if he were holding a baseball bat, ready to hit an oncoming fastball.

The malefic monster suddenly stopped dead in its tracks, and the two men noticed a peculiar, painful look that came over Elroy's face. Loud rumbling noises from deep within the pathologist's distended bowels resonated, as it began to belch and fart out the large collection of flatulence that had formed in the coroner's distressed gastrointestinal tract. After a long stream of repetitive burps and flatus, it began to gag and retch violently. Then the doctor of pathology opened his mouth widely and spewed out a stream of gooey, gelatinous blood. The spray of projectile vomiting heaved out from Elroy's oral cavity, splattering all over the floor.

Sheriff Evans looked over at his emergency room physician friend and asked, "What the hell's going on, Ted?"

"The antiparasitic agents must be finally working...at least that's what I'm hoping for!" answered Dr. Tisdale.

With a frenetic expression of alarm deeply implanted on Elroy's face, the ailing being roared, "YOU HUMANS TRICKED ME...THE BLOOD...WHAT DID YOU PUT IN THE BLOOD?"

"Just a little poison," smiled Ted.

Incapacitated by the toxic potion of the parasite-killing pharmaceuticals, the creature grabbed at the pathologist's abdomen and bent over in excruciating pain. "YOU THINK THAT YOU HAVE KILLED ME, BUT YOU ARE WRONG!"

it yelped.

The humanoid slowly stood up from its bowed position of agony, and then winked at its observing prey, displaying a smug, sinister grin on the medical examiner's face. Suddenly, Elroy's entire body began to shudder and vibrate from head to foot, while the skin of his face contortedly squirmed and bulged—as if a throng of hyperactive worms were wriggling violently under his subcutaneous tissues. Like an overcooked link of sausage, the medical man's integument jaggedly split open along multiple areas of his face, torso, and extremities, exposing a serrated surface of rough green scales beneath Elroy's pulpy flesh. Ted and the sheriff watched in horror while the grisly beast ripped through the encasement of the coroner's body, as if it were an insect escaping the confines of a cocoon. The metamorphosis was expeditious. Like a snake shedding a layer of old skin, the parasiticide-contaminated entity disinhabited itself from Elroy's body, and emerged to reveal its true, shocking image.

The murderous Ebor stood in full view of Ted and Buck, next to the gory discarded shell of human remains that was once the body of Dr. Elroy Dobbs. It easily stood over seven feet tall, and its vulnerable areas were covered in a thick green plate of protective bony scales. The bipedal animal's body form was definitely saurian—similar to one of Earth's prehistoric raptors—except that the length of its hulking arms and legs were more hominid than reptilian. Like its Nalurian relatives, each of its two webbed hands was composed of six digits, which included a pair of opposable thumbs. A curved, scalpel-sharp claw projected out menacingly from the end of each finger. Both of its boxy feet were immense, in order to support the weight of the mutant's massive body, with each hoof being made up of three taloned toes. The behemoth organism possessed a bulky, hairless head that was heart-shaped. A deep furrow extended down the middle of its exposed scalp, which was covered on each side with rows of horny projections. Its evolved ears had no external components, and consisted of a grouping of puncture-like slits that extended interiorly into each side of its oblong cranium. The thing's snout was comprised of a raised, midline vertical orifice, bordered by a set of fleshy lips that opened and closed, as it sucked in and blew out huge lungfuls of air. In addition, it was equipped with an auxiliary breathing apparatus made up of a cluster of sloping gill-slits, situated on each side of its neck, and enveloped by moveable flaps of tissue. An elliptical-shaped pair of piercing black eyes—each highlighted with a centrally located emerald-green vertical slit, sat wide-spaced above its bizarre nose. The alien's organs of sight hostilely glowered out like the malevolent stare of a coiled rattlesnake, ready to strike. Its deep-set, sinister eyes lacked any lids, but possessed overlying, clear nictitating membranes that protected its eyeballs and kept them moist. Positioned directly below its nasal organ laid the entrance to the lizard's oral cavity, concealed by opposing gargantuan green lips that extended horizontally across the extraterrestrial's entire face. The voracious carnivore stretched open its massive mouth and savagely snarled at the two men, revealing bulging upper and lower jaws that were crowded with a complement of sharp, serrated teeth. Fierce, bilateral canine fangs, bathed in stringy yellow saliva, curved out from the alien cannibal's oral cavity, as rivulets of glutinous drool trickled down its chin.

"That goddam creature is impervious to everything!" exclaimed Ted. "Somehow, by leaving Elroy's body, it has protected itself from the lethal effects of the ingested antiparasitic agents."

The ferocious megasaur took a step towards them and growled through its daggered dentition, "NICE TRY, HUMANS...BUT YOU LOSE!"

"Get ready with that axe," warned the sheriff. "Here it comes!"

Ted glanced over at his fellow companion and said, "Give'm hell, Buck!"

As the storming Ebor advanced, the sheriff pumped his remaining three shotgun shells into the relentless fiend, but the pellets just bounced harmlessly off its protective bony plate of body armor. Buck took the barrel of the scattergun in his right hand, and desperately swung it at the huge being as hard as he could. The alert monster grabbed the handle of the advancing weapon in midair with its one clawed hand, and then used the other to take a swipe at the sheriff. As if swatting an annoying insect, the blow from the back of its powerful paw flung the lawman several feet through the air—causing his body to crash violently against the wall, plummeting Buck helplessly to the floor. The Ebor held up the shotgun and looked at it, taking a few moments to examine the primitive human weapon. Then, the alien snapped the heavy, steel barrel into two jagged pieces, as if it were a pencil.

Realizing that his fire fighter's tool was about as useless as tits on a boar hog, Ted still took a full swing at the alien, striking it solidly in the chest with the cutting edge of the stout axe. A *clunking* sound was produced, as the sharpened blade innocently bounced off the being's protective shield of green flesh. The behemoth snatched the pickaxe from Ted, and like a flimsy toothpick, snapped its wooden handle in two. Then it grabbed the powerless physician by the throat with one of its paws, and effortlessly lifted the strangling man's body high off the ground. Not wishing to die by hanging, Ted immediately clung onto the seizing appendage with both hands, in order to prevent his body weight from dislocating any cervical vertebrae. The texture of the mutant predator's skin was rough and scaly — cold and clammy to the suspended doctor's touch. Just as the immortal extraterrestrial was about to snap the neck of the dangling M.D., the side door burst open, and Joshua and Tara rushed in.

"Leave him alone, you bastard...come and get me, I'm the one you want!" shouted the boy.

Startled by the interruption, the vicious brute released the chokehold on its victim and turned around to face the two teens. Ted fell helplessly to the floor, his opened mouth gasping for air after enduring the callous embrace of the creature's suffocating grip.

It looked over at Joshua and grunted, "I WILL KILL YOU FAST, BOY."

"You kids get the hell out of here!" Ted coughed out.

Buck, who still lay on the floor recuperating from the injuries sustained from his toss through the air, yelled, "Run, fast, you two...before that thing rips you to pieces!"

"Daddy...Sheriff Evans...stay where you are...we know what we're doing!" answered Tara.

Ted sat up and pleaded, "Don't be heroes...get out of here while you still can!"

"Trust me," said Joshua.

The reptilian assassin from the planet Chimea yawned open its great mouth at the teenagers to reveal an oral cavity that was lined in white, rippled mucosa—resembling the gaping orifice of a cotton-mouthed water moccasin. Sneering its upper lip, the monstrosity maliciously flashed a jawful of its jaundiced incisors at the defenseless pair of adolescents. The alien then slithered out a black, forked tongue, and licked its chops. Suddenly, it gave out an eerie howl, and charged relentlessly towards them. Joshua deliberately backed into the corner of the room, while Tara cautiously moved away from the advancing attacker.

When the formidable Ebor extended out its pair of green extremities to crush the cornered boy, Joshua quickly reached out and grabbed its clawed appendages with both hands—discharging a visible flow of brilliant blue energy into the assaulting animal. The stunned alien tried to pull its arms away, but was unable to free itself from the teen's unyielding, electrical grip. Suddenly, Joshua's blue eyes transformed into luminous globes of golden light—glowing beams of gilded luster brightly radiated out from his face.

"It's Teirken...he switched bodies...now he's inside of Joshua!" screamed Ted.

The extraterrestrial's goliath arms began to quake violently. "WHAT ARE *YOU* DOING IN THE BOY, NALURIAN...YOU CANNOT POSSESS THIS KIND OF POWER...YOU ARE INFECTED!"

From within Joshua, Teirken responded sarcastically, *"YOU HAVE UNDERESTIMATED ME, EBOR...I AM FULLY HEALED NOW!"*

The struggling, mutant behemoth attempted to pull itself free, but was unable to budge either of its arms. "I AM PERPETUAL...I AM UNDYING...YOU CANNOT DEFEAT ME!" it roared.

The powerful current of Teirken's life force continued to flow from Joshua's hands into the bewildered creature. "*NOW YOU WILL KNOW HOW IT FEELS TO BE PARASITIZED, EBOR!*"

"I CAN FEEL YOUR PRESENCE...GET OUT OF ME, NALURIAN!" yelped the possessed predator.

The anguished entity's titanic body began to furiously convulse, as the essence of the invading Nalurian took it over. Observing the bizarre event from across the room's floor, the wounded lawman vehemently cried out, "Die, you alien bastard...die!"

A pair of luminescent eyes stared at the condemned Ebor, as Teirken's voice emanated from the boy's vocal cords. "*AFTER I INHABIT YOUR BODY, I WILL TERMINATE YOUR LIFE FUNCTIONS AND YOU WILL CEASE TO EXIST!*"

Still in denial, the disbelieving monstrosity screeched, "NOTHING CAN KILL ME...I AM INVULNERABLE...I WILL COME BACK!"

"*NOT THIS TIME, EBOR!*" retorted Teirken.

The two orbs of golden fluorescence slowly faded from Joshua's handsome face, reinstating the boy's normal pair of colorful blue eyes in their place. Following the telepathic instructions from Teirken, the teenager released his hands from the being's massive appendages, and stepped away from the Ebor's frozen body. Tara immediately rushed over and embraced her brave boyfriend with a loving hug, squeezing him tightly with her opened arms.

Teirken, having taken over full control of every biological function inherent to the murdering monster, began working his wondrous magic. Everyone watched in awe, as the Ebor's protective shield of green epidermis gradually began to disintegrate—melting away into thin air. The megasaurian's demise was occurring in conjunction with the Nalurian's destruction of its biochemical makeup. A succession of agonizing, ear-piercing howls emerged from the grossly contorted mouth of the disappearing behemoth, reverberating dissonantly throughout the maze of hospital hallways. The remainder of the dreadful carnivore's hideous body slowly dematerialized, as Teirken continued to systematically ravage its internal molecular structure. Upon completion of the fantastic decomposition process, the imposing figure of the Nalurian vanquisher mystically appeared in place of the vanished Ebor.

"You did it, Teirken...you saved our lives!" Ted exclaimed.

The Nalurian looked over at the physician with his glowing golden eyes and telepathically communicated to all of them, *"I COULDN'T HAVE DONE IT WITHOUT JOSHUA'S HELP. IT WAS THE BOY'S IDEA THAT I TRANSFER FROM TARA'S BODY TO HIM. HIS ANTIBODY TO THE MICROBE RESPONSIBLE FOR MY TRISOMY STATE DESTROYED THE EXTRA CHROMOSOME IN MY CELLS, AND REVERSED THE WEAKENING EFFECTS OF THE INVADING INFECTION. COMPLETELY HEALED BY JOSHUA, I WAS ABLE TO DRAW UPON MY INNATE POWERS TO DESTROY THE EBOR."*

"My brain cancer was nearly healed by Teirken, so Joshua came up with the idea of switching identities...we couldn't leave you two alone to fight that thing," smiled Tara.

Joshua humbly added, "I knew that Teirken would be our only hope of killing the alien, so I thought it was worth a try to see if his powers could be restored by my healing antibody." Ted walked over and helped Buck to his feet. "Hell of a good idea, if you ask me," said the bruised lawman.

"It's imperative that I travel back with Teirken to his planet, in order to isolate and clone the antibody from my immune system that will be needed to produce the vaccine," said Joshua.

"That's right, we don't have those scientific capabilities here on Earth yet," agreed Ted. "And there are millions of lives to be saved."

"THE TRIP TO CHIMEA WILL BE FAST, MY FRIENDS... IT WILL TAKE LITTLE TIME TO PROCURE THE ANTIBODY FROM JOSHUA'S BODY...THEN I WILL BRING HIM BACK HOME," Teirken telepathied to them. *"PLEASE EXCUSE ME NOW...I MUST RE-ENTER TARA'S BODY AND COMPLETE HER HEALING PROCESS...SHE WILL BE COMPLETELY FREE FROM CANCER BY THE TIME WE REACH MY PLANET."*

"Now, hold your horses there!" interjected Ted. "No way that you're taking my daughter and her boyfriend away to another galaxy without me tagging along...got room for another passenger on that flying saucer of yours?"

"I HAD ALREADY PLANNED ON YOU COMING WITH US," communicated Teirken. *"I WILL NEED YOUR HELP PROCESSING THE VACCINE."*

"Well, what are we waiting for then?" said Ted. "Let's make like the wind and blow out of here!"

"Please, Daddy!" squealed Tara. "Haven't we all been

through enough already?"

Joshua laughed and said, "Be prepared, Tara...just think of all the puns your dad will think up during our flight to Chimea."

"*ARE YOU READY FOR ME NOW?*" the Nalurian's brain asked Tara.

"Let's do it," replied the teenager. "I want to be completely free of my disease." Teirken positioned his huge saurian frame next to Tara, and then magically stepped forward into her body, supernaturally transferring the quintessence of his alien being into the beautiful young girl.

The sheriff looked at everyone, and then proclaimed with a wily grin, "You all fully realize that no one out there in their right mind is ever going to believe any of this!"

Ted winked at the lawman and replied, "Buck, I once knew a brave, wise old man who would answer your question something like this—who gives a rat's ass whether anyone believes us or not...the important thing is that *we* know it's true!"

"God bless Henry Pickridge!" exclaimed Buck.

Still somewhat dazed by the recent electrifying, ephemeral events, the weary foursome headed out of the hospital towards the sheriff's truck. Tara and Joshua held hands, and leisurely walked in front of everyone, while Ted and Buck trailed slowly behind. The harrowing life-and-death experiences they shared together that day would form a lasting bond between them that could never be broken. Sheriff Evans would later drop them off by Fletcher's Pool, at the site where Teirken's scientifically camouflaged spacecraft was moored. There, they would say their goodbyes to Buck, and board the gigantic alien saucer, bound for the distant Nalurian planet of Chimea. The brave group of space travelers would unselfishly risk their lives, journeying beyond the speed of light in order to save a race of dying aliens. Mother Destiny would have additional adventures in store for them, as well — but that's a whole other story. As Yoda would say, "Impossible to see, the future is!"

Mary Allen would have been proud of her only son. She was right — he *was* destined to do wondrous things, and he *would* positively affect millions of lives around him. God, in His infinite wisdom, had preordained Joshua for greatness.

"So the Lord was with Joshua; and his fame was noised throughout all the country." *THE BOOK OF JOSHUA,* 6:27.

THE END

Before You Go...

HELP AN AUTHOR

write a review

THANK YOU!

Share your voice and help guide other readers to these wonderful books. Even if it's only a line or two your reviews help readers discover the author's books so they can continue creating stories that you'll love. Login to your favorite retailer and leave a review. Thank you.

G.A. Minton has been an ardent fan of horror and sci-fi his entire life. Growing up as an Air Force brat, he's lived in different cities across the U.S., thus allowing him to observe a variety of cultures. When he isn't writing, you can usually find him out on the golf course, chasing after a little white ball. His other hobbies include reading, traveling, fishing, snorkeling, working out, listening to hard rock music, and watching great movies. He has a wife, a son and daughter, and two Bengal cats.

Weirdly enough, it was only after G.A. was rear-ended by a drunk driver and suffered a closed-head injury, that he developed a newfound passion for writing (a true story, even though it sounds like a fictitious plot for a horror novel). He pens his novels freestyle, almost in a stream of consciousness, relying on no outlines, formats, or templates for assistance— the narrative is able to flow freely from his imagination, ending up with a storyline that contains an ordered sequence of events. One might surmise that the damaged neurons in his frontal cortex had rearranged themselves into a different pattern, thereby enhancing the creative elements in his brain. Who knows? Stranger things have happened! Currently,

G.A. is in the process of completing his second novel, a dark, supernatural tale of horror that takes Good vs. Evil to a whole new level.

CPSIA information can be obtained
at www.ICGtesting.com
Printed in the USA
LVOW11s0928041216

515735LV00003B/515/P

9 781629 894447